# HUSBANDS

## LOVE AND LIES IN LA-LA-LAND

# MO FANNING

spring street books

*First published by Spring Street Books 2024*

Copyright © 2024 by Mo Fanning

ISBN: 978-1-7392903-1-3 (Paperback edition)

ISBN: 978-1-7392903-0-6 (Ebook edition)

Book Cover by Mecob

Illustrations © Shutterstock.com

*mofanning.co.uk | springstreetbooks.co.uk*

*For Mark and Ernie*

To the silenced voices and hidden tears.
The survivors whose abusers walk free.
May this narrative echo the justice you deserve.

**Mo Fanning**

# ACKNOWLEDGEMENT

Sometimes, I look at the acknowledgements page in a book and convince myself that the author would be played off the stage at any self-respecting award ceremony. It can take that many people to write a book. Yes, there's the author, an editor, and maybe a way-too-picky proofreader.

And then I wrote my first book and realised Michelle Obama was right. Everything about creating a novel takes a village.

The older I get, the more I rely on others. So, here are just a few of the *many* people who deserve huge thanks for their generous support in helping this particular book come together.

Thank you so much to all the fabulous people at Faber and the many (far better) writers I met there who helped me refine what was mush. It's rude to pick three out from such a great gang, but Merl, Claudia, and Steve hung on to the grim end, pointing out the somewhat convenient plot twists while staying relentlessly upbeat and positive any time I got needy.

And to Peter Benson, who pulled a confused face when I said I was writing a novel about abuse but making it into a dark comedy. See! It can be done. Thank you for steering this ship forward in the early days.

Special thanks to my *take-no-prisoners* editor, Caroline McKee, who tore my manuscript apart but helpfully provided notes for reassembly. To Hannah Hargrave, my publicity maestro, who made people take notice, and to Mark Ecob for creating a cover that made me cry. You all just got me. Tina Baker took my *blurb-by-someone-famous* virginity and was remarkably gentle, considering the state of the edit. Josh Lanyon was second. Both gave so freely and generously of their time, and if karma works, will surely buy a winning lottery scratch card this year. Or win a yacht.

My amazing husband, Mark, deserves enormous thanks, not only for all the extra dog care, plumbing, painting, and risk-taking re-wiring of our tumbledown house, but also for being willing to listen to me bang on about nothing in particular. All the fucking time. Ernie gets a *good boy* pat on the head for minimal mouse hand nudging during writing time.

Most of all, I want to acknowledge and thank the men who agreed to talk to me about their experiences in the entertainment industry. I hope you feel that justice is done, especially for your Carlton Duprees.

But also, thank *you* for buying, nicking, finding or borrowing this book. I hope you don't decide it's shit.

# PROLOGUE

## 4.42 a.m. April 10, 2016 - Las Vegas, USA

Fried chicken grease stains my wrinkled white shirt, and undone buttons reveal my pale skin. The world spins as I lean on a pillar in the fancy hotel lobby. My date slips a matt black card into the lift, gesturing for another couple to wait.

As we ride to the penthouse level, he pushes me against the mirrored wall and kisses me hard with lips that taste of whisky.

In the penthouse suite, translucent curtains flutter at windows overlooking garish casino signs lining the strip below.

A bartender with piercing blue eyes pours champagne.

My date is handsome in a craggy, daddy-bear way. Not that I buy into the whole gay men as woodland critters thing. Every online hook-up describes themselves as a bear, an otter or a pup, and I've yet to find the animal that chimes with what my Spotlight Casting Directory profile calls '*an average build, Hugh Grant type*'.

He lifts his glass in a toast. "Should we hyphenate our last names, or are you taking mine?"

Shit!

I didn't imagine it. There *was* a wedding chapel, dingy and worn, with stained beige carpeting and rows of plastic chairs. And some campy older guy dressed as Elvis crooning, 'Love me tender'. Cheesy organ music played on a loop, and we gave money to a woman who promised our marriage certificate tomorrow. I made jokes about getting it framed to hang in the loo.

"We're not married, though, right?"

He winks. "I'll call and explain it was a mistake."

Stressed whispers carry from the other room. I steady myself against the wall as the floor lurches—time to leave. Stop being so polite and so British. Be direct. Tell him to order you a taxi.

"Do you have company?" I say, in the sort of voice my mother might use when asking if the local branch of Waitrose stocks oven chips.

"Just friends."

The room spins, and my mouth waters. My head is banging, but his hands are on me.

"Shame to waste our honeymoon." He kisses my neck. "The bedroom is through there."

"Yeah, great, but I need the bathroom."

A door opens at the end of a low-lit hallway, and a guy stands staring. Young. Handsome with a tiny scar below one eye. Bare-chested. Bold. But mostly young. The floor lurches, and I reach for a wall to steady myself.

His fingers brush my cheek. "Stay, baby. I'll get you home safe."

I pull back. "Call them. Tell them we made a mistake."

With a grin, he pulls out his phone and pushes a button.

"Siri, remind me to annul the marriage."

# 1

I've always believed that winning at life comes down to achieving the holy trinity: a fabulous job, great (and regular) sex, and a Sunday supplement-worthy home. I'm a supply teacher in an inner-city Birmingham school, single again at 28, and sleeping in my childhood bedroom beneath a 'Hard Candy' Madonna poster.

In some parallel universe, another version of me lounges in a daytime chat show green room, reaching past Dame Joanna Lumley for freshly baked pastries while trading stories of our respective recent sell-out West End productions. Joanna would call me *darling* and praise my courage for risking a one-man coming out confessional, and I'd explain how much it mattered to my art that I prove to all young gay men they too can evolve from a shy, acne-ridden ugly duckling into a graceful swan with good hair. A budding national treasure. Tipped to win the *Evening Standard Most Promising Newcomer* award.

A football hits my head.

It's my turn for playground duty at Oak Park Juniors, sheltering from the mid-morning drizzle next to a mildewed concrete fountain that Birmingham City Council drained for health and safety reasons.

"Sorry, sir."

The apology comes from a Year Four boy, Lewis something-or-other. The Head of Year calls him a twat. His rough-as-a-bear's-arse father texts the school with illiterate complaints about his little prince's unfair treatment. Last week, his little prince broke a kid's arm and locked two dinner ladies in the netball cupboard. One of them has claustrophobia. Lewis grabs his ball and backs away, giving me a shit-eating grin. I'm ten years old again, hiding how I'm not like all the other boys, pretending not to mind when they call me poofter.

An uneaten sandwich sits on my lap. Cheese and beetroot. Mum started making the same packed lunch every day after I mentioned liking it. As the early evening weatherman finishes his forecast, she turns off the TV and totters to the kitchen to slice mild cheddar, and fish Sainsbury's own-label beetroot slices from a jar.

I liberate the sandwich from its cling film shroud. Damp white bread stained pink and curling at the edges, with a cloying note of sweet vinegar. I'll toss it in a skip near the sports hall extension and buy something from Pret. One more loyalty stamp, and I score a free coffee.

Except tonight, I'm not going straight home. I'm meeting a Grindr date for drinks—a twenty-one-year-old Taiwanese kickboxer who thinks I look 23. I'm wary of anyone who suggests a late afternoon hook-up. They avoid evenings because they have a wife and kids or an electronic tag that puts them under post-sunset house arrest. This guy is cute, though, and mentioned having had a part in a recent action film.

Five years of teaching is enough. My true calling is acting, not sitting in a classroom that may or may not have asbestos in the walls. Last year, I scored a minor role in a period drama and worked as a body double for a soap star. A prosthetic nose fell off during a sex scene, and the intimacy coordinator lost her shit. I've played a mysterious monk in a gentle whodunnit and once featured in the audience for a taping of *Britain's Got Talent*. The producer zoomed in twice on my appalled face as an octogenarian crooned 'Danny Boy'.

Today marks three months of being a single man after ending a disastrous relationship with a compulsive liar who cheated on me with our Brazilian cleaner, Joaquim.

July is my month of saying yes. This evening, I'll lose myself in someone else's life.

Perhaps he'll introduce me to his agent.

Walking across the playground, I mutter a pep talk about how dreams are worth chasing and tonight's hot date could start a new chapter. The school bell signals the end of break time, and kids form reluctant lines to head inside. There are three weeks until the summer holidays, and they're as sick as me of introductory algebra and hearing about the Irish potato famine.

Tonight, I'll step out of my comfort zone, embrace

the unknown and inch closer to the life I've always wanted. I'll say yes when opportunity knocks.

————

A warm bottle of Czech lager sits on a rickety plastic table beside my phone, and I contemplate leaving a third message for my date. But how would that make me sound? Desperate? Needy? Pissed off? The sun beats down, turning my face the colour of boiled ham. Why do I never pack sunblock? Joan Collins swears by that, and a wide-brimmed hat—which I once tried, but a random woman tapped my arm and asked if I'd lost my carer.

The bar opposite is bathed in soothing shade, but I chose The Pink Flamingo for its potential networking opportunities——BBC casting directors loiter here and scout for new faces. One of the ex-barmen now runs a second-hand book stall on Albert Square in EastEnders.

Surrounded by empty chairs and tables, I glance up whenever anybody emerges from inside. A cuter guy clearing tables keeps looking over, judging me, and writing me off as a loser. Rummaging through my backpack, I pull out a dog-eared copy of Stanislavsky's 'An Actor Prepares', my place marked by a folded-in-two prescription for lower back pain tablets.

The Head called me into her office as I was leaving.

"Are you happy here?" She peered over a huge round spectacles like a constipated owl.

"Delirious," I said, hoping she had an ear for sarcasm.

She fished a folder from a drawer. "This morning, I had a conversation with Suzanne."

"Right?"

"You're filling in while she takes stress leave." She placed air quotes around the last two words. "Suzanne won't be rejoining our merry band. The doctor recommends a total break, so she's moving to Telford to keep chickens."

I held my breath as she slid papers across her desk—application forms for a full-time position.

"We'd love to retain your services, Kyle," she said. "The kids adore you."

We both knew it was bull. The kids there see me as just another burnt-out teacher in an Ofsted failing school, but I come with Grade 3 piano skills, which makes me invaluable at morning assembly.

Every sensible bone in my body says to apply for the job, but what if my acting break happens? For one thing, it wouldn't be fair for the kids to lose a much-loved father figure midway through the term. And any casting director will ask if I'm employed and pick someone more available.

———

I consider firing off a third message to my date. He's well over an hour late. My first was casual, jokey even.

> Hey there. At the pub. Ordering lots of beer. See you soon.

Should I add a kiss? After all, he's a stranger, and I don't know his real name, though I do suspect it isn't *CumDump64*. Grindr dates are like petrol station milk.

Usually, they're fine, but there's always a risk you might get sick and develop a nasty rash.

I wait another twenty minutes and try again. This time, leaving a voicemail.

> We did say five o'clock, didn't we? Or did I get it wrong? Anyway, I hope you're OK and didn't get injured in a fight...or something. Call me when you pick up.

I considered adding how horny I was, but my sex voice is more creepy than thirsty. We've already traded dick pics, so he gets what kind of evening I have planned.

By the time I've drunk one and a half more over-priced bottled beers, the pub is getting busy for happy hour, and topless, tattooed bartenders have replaced the afternoon shift. A DJ takes over, and it's bottomless jugs of margaritas all round. Office girl gaggles descend, and a random asks to 'borrow' chairs from my table. Soon, it's just me, one empty chair, and two tall, skinny guys in shiny blue suits cut tight on the leg with estate agent hair, giving me stink eye, willing me to move.

I grab my phone.

"Milly," I say when she answers. "The tosser stood me up, and there's a half pitcher of watered-down cock-tails with your name on it."

———

Milly reaches for the jug, and ice cubes clink. The background music has reached shout-to-be-heard levels, and the after-work crowd is drunk-dancing and singing along with Kylie.

"The man is deformed." She returns my phone. "You had a lucky escape."

A part of me wants to believe her. For one thing, she's right. Something weird is going on with his penis, but it could just be bad lighting. Nobody ever looks their best without an LED halo lamp.

We've moved inside and bagged seats at the bar. The Flamingo tries to pass itself off as a Birmingham gay institution, but it's seen better days. The walls are painted the same garish shade of purple as when I summoned the courage to duck past bouncers and order my first gay pub drink ten years earlier. The place even smells the same. Say what you like about Lynx Oriental body spray. It's a classic.

Kylie gives way to a four-on-the-floor beat of loud, distorted guitar and pounding bass.

An unread text notification appears on my phone. Most likely *CumDump64* rescheduling.

Milly pays for our drinks. She never lets me settle bills because I'm a supply teacher, and she's a partnership fast-track lawyer with an expense account.

"Let me guess," she says. "His wife has COVID, and he's in charge of making sure the kids get their fish fingers and oven chips?"

I stuff the phone back into my pocket, wounded not from Grindr rejection but by a ten-word text from Montgomery Casting. Two days ago, I auditioned for a non-speaking role of 'man at party'. The brief said: male, 18-

30, six-foot-tall, dark hair, not too fat, not too thin, any ethnicity. It should have been a formality.

"They gave some other pretty boy actor the part," I say, and she reaches to stroke my arm.

"You'll land the next one."

"You said that last time and the time before. And when I made the final three to play a headless corpse in Silent Witness."

"You did that play."

She means an experimental theatre piece I let myself be talked into by a man with swimming pool eyes and super tight jeans. My character spent an hour on a stage locked in a box, making animal noises while someone dressed as Bo Peep called for lost sheep. On the opening night, we played to an audience of seven. There was no second performance.

My phone rings, but I don't react.

"Shouldn't you answer that?" Milly says. "What if the casting people sent the wrong message?"

She's a proper glass-half-full kind of friend. We agreed if we're both still single at 35, we'll buy matching fuchsia sweaters and a bungalow. We'll join a choir and start rumours about the neighbours being swingers.

Tomorrow, she'll call and say she's booked us in for La Mer facials, followed by lunch at some fancy place with a two-month waiting list run by a TV chef.

She puts up with my wannabe actor shtick on the whole, but never shies away from suggesting the grass might not be as green as I imagine on the other side of fame.

The phone stops ringing, and she peers at the screen. "That was a US number."

Seconds later, a ping signals voicemail, and I act like it's no big deal. "Problem some bloke to ask if I'm happy with my doors and windows."

"Calling from America?" She lunges for my mobile.

"Fine."

I play the message on speaker.

"This is Carlton Dupree. I work for Aaron Biedermeier. I must speak to you. Today, if possible."

Milly wrinkles her nose, and I scratch my head, running through a long list of the men I've slept with since discovering my husband-to-be was a lying, cheating bastard. Had there been an American? I half recall an air steward with a New York accent.

"Biedermeier," I say. "Why do I recognise that name?"

She taps it into a search engine on her phone. "Is this him?"

The face is familiar. Handsome, square-jawed, and rugged with dark brown eyes.

"He's a director," she says. "Remember that artsy bollocks film we watched? The one set in the French civil war? Everyone in the village lost their memory after aliens invaded."

The pair of us sit through so many terrible films. It's our thing. A perfect Saturday night involves way too much Chinese food while streaming something that scored zero on *Rotten Tomatoes*, ideally with subtitles.

"Paper Tiger," she says.

"That was him?" I stare at the picture. "I figured the

director would be Italian, with a bulbous wine-drinker nose and a penchant for underage girls."

"Close." She takes back her phone. "I read in *Popbitch* about how this guy trades roles for sexual favours from wannabe movie stars. Male wannabe movie stars."

I snort. "Perhaps this is my break."

"Except he prefers younger men."

I'm at a loss for words. "I'm 28, Milly. That's hardly old. CumDump thought I was 23."

"So, you'd sleep with a man for a part in a film?"

I'm about to reply that yes, of course, I would. Who in their right mind wouldn't, when my phone lights up. It's Mum. For over a week, I've ignored hints the size of a boulder about how her choir group needs someone to fill in since their regular pianist booked a late saver deal to Lloret de Mar.

———

Early evening Birmingham city centre is always the same. The smells of food cooking fill the air, and music plays from open windows, a woman's soulful voice crooning, bass notes thumping. Crowds mill, talking, laughing, drinking, and enjoying good weather. A setting sun pastes warm shadows between high-rise buildings.

Someone calls out, and heads turn. A guy in his thirties with shaggy hair and a worn leather jacket raises a hand in greeting and forces a crooked grin. He plays an alcoholic doctor in an afternoon drama. Once, we got chatting online, and he sent a photo. Not of his face, obviously. I recognise a tiny tattoo on his wrist—Sanskrit for *eternal flame*.

"Where are you? Is that music playing?" Mum interrupts my pondering whether to go over and say hi, invite him to join me for a margarita, and swing the conversation on to whether the producer of his soap might need a six-foot-tall, moderately handsome geek.

"Drinks with Milly," I say. "Sorry, I missed your calls. We had a staff meeting after work."

Mum holds a huge candle for Milly and me getting together, always pointing out how much we have in common. When I first dated Dave, Mum showed him photographs of our joint graduation, making him agree just how happy we looked. How well-suited we appeared. Two eggnogs later, and she was debating whose nose any future grandchildren might inherit.

"A man keeps calling." The wobble in her voice suggests she hopes this doesn't mean a new boyfriend. "I gave him your mobile number."

"Did this caller have an American accent?"

"Yes, but he sounded friendly."

"If he calls again, hang up. It's a scam."

There's a long silence. Mum reads the Daily Mail and stays alert for scammers out to swindle away her meagre savings. She bought a special pen to obscure the address on envelopes and a commercial paper shredder for bank statements. She's ex-directory and has a device attached to the phone to show who's calling before picking up. If anyone knocks on the door, she demands identity and refuses to shop online.

"There's a number you call to report them," she says. "Hang on while I find it for you."

The line muffles. She'll be searching through the drawer in her special hallway telephone table.

"I'm about to jump on a bus." Sometimes, I worry just how easily lies spring into my mind. "I'll be late home. Don't bother doing me anything for tea."

————

After typing Aaron Biedermeier into my phone, I scroll through photos of him and his super-buff husband-to-be, actor Noah Winters, frolicking in Venice Beach waves. Winters was tipped for an Oscar three years back for 'Walter's War', a Biedermeier Pictures production. The bastard was nineteen, and now he's 22 and engaged to the guy who made him famous.

The crowded city centre street feels too loud, too exposed for what could become my pivotal step on the yellow brick road to fame. Everything hangs off first impressions, and I need to sound like I get calls like this all the time. I glance around, seeking somewhere private. Somewhere that might pass for my dressing room on the set of a prestige BBC drama.

Narrow concrete steps lead to the nearest canal. Below street level, the air is musty and dank. Water laps against lichen-coated walls while early evening traffic rumbles overhead. Carlton Dupree's number rings and the voice that answers is high-pitched and nasal.

"Who the fuck is this?"

"Kyle Macdonald." I try to sound chilled. "You left a message on my voicemail."

Static crackles.

"Oh, hey...Kyle." He sounds less frosty. "Thank you for getting back to me. Especially given the circumstances. Kinda shitty, right?"

He's got the wrong guy. It's happened before. There's a Glasgow Kyle McDougall listed in Spotlight, and he's doing way better than me. Last month, he auditioned for a Jennifer Aniston show.

I clear my throat. "When you say circumstances..."

"We here at Biedermeier Pictures can't begin to imagine what you must be going through. It has to be hard to hear your husband was attacked. Let alone that he's in a coma."

"Can I check something?" I say, but he's not listening.

"You have such a great voice, Kyle. So distinctive and memorable."

"Tell me again about the attack."

He exhales. "Aaron is in a bad way, and the doctors aren't sure if...well, I'm getting ahead of myself." He leaves a pause. "There's a flight leaving Heathrow in three hours, and I figured if I booked you a seat..."

"You've got me confused with someone else," I say. "I don't know anyone called Aaron."

Papers rustle down the line.

"Am I talking to Kyle Rupert Macdonald? Born on the fifth of September in Stourbridge." He pronounces it to rhyme with drawbridge. Americans always do.

"Yes, but..."

"Jeez, you're hard to track down. Clark County gave

me your name, date of birth, and the wrong telephone number. I spoke to some woman who kept asking if I was trying to sell double glazing. She passed on your details. It's not like I can ask your husband."

It's the second mention of a husband, and now he's done the whole name, date of birth and embarrassing middle name. I feel I should ask quite what the hell he's talking about.

"You keep talking about me being married," I say, and then snort like a cat coughing up a furball.

There's another long silence—more keyboard taps.

"Six years ago. You were in Vegas. April 2016."

I think back. Vegas just isn't my kind of town. I've only ever been once for a stag weekend. One I got talked into and regretted within ten minutes of arriving at a hotel that made Blackpool Pleasure Beach look classy.

"Do you remember what you did on Saturday, April 9, 2016?" he says. "To be fair, it was more like the small hours of Sunday, April 10."

Like any Vegas stag weekend, things got messy fast. There were six of us and we emptied three hotel room minibars, and proved the bottomless cocktails had a cut-off point, before hitting the casino, where I accidentally-on-purpose ducked into a gift shop to avoid being dragged to a strip club.

"Do you recall visiting The Little Less Conversation Wedding Chapel?"

My mouth runs dry, and I grab a railing to steady myself as my stomach rolls. I've long since buried the memory of agreeing to joke-marry a stranger I met in a casino. We were both falling-down drunk, and no overweight Elvis impersonator could join us in any legally binding way. Surely.

"We never collected the marriage certificate," I say. "So it didn't count. And the guy..." His name might have been Aaron. Or Alan. Or Adrian. "He was going to call the chapel for an annulment."

"I'm not here to judge. My job is to help."

"Help with what?"

A bubble of sick rises, and at the back of my mind, a nagging voice points out how I should have double-checked that nothing ever came of that drunken half-night stand.

"Here's the deal. I work for Biedermeier and six years ago, you married my boss. Aaron loves doing impulsive things. It's a total ball ache keeping track of his lunch order."

There's a pause. I should demand proof. A copy of the marriage certificate. The one that was going to be annulled.

"Are you certain about any of this?" I say. "Because I never actually signed anything."

Carlton Dupree sighs. "Aaron just got engaged to some twink actor called Noah Winters. You may have heard of the guy. Nominated for an Oscar. Yadda yadda. And then...what with the attack and everything..."

"Hang on," I say, "tell me more about that."

"A bunch of guys. Early morning. Downtown. I keep telling him to use studio drivers and security, but Aaron's a free spirit. Now he's in Cedars Sinai, hooked up to a bunch of machines. A guy from Legal was going through paperwork, and...well, that's how come we're talking."

There's every chance I'll vomit. Like people do in TV shows when unexpected bad news breaks. Mum's biggest moan about Coronation Street is how, at the slightest hint of something going wrong, someone ends up bent double over a toilet bowl.

"Should I have changed my name?" I say, punch drunk, confused. "Should I be Kyle Biedermeier?"

"About that flight." He ignores my questions. "It's showing one seat remaining in First." Clicks suggest he's typing again. "You want me to specify a meal preference?"

Things are moving too fast. Why fly anywhere?

"My friend is a lawyer," I say. "You could courier the documents..."

Dupree sighs. "You think I wouldn't be doing that if it was a possibility? The marriage was in Nevada. California has different laws."

"I can't just drop everything." I step to one side to let a couple with a border collie pass by. "I have a job. Perhaps if I make some calls..."

"You've got a husband in the ICU." Carlton's breathing gets heavy and unsteady, like a hissing kettle set to boil over. "I'll take care of everything once you're here."

Heathrow is four hours away. Tomorrow is sports day at school, and I'm in charge of the stopwatch.

"Are there no flights out of Birmingham?" I say.

"Birmingham, Alabama?" He sounds surprised.

"Birmingham, England."

More clicks. "OK, so I can route you through Amsterdam in business-class, with lounge access. How does that work for you? Can you make a ten-thirty flight tomorrow morning?"

I scan nearby bridges and buildings for TV cameras, suspecting a prank. Any minute, some minor daytime presenter will leap out and yell "surprise".

"This is a joke, right?" I say. "Milly put you up to it."

He ignores me. "When you land in LA, look for a guy holding a board with your name. He'll bring you to the hotel."

My phone pings with an email containing ticket details. Business-class seats and an executive suite at the Beverly Hills Hotel.

In Hollywood.

———

Milly narrows her eyes. "You're married to Aaron Biedermeier, and he's in a coma?"

I nod. "This Dupree guy made it sound super urgent...like he could die any minute."

She's tapping at her phone, checking the story. "The coma part checks out. But I don't get why you need to be by his bedside. It's not like you stayed in touch."

"We're married."

Out loud, the phrase sounds dumb.

She folds her arms. "You can't drunk-marry anyone. Not even in Las Vegas. It's the same the world over. Both parties must be of sound mind and able to exercise free judgement."

A memory pops up. Of a hotel suite. Of some kid in another room. Bare-chested. Scared. Young.

"The woman at the wedding place said to go back the next day for our certificate," I say, recalling fuzzy details. "But my ticket was non-refundable, and I had to get to the airport. The guy...Biedermeier, I guess...he promised to sort everything out."

"Jesus." Milly slaps her palm on the counter. "All this time, you didn't think to check? You get how I'm a lawyer, right?"

I stare at the floor, face burning. "Isn't it like here where you get to divorce on the grounds of desertion? It's been six years."

"How would I know, Kyle? I trained in UK criminal law. You need to speak to an expert in what to do when some feckless twat gets wasted in Vegas and marries a total stranger." She pulls out her phone. "I have a girl-friend in San Francisco. Her boyfriend is a family lawyer."

Milly always comes through, no matter how deep I wade into crap. She once convinced a furious Italian chef that I was a rare cheese connoisseur after I called his lasagne greasy. After the place closed for the evening, we sat through a tense cheese-tasting in his overheated kitchen, with me praising the Gorgonzola like it was the holy grail.

"Biedermeier's guy booked me onto a flight, leaving tomorrow morning," I say.

She looks up. "Don't you have to work?"

"I was going to say I tested positive for COVID."

Milly's lips form a grim line. Her eyes narrow. "How do you plan on explaining to your mum why you're taking a change of clothes and that you might be gone a while?"

"Last-minute inset training?"

I shift, avoiding her glare. This is my chance to prove the school bullies wrong. Revenge for every poofter, fag or queer jibe.

"Is it wrong of me to want this? How often does a Hollywood director need you at their bedside?"

"What if all you get is hurt? Block the number. Move on with your life."

Coma or no coma, Aaron Biedermeier has connections, and when he wakes, who's to say he won't remember our wedding night? And then, we'll catch up, and I'll let slip about having acting experience, and he'll call in favours. Things will start small. A background role with no words. Or one line. A scene-stealing valet parking attendant who gets slapped by Julia Roberts. Milly waves a hand in front of my face.

"I got a text back from my friend with the lawyer boyfriend. He's going to call you tomorrow evening."

"Does he need the hotel phone number?"

She looks crestfallen. "So, you've decided?"

# 2

Our taxi joins a long line of cars waiting to offload passengers at the airport terminal. In front, two kids pull faces and blow kisses from the rear window of an oversized SUV. Milly's body language suggests there's something she's aching to get off her chest after sitting for half an hour, chewing her lower lip, staring through rain-spattered windows, and drumming purple-painted fingernails.

"At least they would have cancelled Sports Day," I say. "And look at those brats in front. I bet their parents lied to their school so they could get cheaper flights."

Milly clicks her tongue.

"I wish you were coming with me."

She grunts.

"Think of all the fun we'd have."

She stops drumming her nails and inspects her fingers. One by one. "Sure. I could sit by the pool like Billy-No-Mates while you flog your golly around film studios."

"That wouldn't happen."

Her brow furrows. "Come on, Kyle, what are the chances of this working out?"

I keep my voice even. "You'll need to be more specific."

Does she not see how huge this could be? Last night, I lay awake, telling myself nobody gets phone calls from people who work for Hollywood directors. This is fate. Playing it safe has got me nowhere. I had my perfect life mapped out. By 30, I planned on sharing a Farrow and Ball-painted Soho loft with my game-show-presenting husband and a golden Labrador called Ernie. In between Bafta-nominated dramas, my industry-leading agent would score me gigs narrating 'Book of the Week' on Radio Four.

"Let's say Biedermeier wakes from this coma," Milly says. "You're the first face he sees, and he begs you to star in his next film. What then?"

"I call around real estate agents, rent a place with a pool, and extend my stay."

Her shoulders drop. "You already plan on quitting your job?"

I've kept every option open with work, calling the head to say I tested positive for a new COVID variant that had scientists puzzled, stressing how it makes me super infectious, and the doctor was signing me off for days.

Milly's not done. "Let's suppose miracles happen, and you become a huge star and move to Hollywood. Where does that leave me?"

"I'd rent a condo with a spare room, and you can stay any time. I'd even remember to put the loo seat down."

Our taxi driver glances in his rearview mirror. The cars in front haven't moved in ten minutes. "Mate, I'd get out and walk if you want to make your flight."

I lean forward to open the door. Chinos crease, and there's every chance I'll look like a bag of washing before reaching LA as it is. It's still raining, but not so heavy that we'll be soaked, and I need a break from hearing about how I'm making a mistake. I hand the driver more money than his meter shows and open the door. Milly stays put, her lips forming a grim, defiant line.

"I guess I'll call when I reach the hotel," I say, patting pockets for my passport.

"Whatever."

I lean into the car. "You're going to abandon our friendship like this? The next time you see me, I might be on stage at an awards show, thanking Jesus and everyone who believed in me. Thanking you."

She stares straight ahead, pretending not to hear.

"What if I agree to buy coffee and doughnuts?"

Milly groans and climbs out of the cab while I mutter thanks to the God of sugar-coated, deep-fried dough.

---

Birmingham airport is noisy and stale with sweat. A disembodied voice details flight delays, causing groans from long lines of people trying to make sense of auto-mated check-in machines. I should be excited. In half a day, I'll be in Hollywood.

Milly takes my hand and drags me to the Business-

Class desk, where a woman with dyed blonde hair and piggy eyes looks me up and down.

"That's all your luggage?" Her voice has all the personality of a vanilla protein shake.

I'm a chronic over-packer, so cramming everything into one Fjällräven Kånken backpack had me on edge. Mum had to believe I was heading to Manchester for a teacher training course, not jetting to LA to be reunited with my comatose husband.

The check-in woman taps a keyboard. "Are you travelling alone?"

"Yes."

"Aisle or window?"

Milly answers for me. "He always sits by the window."

My theory is that if the plane loses one or more engines, I'll have time to scan the approaching ground below and plot a path to safety. And if we're likely to land in a jungle, I'll have scoped out who to eat when push came to shove.

As my boarding pass prints, a terrible thought makes itself known.

"Mum and Dad are my next of kin," I say. "Their names are in the back of my passport."

Milly stares like I spoke a foreign language. "And?"

"If the plane crashes, the police will contact them, and then they'll work out I lied about the training course in Manchester."

Her eyes roll. "Should the aircraft tumble from the skies, it'll be an orgy of twisted metal and burning flesh. Your passport will be at the bottom of the Atlantic."

I pull her close for a hug. "You say the nicest things."

Behind the counter, manicured nails tap a staccato beat on a grubby computer keyboard.

"Not so fast," the check-in dragon says as I bend to retrieve my bag. "You have an ESTA?"

My phone displays a permission to travel certificate, refreshed for what should have been a New York weekend with my now ex-boyfriend. Dave and I planned on ice skating at 30 Rock and a horse-drawn carriage ride through Central Park. I laughed when he told me the hotel refused to refund his deposit and hung up when he tried to make me pay half.

"Express security is at the top of the stairs." The dragon doesn't stifle a yawn. "Follow the yellow signs."

There's no queue at the first-class checkpoint. I could walk straight through, except reality has bitten, and I need to be sure this isn't my worst decision yet.

"Here we are, then," I say. "I'll call you as soon as I reach the hotel."

Milly glances at a screen. "You have two hours. Should we have that coffee?"

"Caffeine dehydrates your skin, and I have to look my best. There is a chance of press waiting at LAX."

She gives me her *get-over-yourself* face.

———

As we stand in line at the Red Rooster Roaster, I calculate how many calories there might be in a triple choc latte with whipped cream, and the number of star jumps I'll need to do in my hotel room tonight to work them off.

All-day breakfast detritus litters the coffee shop counter. What gene makes otherwise sane people abandon all reason in airports and spend eleven quid on reheated bacon sandwiches, which they eat without talking like it's their last meal?

It takes an age to get served, and then every table is taken, so we sit on the floor with our backs against a bookshop window.

"I still don't think you should be going," Milly says. "Not until you've checked this Carlton Dupree out."

"What did we agree on the day we got our A-level results?"

She wrinkles her nose. "That I should have offered Monsieur Leblanc a handy for a better grade at French?"

We were eighteen, with life stretching out ahead. Milly had an offer to study law in Leeds, and I was heading to a teacher training college. Although we'd be apart in term time, we had agreed to spend most weekends together. We celebrated our exam results with a Broad Street pub crawl that ended in A&E. I broke my wrist, and she cut her leg open after table dancing in a pub where nobody dances, let alone on tables. I'm still not sure there was even any music playing.

"Stop worrying," I say. "If nothing comes of this, I spend a few nights in the Beverly Hills Hotel. There's a chance I'll spot someone famous."

She puts down her coffee and stares straight ahead.

"Look," I say. "I know how you think this is a bad idea, and yeah, perhaps it's ridiculous to hope it leads anywhere, but I'm sick of floating along. How many more Hollywood directors am I going to marry?"

"Did you Google him?"

"Obvs. He's still cute. For an older guy."

She shifts awkwardly. "I don't mean, did you look at the photos? Did you read anything about him?"

"Such as?"

She taps at her phone and hands it to me.

### Teen Actor Dies After Vegas Trip

*Los Angeles—Tim Larson, a fifteen-year-old actor best known for his role in the hit teen drama 'Bright Futures,' was found dead in a Las Vegas alleyway over the weekend. The cause of death has not yet been determined.*

*Larson was in Las Vegas following CinemaCon. His mother, Jean Larson, says he was not known to use drugs or alcohol. "Tim was a good kid. We're shocked and heartbroken," she said in a statement.*

*Las Vegas police are investigating the circumstances of Larson's death, and autopsy results are pending. He had recently been cast in an upcoming Aaron Biedermeier movie. The director called his death "a tragic loss of an immense talent."*

"OK," I say. "So...that's sad, but how is this a red flag?"

She shows me another story. This time on a lurid gossip site with more pop-up banners than content. Another young actor claims Larson was a regular at LA pool parties. Parties where older men hung out with younger guys.

"It's not exactly The Guardian," I say, returning her phone. "And none of this mentions Biedermeier by name."

She holds up her phone again, but I wave it away.

"Stop trying to rain on my parade, Mil. I'm not about to be sold into slavery. I'm 28. Do you know what that is in gay years? As for whether this works out and somehow I talk my way into an audition, well, sure, you're right. It's a long shot, but can't you pretend to be excited for me?"

She turns off her phone. "I am. But there are all these things. Rumours. About Biedermeier."

"Exactly, Milly. Rumours. Gossip. The stuff he now can't deny because some thug put him in a coma. I don't need to hear what fame-hungry ghouls want to say about what he did or didn't do. Are any of those guys starring in his movies?"

She makes the signal of zipping her lips.

"I can look after myself," I say. "One ball gag, and I'm on the next flight home."

Milly gets up and goes to use the ladies. I wait until she's out of sight before pulling up the Larson story. I need to be sure of something. Just to set my mind at rest. In a photo, Larson is a bright-eyed, blonde kid, holding fingers to his temple in a mock salute. I pinch the screen and examine his face for any hint of a scar under his left eye. There's nothing. I scroll back up to check the date: April 10, 2016. I gave a best man speech on April 17, 2016.

We were in Vegas the night Tim Larson died. If

anything, that proves Aaron Biedermeier had nothing to do with what happened to this Larson kid. He was otherwise engaged. Marrying me.

Milly is back, complaining about wet toilet seats and a lack of hand wash. I give her one of my post-pandemic stockpiled bottles.

"I was with Biedermeier the night that kid died," I say. "If anything, I'm his alibi."

"Fine." She holds up surrender hands. "I was just looking out for you."

I pull her close for a hug and kiss the top of her head. The departure screens flash up a three-hour flight delay.

"What now?" I say. "Socks or perfume?"

This is what we do at airports. Milly and I reach past the most hostile shop assistant for the most expensive fragrance, douse ourselves, and when asked if we intend to buy anything, speak in a made-up language, often staging an argument between a fake man and a fake wife. One time, she forgot herself and slapped me. Hard.

"You've got access to the posh lounge. I don't want you to miss out on something somebody else is paying for, but if they have fancy magazines, grab me a copy of *Vanity Fair*. I forgot to renew my subscription. Just make sure nobody has already nicked the samples."

———

The seatbelt light pings twice, and the plane banks as the pilot's reassuring voice confirms it's eleven-thirty in Los Angeles. I've been in the air or on airport tarmac for twelve hours. My default setting of *Born Worrier* kicked in when my connecting flight left Amsterdam. Was Milly right? Is this a terrible idea? As exciting as business-class flights and a suite at the Beverly Hills Hotel sounds, there's no such thing as a free lunch. The man I drunk-married is in a coma, and I don't understand why anyone needs me by his side. Carlton Dupree didn't come across as the sort of guy who enjoys reuniting husbands.

I take out my phone. Despite garish airline leaflets boasting about how I'd never be 'out of touch' onboard, there's no signal, so I flag a passing steward. A Dutch air steward. Tall, blonde, and tanned with perfect teeth and cold blue eyes. He sighs when he sees it's me again—that annoying passenger in 3A who keeps wanting stuff.

I hold up my mobile. "This isn't working."

"Did you buy a voucher?"

"Is that a thing?"

With a tight smirk, he leans across the guy in 3B, who's been sleeping much of the flight. One tap at my seat-back screen and a form appears demanding credit card information.

"Business-class passengers have to pay?" I say, unsure if he heard me. "I only want to make one call."

"Complete your details and hit send. You'll see a passcode. Type that into your cell."

There's no way I'm forking over a ridiculous sum of money for one phone call. I thank the steward, but he doesn't move away and arches one plucked eyebrow. "What kind of card do you have?"

Red-faced, I fumble for my wallet. Did I leave it in my bag in the overhead locker? That means nudging Rip van

Winkle in 3B. He growled in my face when I asked to use the loo an hour ago.

"It can wait," I say.

The steward grins in a way that suggests he won this prissy stand-off.

As clouds part, Los Angeles shimmers below, and I shut my eyes, picturing my cramped childhood bedroom, the faded posters, and a ragged, stuffed animal Mum refuses to throw out and still positions on my pillow each morning after I leave for work. Teaching isn't where I thought I'd be by 28, but it brings familiarity. And sure, I hate the constant Education Authority inspections and orders from above about what to do if a kid has a bruise on his arm or decides he wants to be known as she, but those rare seconds when a spark of interest lights up a kid's face are what I live for.

Soon enough, I'll be in a limo heading for the Beverly Hills Hotel and able to make all the phone calls I want. Me. Kyle Macdonald. The guy, the Birmingham Evening Mail, described as a handsome aspiring actor. They sent a reporter to the school to cover the unveiling of a plaque for some bloke who designed a nearby clock tower. The reporter was cute, and we got talking. As he pulled on his jeans and called an Uber the following morning, he promised to put those exact words into his write-up.

It hits me. I have no friends in LA. Nobody to call if things go wrong. No safety net. I breathe deeply, in through the nose, out through the mouth, and tell myself this will be an experience. Despite a nagging fear that it's a colossal mistake.

"Your seat needs to be in the upright position." A

cloud of sweet aftershave signals that the snitty steward is back. "We've already begun our descent into Los Angeles."

My knuckles pale as I grip the armrests. When most people think about aviation disasters, they envision a plane plummeting from the sky and trailing smoke over an empty ocean. But I read once about how most accidents happen during take-off and landing, on account of how planes fly closer together. Especially at congested airports like LAX, where the chances of a collision more than double. And don't start me on overworked air traffic controllers, who could extinguish lives with one wrong call. A BBC documentary described the job as the most stressful in the world. Worse than keeping track of nuclear warhead codes. Guys blackout and forget where they are. The person guiding this aircraft to the runway could be staring at a blinking screen, unsure what to do or say next.

"Sir, your seat-back..."

I force my eyes open. "Sorry, I..."

He pouts and moves on through the cabin.

The guy in 3B belches himself awake, reminding everyone in nearby rows that he ate garlic chicken for his in-flight meal.

Jet engines roar, and there are too many bumps for my liking. Noises that sound a lot like a wheel breaking loose or something vital falling off. Both eyes stay shut as my ears pop and my stomach plummets.

"Welcome to Los Angeles," the captain chimes through the speakers. "It's 86 degrees and sunny. We should be at our gate in eleven quick minutes."

I rub clammy hands together. Passengers are already on their feet, rummaging in bulkhead storage. The air steward has a purple-faced fit, screaming over the PA about remaining in our seats until he says otherwise.

So here I am. Sweet dreams, my LAX.

———————

Fellow zombies squint at phone screens, pinging with *Welcome to the USA* text messages as automated voices drone that this is a non-smoking airport. We move as one, following the leader. Now and then, weaker herd members peel away for toilet breaks. Our herd merges with others, filling gaps in the formation and moving as one. The baggage reclaim area is like a Black Friday sale on wheels, with anxious faces scanning conveyor belts like they're waiting for the last chopper leaving 'Nam. My bright yellow backpack stands out, jammed between oversized silver cases.

A six-deep line for passport control snakes around an airless hall lit by harsh fluorescent tubes. Impatient security officers bark orders, itching to pounce on any wrong move. I'm photographed, fingerprinted, and treated like a criminal before being waved through a metal detector and sent on my way.

No matter how hard I try, in any airport, the second I come face-to-face with officialdom, everything about me screams international drug smuggler. I'm the guy you see being frog-marched into side rooms for a sadistic strip search. A gaggle of older women in nylon tracksuits power-walk for the exit, and I hide in their wake. An officer with grey hair and a calm demeanour waves us through.

Doors swish, and anxious faces crane for friends and family. I scan left and right for a smart-uniformed driver ready to whisk me away to the five-star glamour of the Beverly Hills Hotel. Tanned and toned, he'll address me as sir and insist on carrying my bag. There will almost certainly be a fridge in the back of the car, stocked with those tiny bottles of champagne you pay a tenner for at theatre interval bars.

Eager drivers hold up signs—a buffet of names, from Smith to Princess Sparkle Diva. A pale hippy with shoulder-length greasy hair holds a piece of torn cardboard with my name scribbled in Sharpie.

I hesitate. Perhaps another Kyle Macdonald just touched down. My actual chauffeur could be running late, and sent this guy to let me know. I hang back, making every kind of deal with every brand of God, but the hippy guy is still waiting.

We lock eyes, and I walk over, offering a handshake.

"I don't do skin-on-skin contact," he says with a sniff. "You might have dermatitis."

"Are you from Biedermeier Pictures?" I'm crossing my fingers he's been sent to meet and greet and show me to my limo—the one with the mini fridge and liveried chauffeur.

"Sure am. My brother does this run, but he bust his arm, so I offered to step in."

Questions flood my mind: is this stand-in guy insured? Is he driving his brother's car legally? If we have an accident, what happens? Should I call Dupree and insist on someone who looks less like he spent last night in a skip?

He's already taken my bag and is pushing through the waiting crowd.

Outside the terminal, cool, sanitised air turns hot and humid. The heavy scent of aviation fuel overlays a pungent tang of tarmac. It's all honking horns and the intermittent screams of jet engines. People drag luggage, and intercom announcements blur in a constant drone.

"Buddy. Over here."

I shade my eyes and see the guy with my bag waving from a concrete platform in the middle of three lanes of slow-moving cars. Next to a gleaming blue limo, he looks plain wrong. A traffic cop blows his whistle, jabbing an angry finger at a sign saying *LAX Shuttle Zone Only,* so I pick my way between vehicles. There is a fridge. But no champagne. I open a bottle of chilled water. The engine rumbles, and we pull away.

"Lunchtime traffic." Bloodshot eyes meet mine in the rearview mirror. "You picked a bad time to arrive, man."

I swallow every British urge to apologise as we join six-deep lines heading for the airport exit. Giant billboards advertise places to eat all you can, low-cost hotel rooms, movies you don't want to miss, half-price haircuts, teeth whitening, and facial fillers.

"I'm Mike," my driver says. "You in the business?"

"Not really."

"But Biedermeier is paying for this?"

Do I explain how six years ago, I got blind drunk and decided to marry a stranger I met in a Vegas casino, or lie about Aaron being a close family friend?

Mike holds up a finger to signal he's talking on his headset.

"Sure...doors to the kitchen. No problem."

When we stop at traffic lights, he half turns in his seat. "So then, Kyle Macdonald. You must be somebody. Sneaking in through the back entrance of the Pink Palace."

I fake a cheerful expression.

"I kinda think I recognise your face." He points to his head and screws up his eyes. "It's in here, somewhere."

Despite a blast of cold air, my face flushes. There's every chance he saw my career-defining 'man in crowd' in an early Harry Potter. I affected a limp until the director called cut and demanded I walk just like everyone else.

"You mind if I sleep?" I say. "It was a long flight."

Mike pushes a dashboard button, raising a bullet-proof glass screen.

The lights change, and narrow lanes give way to a wide boulevard lined with tall, skinny palms, car dealerships, strip malls, and apartment buildings. Horns honk whenever slow-moving buses nudge into traffic. The sun causes the road ahead to shimmer. There are more cars than I've ever seen in one place. Motorcyclists squeeze between, playing real-life Tetris.

I check my phone—still nothing.

———

"This is where we part company." Mike parks in a tree-shaded area. Somewhere, a radio plays soft rock. The engine ticks before falling silent, and he pops the door.

All the online photographs of the Beverly Hills Hotel feature a beaming doorman holding out his hand for luggage. We're outside a grimy loading bay.

"This is the right place?" I say, hoping he'll admit to a prank. The sort of joke every LA driver plays on every dumb English guy.

"Orders from Mr Dupree," Mike says. "Can't have the press knowing you're here."

The press? What have I gotten myself into?

"So...I go in through those doors?" I point to an entrance marked Staff Only.

"Someone will be there to meet you."

I ponder if being found dead in the basement of the Beverly Hills Hotel might one day inspire an award-winning true crime podcast or even a TV series. Who would they cast to play me? Hugh Grant is old, and Jackson Rathbone has too many teeth.

Mike skids away in a cloud of dust after I retrieve my bag.

"Pull yourself together," I mutter under my breath as I push a button marked ATTENTION near the doorway. "Aaron is a big deal. And if I am his husband, my profile has to stay low."

A silver-haired man in a dark suit appears.

"Mr Macdonald?" He speaks with a soft Scottish accent. "My name is Edward. I am the concierge. Follow me."

He leads me through winding corridors, past a

kitchen and a laundry, and to a door that opens onto an airy lobby where heavy-framed modern art hangs on pink-washed walls and opulent chandeliers swing, casting rainbows on the floor. Uniformed bellhops wait to whisk away bags, and well-dressed guests confer with receptionists behind a polished wooden counter.

This is the Beverly Hills Hotel I expected.

When we reach a heavy oak desk, Edward collects a room key. "You're in Suite 602. A bellboy will deliver your luggage."

I try acting unfazed, but only muster an awkward head bob.

The screen of my phone flashes a local number.

"Hey there." The voice is husky. "This is Kyle, right? I'm Bryn. Andrea said you needed help."

My mind is an exhausted, fuddled mess. "Andrea?"

"You know me better as the hot-shot lawyer guy."

There's a pause as I connect the dots. My body switched to reserve power an hour ago.

"Aaron Biedermeier is your husband?" Bryn says.

"That's what I've been told."

He whistles, and I can't decide if that's because he's impressed by my starfucker status or my apparent stupidity.

"We should meet this evening. I can do drinks at eight. What if I swing by your place about then?"

———

An enormous bed with a white comforter fills half of my executive suite. Yellow roses in a large vase sit on a mahogany dresser. Massive balcony doors reveal a panoramic cityscape view.

"You're not in Birmingham any more," I tell my reflection in a gold-framed bevelled mirror.

Cool, conditioned air caresses my face and hands as I sink into a soft suede couch, let out a slow breath, and tug my toes from a pair of Allbirds, resting my bare feet on a footstool.

This isn't my world, this larger-than-life place that performs 24/7. It's too perfect, too staged. And yet, wasn't it a dream of mine to one day be a part of this? As a kid, I spent Sunday afternoons at my Nan's house, glued to black and white classics as she slept off her lunch. I envied Rosalind Russell, Bette Davis and Leslie Caron their poise, grace and effortless charm, and would mimic every move and line.

"Kyle Macdonald, a tough old broad from Birmingham," I muse out loud.

I should be happy.

It takes six whole minutes to pin down how I actually feel.

Lonely.

Horribly, desperately lonely.

A foggy head refuses to settle on what time it might be back home, so calling Milly is out. Three in the afternoon here, and she's eight hours ahead. Nobody calls anyone after nine at night unless it's to say they're in hospital or police custody. My furred tongue touches my equally furred teeth, finding bumps and ridges. In the bathroom, I fill a glass with water. It smells of chlorine but goes down in one tall gulp.

What now?

I fire up Grindr, finding comfort in hot guys wearing tank tops and muscle shirts, showing off sculpted pecs and six-packs. Grindr LA, though, is different to Grindr back home. Everyone here is an actor-slash-model-slash-influencer. They post links to their showreel, and there's a preoccupation with body fat percentages. I have no idea how much of me is perma-lard, but suspect it doesn't come close to the local average of nine per cent.

Dupree's number rings three times before going to voicemail, and I'm about to leave a message when Grindr pings. A guy nearby wants to meet.

Pics?

He isn't up for small talk. This is online banter for *'show me your cock'.*

Hey there. New in town...

I type, hoping to engage. There's a lengthy pause, and I flip to his photo. Pale green eyes and golden-tanned skin. He's 28 and waits tables. Is into NSA. No Strings Action: Gay shorthand for *I have a dumb boyfriend/husband who believes me when I say I went shopping with friends, not screwing strangers.*

Does it make me a bad person to admit I'm tempted?

He posts again. This time with a filter-heavy shot of his arse and the kind of thing that passes for poetry on gay dating apps...

Fuck me, Daddy.

Daddy? How old does this guy think I am? Milly spent hours polishing my profile pic, adding filters, and airbrushing acne scars. I look hot. And I look young. I'm nobody's Daddy. My reply is polite.

No thanks.

His response is immediate.

Screw U

And then, just like a generation of baby gays before him, *NSA-28* does the right thing and blocks me.

Part of me is shaken, and part of me is wounded. I push my feet back into trainers and head for the door in search of affirmation.

Raucous laughter drifts over as I step from the lift and into the lobby. Tinkling piano music plays through hidden speakers, and the art on the walls screams money. I slow my pace and lift my chin, pushing back my shoulders to radiate confidence.

At the front desk, a receptionist smiles.

"I plan on exploring," I say. "Can you help me with that?"

"Of course." She reaches for a map and a visitor's guide. "What is it you're looking for?"

The obvious answer is someone who works for a movie studio, who'll take one look at my face and insist I sign a three-picture deal.

"Local colour?" I turn my answer into a question.

"O...K..." She draws out the word. "Hollywood is one of the leading tourist spots in the world, so we're kind of spoiled for choice."

"A bar?" I lean in. As if to share a scandalous secret. "A gay one, perhaps?"

She laughs. "Hot or divey?"

"Divey?"

The receptionist scribbles an address. "Go talk to Edward at the concierge desk. He'll fix you up with a ride."

———————

A chatty driver fires questions as we pull away from the hotel: Am I famous? Do I have an agent? Have I met the royal family?

"I'm a junior school teacher," I say, relying on a never-failed-me-yet conversation killer. "Nobody special."

With a roll of his shoulders, he turns on the radio, tuning in to a station playing country music. Just my luck. He's a whistler.

We take Santa Monica Boulevard, driving along endless tree-lined avenues past mismatched millionaire mansions with tended lawns, tall palms, and last-forever gardens. Cars the size of tanks move from lane to lane, some with windows rolled down and driven by identikit beautiful people with faces made of plastic. As we reach a *Welcome to West Hollywood* sign, the houses become apartment buildings sandwiched between offices and nightclubs. Giant billboards tower between swanky sex shops called names like The Blue Orchid and Hot Stuff Entertainment. 'Drug stores' hide behind shutters, and hustlers prowl the streets. A row of makeshift tents lines the pavement near an intersection—home to men and women literally living on the street. A man in a torn shirt screams at the sky. We pull away from the lights, and I spot my first rainbow flag above Garland's Bar. The part-shaded window promises *Boyz Boyz Boyz*.

"You sure this is where you want to be?" The driver squints.

"I'm positive."

Once through the door of Garland's, my eyes adjust.

A dusty mirror ball hangs from a tarnished chain above the dark wooden bar, which has a brass footrail and a mirrored shelf adorned with half-full bottles and framed photographs of Dusty Springfield and Liza Minnelli. Candles flicker in small, red sand-filled glasses. The kid serving has short, sun-bleached hair and a clean-shaven jaw. He wears a white cap backwards and a green apron. I order a beer, and he opens two bottles.

"It's happy hour."

The music is 80s-lite. Meat Loaf meets the Doobie Brothers. A perky, blonde newsreader is laughing with a perky, dark-haired newsreader on a muted TV above the bar. The sun ducks behind a cloud, plunging the bar into shade, just as Aaron's photograph appears on the screen. It's an old picture. He's handsome, tanned, and happy in his skin. The perky blonde does sad face, and my first thought is that Aaron died, and she's paying tribute. I ask the bartender to turn up the sound, and he reaches for a remote without looking away from his phone.

"The allegations date back six years, to when Eisenhart was just fifteen," the newsreader says. "Biedermeier is alleged to have cultivated a system in which young boys were brought to the director and his friends for what the actor's attorney calls sex parties."

"Asshole," the guy with the empty wine glass mutters. "Paedo asshole."

I take a slug of beer. I am married to a monster.

# 3

One minute, I'm an angel of mercy, dropping everything and lying to my parents to board a plane and sit vigil at the bedside of an unconscious husband. The next, I'm about to become the sort of guy who gets bundled out of buildings covered by a fleece blanket and surrounded by security while an overworked PA screams, 'no comment'.

The phone line crackles, but Milly doesn't speak. In under an hour, hot-shot lawyer Bryn is meeting me to talk about how to divorce my comatose husband, who may or may not be the gay Harvey Weinstein.

"Some of those kids were teenagers," I say. "That's sick."

"Did you ever think this might be some loser trying his luck because Biedermeier can't answer back? I looked Judah Eisenhart up online. He makes Andrew Tate look like a member of Mensa."

I'm on my feet, pacing. "What if they suspect I'm involved?"

Milly sighs. "Your honeymoon lasted six hours. He never stayed in touch. Did you speak to Andrea's boyfriend?"

"We're meeting for drinks."

"Make him talk to that creepy PA guy who gets paid squillions to eat whatever dirt his boss creates."

I know she's right, but anxiety still gnaws.

Milly seems to read my mind. "Take it one step at a time and try not to panic. I'm here if you need me."

After hanging up, I do what Milly more or less insisted and type Judah Eisenhart into a search engine.

He's a good-looking guy. Almost too perfect, like someone used an AI app and requested a bad-boy shirtless hunk with icy blue eyes. Tribal tattoos cover his arms and chest. Angel wings spread across his back.

Eisenhart was dropped by his management company and reduced to being a competitor on reality TV, where his status relied more on how much skin he showed than acting talent.

In the sidebar of a gossip website, a photograph of Aaron catches my eye.

**Biedermeier lawyer rejects abuse claims as allegations multiply.**

The lawyer acting for Hollywood movie mogul Aaron Biedermeier has rejected further claims of sexual abuse made against the 'Sudden Loss of Faith' director.

In a statement issued late last night, attorney Odell Haws dismissed the latest claim by reality star Judah

Eisenhart, calling it 'vicious, defamatory, and moti-
vated by greed'.

The rejection came after Eisenhart filed papers
claiming to have been abused on the set of the 2018
movie 'Crosstown Limits'.

Mr Biedermeier remains in a serious condition in
hospital following a vicious attack last weekend that
some claim to be related to the allegations.

—————

Bryn texts to apologise for running late. Traffic, he tells
me, is hellish. By the time reception calls to say he's here,
I'm climbing the walls.

In trainers, jeans, and a T-shirt, I don't fit in with the
gleaming polished marble floors and gleaming polished
hotel guests. The concierge asks if everything is to my
satisfaction.

"Everything is great," I say, and heat crawls up my
neck. Does he know who's paying for my room? Has he
heard the Eisenhart claims?

"You just call down and ask for Edward if that changes."

Of course, it's going to change. At some point, a
police car will arrive, and I'll be hauled away for questioning. They'll want to know if I had anything to do
with what the guy I drunk-married was doing right
before someone put him in a coma.

"Absolutely," I say, with yet another smile, and scan

for someone in a sober suit with slicked-back hair and no soul.

"Kyle?" I turn and see a *Men's Health* cover guy. All muscle, and looking like he could snap an iron rod with one hand. "I'm Bryn."

I sat through seven seasons of '*The Good Wife*', and not one of the lawyers in that show turned up for a meeting dressed in tight jeans and an even tighter white t-shirt. And yet, his imposing physical presence puts me at ease rather than on edge.

Bryn's handshake is firm. His grip is warm.

"This place is fancy." He gazes around at pink marble columns and high ceilings. "I drove by so many times. Always wanted to see inside."

Until two days ago, I, too, had dreamed of mixing with people who could afford rooms at swishy five-star Hollywood hotels. Be careful what you wish for.

He signals over to the hotel bar. "We should get a beer. I'm paying."

Bryn's stride is confident. Shoulders squared, head high. I fiddle with my untidy hair.

Like every part of the Pink Palace, the Polo Lounge is stunning, with a canopy of glass lampshades and a white marble countertop inlaid with a mosaic of brown malachite and onyx. Photographs of screen legends stare from lacquered frames. Amber-hued sconces bathe everything in a soft, flattering light. Bryn zeroes in on the one empty table and signals for two beers.

"It's so good of you to make time for me," I say. "Did Milly bring you up to speed?"

He pulls out his laptop but leaves the lid shut. "Eisenhart strikes me as a piece of work."

He keeps his voice low, not that anyone nearby cares. They're all too busy making sure they're seen. Cocktail glasses clink, and the laughter stays subdued.

"Someone at the LAPD owed me a favour," he says. "I downloaded a copy of Eisenhart's file. A couple of DUIs and a record of violence. Alcohol-related. One time, he wrecked a diner, but told the judge he was sorry and got off light. They made him pick up trash for a week. I guess money talks."

My head jerks. "I figured he must be broke."

Bryn leans back in his chair. "Family invested in oil. One thing you can never call the guy is cheap."

"Then why is he out there talking dirt about Biedermeier?"

"The dots don't connect for me, either. I want to say it's because he developed a conscience, but Judah's not that kinda guy. Maybe he's trying out for some new reality show and needs to create noise."

"By badmouthing someone in a coma?"

"Like I said, dude's a piece of work."

I'd been looking forward to meeting the friend of a friend who'd make everything right, but now I'm unsure. Can lawyers *be* super cute and have a killer instinct? It's difficult to picture him pacing around a courtroom, looking like a swimwear model, winning over the jury with hard-boiled anecdotes.

He leans back and surveys me, smiling. "You already checked Eisenhart out online?"

I blush. "I sort of felt I should."

"Did you also check out the pictures from back when he first hit town?"

Bryn taps at his phone. The guy in the photo he shows me is nothing like the ten-a-penny-tanned himbo currently raging against my comatose so-called husband. He's skinny, blonde, and slight.

And more than slightly familiar.

I pinch the screen to make the picture bigger. "I kind of think I recognise him."

Bryn's shoulders rise and fall. "My high school year-book has a hundred kids like him. People change. I was the original nerd who got sand kicked in his face." He takes a slug of his beer and leans in close. "Don't take this wrong, but why come here? To LA, I mean. We have this thing called the Internet these days."

How can I tell a stranger I jumped on a plane even though my best friend warned against it because I figured being married to a big-shot director might lead to a movie break?

Bryn flashes LA teeth. "I'm messing with you, Bro. If someone offered me a suite at the Beverly Hills, I sure as hell wouldn't refuse."

I glance once more at the photograph of young Judah. Pre-tattoos, pre-facial piercings. I know him. But how?

"OK," I say. "Million-dollar question. How easy is it to end my marriage? I haven't laid eyes on the guy in six years."

He shifts in his seat. "If either of you had stayed put in Nevada, we could apply for an annulment, but here in California, there's a four-year cut-off. That boat sailed."

"But I just have to sign papers, right? No big day in court."

The way Bryn leans back and lets his eyes soften suggests good news, and so I allow myself to relax.

He takes a breath and cracks his knuckles, not breaking eye contact. "First step, I fill out a bunch of forms and have someone serve them. We'll see if he responds."

I shift in my seat. "He's in a coma."

"Rich people appoint a power of attorney." Bryn drums on the table, making the beer bottles rattle. "The law gives whoever thirty days to put together a reply."

My stomach churns. I've already transformed a cocktail napkin into confetti. "Can't we ask a doctor to sign something and say he's unavailable?"

"That would be my next angle." Bryn's smile is back. "Tell whoever's in charge of his care to prepare a written statement and confirm the dude is not expected to regain consciousness any time soon." He spreads his fingers on the table, and I sense bad news. "None of this is going to move fast."

"OK." I force myself to stay calm. "How much is this going to cost me?"

He shrugs. "I was told my girlfriend owes your best friend some huge favour, so it's pro-bono."

"That means free, right?"

His lips curl into another smile. "I'm no angel, Kyle. There are all kinds of tax breaks and professional reasons for doing work for free. One way or another, I get paid."

I stare down at the floor. "When you say this isn't going to move fast..."

"We're talking several months. Could spin out to a year."

"I guess I'll go home then. Wait for news."

He looks less comfortable. "Some judges could see that as you choosing to walk out of the marriage. They might decide to award costs to Biedermeier."

"What the actual fuck?" I'm stunned. "I was off my tits in Vegas, and now a millionaire gets *me* to cover his legal bills?"

The room goes dark, and the walls move a little closer. The thought of being made to pay costs for a Hollywood director has me short of breath. There's no way Dupree will stump up for me to spend a year swanning around the Beverly Hills Hotel. My overdraft could just about cover a week in a Holiday Inn. A while longer in those pod places near the airport or some tumble-down motel on the far outskirts of town, maybe sharing with a guy who cooks meth.

"Dude." Bryn waves a hand in front of my face. "I'm giving you the worst possible. We gotta follow processes."

"Say Aaron wakes up. Say he agrees to the divorce. Can you file papers without me being here?"

"Sure..." His big smile returns. "We're talking a mutually agreed separation, and since his lawyers already have their hands full with Eisenhart, chances are they'll skip going to trial, but you never know."

My pulse gallops once more.

"Would it be OK if I signed something to indicate I don't *need* any of his money and this marriage was all a mistake?"

Bryn rocks his head from side to side. "I'll get a certified copy of your ID. That way, I can act on your behalf and countersign anything they send over. You might still need to have your day in court, but we'll deal with that further down the line. And if you do need to hang out here for a while, don't stress. We have a spare room at our place. I'll talk to Andrea about letting you stay over."

My tensed shoulders relax. I have an idea.

"We should speak with Noah Winters. Aaron got engaged. That has to prove he intended to divorce me."

Bryn puts his huge hand over mine and gives me a gentle squeeze. "Let's keep things simple. You drag Winters into this, and it gets complicated. Please. I know what I'm doing."

———

Back in my room, I do everything Bryn said to avoid and scan websites for photos of Judah. Don't let it bother you, Bryn said. Put it out of your mind. And I agreed, but...come on. He had to know...

Then I track down Tim Larson. He looks so young in the few online photos I find. Then Noah Winters. More than anything, I want to see how they might have looked six years ago. When I drunk-married Biedermeier.

There was a kid. In that Vegas suite.

What if I was the last person to see Tim Larson alive?

I keep searching.

Does Aaron Biedermeier have a nephew?

He doesn't.

Does Aaron Biedermeier have a son?

The Internet all but laughs at me. He doesn't.

So, who was that kid in the Vegas hotel?

I need air. The balcony doors slide open, revealing two wooden loungers and an ornate glass table. The Hollywood Hills lurk in the distance, dotted with movie star mansions. This time a week ago, I'd have given anything to be here.

The night we met, Aaron was drunk, too. I was watching someone lose all their money at a card table, and we laughed about how the casino was rigged. The spark was instant, and we spent the whole evening together, and, at some point, we must have dared each other to get married. Vegas is dotted with wedding chapels. Afterwards, he invited me back to his room. And I went. Because he told me he had coke. And I'd never actually tried it. A guy was serving drinks, and that kid was in the hallway. I try so hard to remember anything about his face while staring at shots of Larson. It wasn't him.

The sun sinks behind trees, turning the sky pink and wispy clouds orange. Birds take flight, and cicadas shriek. My body aches with exhaustion, my stomach rumbling, not knowing if it wants dinner or breakfast. I'm trapped and married to a stranger. A man I can't divorce unless he wakes from a coma.

He might never.

And if he does, what if he's suffered brain damage,

necessitating round-the-clock care? As his legal next of kin, a court might order me to become his keeper. It's not in me to wipe someone's bottom or spoon mush into feeding tubes. Milly's sister has a podgy but cute two-year-old. The one, and so far only, time we agreed to babysit, he held out cute podgy hands for *Spicy Giuseppe* pizza, and then, midway through '*I'm a Celebrity*', the kid erupted from both ends. I panicked and mainlined her sister's artisan gin while Milly ran a tepid bath and decimated a Kai Body Buffer.

Aaron is rich. Biedermeier Pictures racks up hit after hit. He can afford trained medical staff. I'm worrying about nothing. Right?

But if he's guilty of half the things Eisenhart claims, what then? A judge might freeze his bank accounts, and what's to stop the people with power at his studio from throwing me under a bus?

A phone rings, and I scramble back inside.

"Hey Kyle, how's LA treating you?" It's Dupree, his voice slick with fake Hollywood smarm. "I thought we might meet. Perhaps for dinner?"

His tone suggests the invitation isn't optional.

"Sounds fantastic," I say, determined to keep my tone friendly.

"There's this place I know. Rooftop views, great wine, food to die for."

"Works for me. How do I dress?"

There's a knock at the door, and I call out to wait.

"You should get that," Dupree says. "It's my answer to your question."

I'm waiting in the hotel lobby, ill at ease in an electric blue Italian suit tailored to perfection and delivered to my room by a porter. How did Biedermeier's PA know my size? Did driver Mike take pictures?

Expensive perfume mingles with the aroma of fresh flowers arranged in ornate vases, and I scan for my dinner date. In my head, Dupree is a Wall Street banker type. Or a lawyer. The kind of man who power-dresses to get whatever they decide to want.

A guy is pacing by the entrance. He's tall and skinny, pasty and cadaverous, wearing ratty jeans, a white polo shirt, black penny loafers, and an oversized gold watch with a thick band that glitters in the light.

My phone rings. It's Dupree. "I'm downstairs. Where are you?"

Our eyes meet, and I hang up.

"Kyle?" We shake hands, and his grip is firm. This is a man who is used to being in control. "Welcome to LA."

I rekindle a smile and mumble thanks, telling him the room is lovely and offering to pay for dinner. God knows why. My idea of splashing out is a Charlie Bigham Ready Meal.

He steers me towards a row of doors and into the humid evening air, where a black limo awaits. He climbs in, leaving the door open for me to follow. I glance back into the lobby, hoping someone remembers seeing this scene when I'm reported missing. Not that anyone will miss me. Mum and Dad think I took a train to

Manchester, and Milly will assume I'm sleeping my way through Southern California.

The limo door closes with a soft click as locks engage.

Dupree fixes me with a thin smile that never quite reaches lukewarm. "Tell me more about your crib."

"My crib?"

He laughs like he made the best joke ever. "Your room, dude. I keep forgetting you're not from around here."

"Oh," I say, remembering my manners. "It's great. You've been so generous."

---

We're shown to a quiet table in a dimly lit part of a high-end eatery perched atop a glass-and-chrome tower. Los Angeles sprawls out below, a network of lights and still-gridlocked traffic. Subtle hints of grilled meats and exotic spices waft from an open kitchen. Piano music plays, and clinking glasses punctuate carefree chatter. The waiter appears, ready to take my order, and I stumble over the unfamiliar menu.

"How is Aaron?" I'm determined to make conversation. And given that this is all we have in common, the question works.

Dupree raises an eyebrow, a smug little smirk playing on his lips as he swirls sparkling water in his glass. "I believe the term they use at the hospital is *'comfortable.'*"

I fiddle with a napkin. "So, there's been no change in his condition?"

"Dude's still in a coma, if that's your question?"

I bite the inside of my cheek. Uncomfortable subjects are not my strong suit. The one time Dave took me to meet his parents, I nodded and smiled as his mother talked about how wonderful it was that they'd found a cure for AIDS.

Dupree reaches for a water pitcher and refills his glass, leaving mine empty.

"Kyle..." He's picking his words with care. "I know you must think I'm some heartless Hollywood droid. But keeping the studio running and protecting Aaron's reputation—well, it takes a toll. I can't remember the last time I slept through the night."

I try for a smile. He's being upfront with me. I should reciprocate. "I guess you must get how this has all been a lot for me to take in. I'm a teacher. In Birmingham. A couple of days ago, I had no idea..."

He half-smiles again. "Hopefully, I can help keep everything painless."

"My lawyer says..."

Dupree raises a hand, cutting me off. "You engaged an attorney?"

"He's more of a friend of a friend."

"Biedermeier Pictures has the best legal team in town. If you have any worries or concerns, let me connect you with one of our guys."

I avoid his gaze. "No, no, I'm not worried. I already talked to Bryn, and..."

His brow furrows as much as Botox allows. "You're a smart young man. I see that. Send me this dude's details, and we'll ensure any paperwork finds its way to him."

Our starters arrive. "There's no rush. Tomorrow will be just fine."

Dinner remains awkward. For his part, Dupree plays the consummate host, even though his good humour is patently fake, his laughter too ready, and each anecdote over-rehearsed.

The need to shut my eyes and sleep forever hits like a truck, and I decline dessert, having left almost all of my main, but Dupree insists on coffee. He's determined to prolong the evening.

"We should enjoy this view." His voice sounds softer than before. "I apologise if I was snappy when we met. I've had a crappy day with people wanting impossible things from me. Producers keep calling, demanding guarantees for when Aaron will be able to work."

I stay quiet.

"It's tough on everyone," he says, and sincerity reaches his eyes. "The stuff that went down. Believe me when I tell you, I genuinely want to help make matters as easy as possible. It's not like I was Aaron's bodyguard. I couldn't tell him what to do. So...you know...I suppose when the hospital told me they'd found your name in his medical records."

I stare. "You didn't know?"

Dupree holds up his hands. "What happens in Vegas..."

Now I know he's shitting me. Aaron Biedermeier got drunk and came back with some strange guy to a hotel room, claiming to be married. There were other people there. The guy serving drinks. The men in the other room.

"My sister was sick," Dupree says. "The weekend you met Aaron, I had to skip the Expo."

"And he never told you about me?"

He sighs. "Aaron had a reputation. I'd have been more surprised to hear he spent his time there alone."

"And my name was in his medical records?"

Dupree narrows his eyes. "I don't know how it works where you come from, but when you marry someone, it triggers a whole bunch of admin. Names get added to files."

"But you didn't know about me?"

"I'm the guy's PA, not his fucking geriatrician. I fix meetings. I book hotel rooms. Nobody keeps me posted on the condition of his urinary tract."

There's an authenticity in his voice that I can't ignore, and I find myself nodding. "This whole situation is kinda surreal for me too. I mean, marrying a stranger in Vegas was never on my bucket list."

He gives me a half-smile, enough to signal he gets it.

"I know this is messed up," I continue, "but if you're genuine about making things easier, then I'll do whatever you need me to do."

He sighs once more. "The legal system here can be slow. Attorneys are paid by the nanosecond."

I draw on my strength to let my face brighten. "What are we talking...a week?"

He reaches for my hand. His skin is unnervingly cold. "We could be talking a while longer. But hey, don't stress how much it costs for a room at the Beverly Hills Hotel. The studio will cover everything. Aaron would want it that way."

I feel obliged to nod. Even though I don't know the guy.

Dupree stares through the window at the sprawling city below. "All the same, you must have work commitments, family, and a life back home. Perhaps we could expedite things. But only if you're comfortable with what I'm going to suggest."

I nod, cautious of any trap being set.

"One thing I can promise you is there will be paperwork. Forms to sign. Affidavits. You know the shit."

I nod again.

"And everything you sign gets countersigned. The court needs proof you're who you claim to be."

I say nothing. My head is spinning. This already sounds bad.

"When I say this might take a while...it all hangs on how long Aaron is sick. He could wake up tomorrow..." Dupree's eyes meet mine. "Or never."

"So I could fly home and come back when he's awake?"

He weighs my words. "We get this a lot. Movie stars don't like to be tied down. In between projects, they take long vacations. Far away from this town. But the paperwork never takes a vacation. Contracts still need to be signed. Release forms. You name it..."

"How does any of this matter to me?"

"We employ a legal team. I can have them take a copy of your passport and send it to the nearest British Embassy. It comes back stamped, and the legal team gets to sign anything that comes your way." He holds up a hand. "I'd still run everything by you."

"Can't I get a lawyer back home to do that?"

He chews his lower lip. "You know someone back there who's familiar with California family law?"

My mind is a mess. "How long would this thing with the embassy all take?"

"Normally, we'd be looking at a week or two. But a guy there owes me a favour."

"And I'd get my passport back right away?"

"Kyle, I don't want to pressure you into anything. If you'd rather wait, the team will ensure you're looked after for however many weeks or months it takes."

For one beautiful moment, fate looks to be throwing me a lifeline. A chance to escape this make-believe land and return to being Kyle Macdonald: primary school teacher and occasional bit-part actor. And Bryn mentioned certification too, so it must be a thing.

"I understand if you're uncomfortable letting me have your passport overnight," Dupree says. "We only just met. Like everything else in this process, the decision sits in your hands. If I put it in front of Legal tomorrow, you'll be good to go by mid-morning. We'll book you a flight home tomorrow evening. Unless you want to hang out and see the sights, I'm more than happy to fix up a studio tour."

A voice in my head screams, no. Don't trust this man.

"I need to talk to my lawyer," I say.

Dupree's smile fades for one brief second, then bumps back up to full power. "Sure. The friend of a friend, right?"

"It's not that I don't trust you."

His lips curl. "We have an entire team of guys with

Harvard degrees. But sure, you'd sooner get your advice in exchange for the cost of a beer. Makes total sense. But, Kyle, why would it serve either of us to start bullshitting? Aaron has a reputation in this town."

Now would be as good a time as any to argue that his reputation seems to be tied to abusing young male actors.

"So?" Dupree glances around for a waiter so he can pay. "Are we on?"

"Yeah...I guess...sure..."

He smiles, and this time it's genuine. "Kyle. You're being way too British. Way too polite. Tell me to go screw myself if you don't want to do this. I'm rushing you. Call me in the morning and let me know. You're welcome to run shit past your Howdy Doody lawyer or even spend time with our fully qualified legal team." He snorts. "I'd be insulted if you didn't want to check me out. I got a reputation for being a total slimeball. I'd hate to think I was losing my touch."

It's my turn to smile. "I would like to sleep on it."

He signs a slip to pay for our meal. "We can talk more in the morning."

———

My hands tremble as I struggle to unlock my hotel room. I'm so tired. I could pass out. Dupree was charm personified, but doubt took over on the ride across town.

Twice, I drop my room key, swearing out loud, and across the way, a door opens. A middle-aged woman asks if everything is OK.

"Everything is fine," I say. "Just can't get this card to work."

She rolls her eyes. "So much for technology. This might sound wild, but rub it on your pants. I had the same thing happen. It's static electricity or something."

I try, and the LED on the handle turns green.

"Thanks," I say over my shoulder and step into the darkness, feeling for a light switch, before slipping off my borrowed suit and shoes and tiptoeing to the balcony to breathe in an evening breeze. Neon lights from distant billboards pierce a canopy of trees, the dancing dots of red and yellow like fireflies. I need someone to tell me what to do.

Back inside, I throw myself on the bed and lie still, staring at the ceiling, before closing my eyes to focus on the texture of crisp white sheets, shutting out a whirlwind blowing through my mind.

Where lies sleep?

A half-hour passes. It's midnight—the cusp of a new day at home. I reach for my phone.

"This had better be you telling me you met Henry Cavill," Milly says when she picks up my call. "I need to hear how you showed him my photograph, and he's boarding a flight right now."

She sounds to be on her way to the office. Car horns sound over the constant beep of crossing signals, making me ache for home.

"Henry Cavill is mine." I force a laugh.

"Are you OK? Did something happen?"

"Actually, yeah. Something did."

I explain Dupree's proposition.

"He wants you to hand over your passport." Her voice turns stern.

"It's a thing, though, right? Certification?"

She exhales. "We do it, yeah, but not for anything big like a divorce. But...what do I know? Maybe it's different there. That passport is proof of your nationality and legal status, and if you hand it over to someone you only just met..."

She leaves it hanging—the line crackles.

"They have a whole legal team. It's not like some shady guy from a back street bar."

"Fine...but do you trust everyone else who may gain access to that copy of your passport? Dupree's office, the courier service, and some intern who collects the dry cleaning."

I get how it's Milly's job to see the worst in people. But she hasn't met Dupree, and while everyone in this town is likely out for themselves, he stepped back when he saw how I was feeling pressured.

"So, what should I do?"

"Is there an option to verify your identity through a video call? We do that all the time."

A faint scratching at the door interrupts.

"Hang on." I shift from the bed. "There's someone at the door."

A small, white envelope skims along the polished floor, and my fingers tremble as I tear it open and pull out a handwritten note with a scrawled phone number.

I tell Milly. She laughs. "What if some hunk saw you checking in and wanted to sweep you off your feet?"

"You think?"

"Bugger me, Kyle," she huffs. "Do something about the size of your ego."

"What are you saying? Call the number. Don't call the number."

"You're going to call it no matter what I say. Just text me when you're done."

She's right. Of course, she is. But that doesn't stop me from pacing the room, my mind on double speed. Who could it be? What do they want? When I summon the courage to try, a male voice answers, sounding cautious and familiar.

"Who is this?" I say.

There's a pause.

"Noah Winters. I'm the dude who's engaged to your husband."

# 4

The morning sun streams through the windows of the hotel breakfast bar, where quiet chatter and the clink of silverware on china fill the air. I climb onto a high stool at the bar and signal for coffee. The guy beside me puts down his fork and gets to his feet, leaving behind a copy of the LA Times. A photograph of Aaron stares out at me beside a litany of fresh allegations courtesy of Judah Eisenhart. I read about parties where up-and-coming Hollywood starlets mingled with older studio executives, drinking the best champagne and snorting lines of coke from silver trays.

Aaron's way-back-then face makes me think again about Vegas. Foggy memories haunt me of that young guy, bare-chested and defiant, meeting my gaze, scared, and yet refusing to flinch. Sour bile rises into my throat, and I climb from my stool, swallowing and trying to walk in a straight line until I reach the hotel lobby, where the constant in-house scent of vanilla turns my stomach.

And then things move fast.

Superfast.

I stumble as my fist slams open the bathroom door, and I dive into an empty stall, falling to my knees to lean over the toilet bowl.

Coffee burns my throat, somehow making its way down my nose and causing my eyes to sting. Slumped with one ear pressed against polished wood, I catch my breath and focus on the marble floor.

When I'm sure it's safe to move, I haul myself up and stagger to a wall of mirrors. A sheen of sweat covers my forehead, and I reach for a soft hand towel, running it under the tap.

A voice startles me.

"Hey, buddy...are you okay?"

"Yeah, I'm fine." It comes out husky. "Must have eaten something."

The guy asking is short, stocky, and dressed like he plans a day on the golf course. He washes his hands, and I feel his eyes on me.

"I *am* OK," I say. "But thanks for asking."

Dupree messaged early to say a car would be waiting outside to bring me to the hospital. He figured I might like to see my husband.

I can't think of anything I'd rather do less.

———

Mike is my driver again today; if anything, he looks to have had a worse start to the day than me. His eyes are bloodshot, and he stinks of booze.

"Are you okay to drive?" I ask, trying to keep my voice steady.

He grunts in response and rolls a cigarette as I climb into the backseat, stroking the soft leather.

An already blazing sun scorches the streets, and gridlocked traffic becomes an all-out skirmish with blaring car horns. The limo air-conditioning can't prevent a bead of sweat from trickling down my back. I check my face in Mike's rearview mirror and pluck a tissue from a seatback dispenser.

"You plan on talking to Mr Biedermeier today?" he says. "You know, doctors reckon people in comas can hear everything going on around them. After a car hit my aunt, she spent ten days unconscious. When she came around, she got real pissy about how she heard my sister say she wanted the jewellery."

I feign interest. "I guess that got awkward."

Mike shrugs. "Not so much. Bitch died a week later."

I will him to push the button that separates us with a screen. What if Aaron wakes when he hears my voice? I don't want the first person he sees to be an estranged husband who looks like he's been boil-washed.

Mike turns down the constant yammer of talk radio. "We could take a diversion."

Although I've been taught never to judge a book by its cover, everything about the guy is sketchy. I figure his kind of shortcuts would skim the worst parts of town.

"The regular route is fine. There's no rush. It's not like Aaron is going anywhere."

The engine roars as he presses the accelerator. "If we run the lights at Wilshire..."

I take a deep breath. "Please. No running lights."

Mike's shoulders rise and fall like I've spoiled the one good bit of his hungover day. "Whatever you say."

I ease back into my seat and fan myself with a folded magazine. For a while, we don't talk. I shut my eyes and try breathing exercises, but when I open them, he's staring at me in the rearview mirror.

"I must have stood in for my brother and driven Mr Biedermeier a dozen times. Never gave me a single cause for concern. You ask me. He's one of the good guys." We inch past a Lincoln, taking two lanes. "That punk Eisenhart is talking crap. I mean, come on...Mr Biedermeier is engaged. Noah Winters is cool."

My stomach turns over. I get how people invent stuff about the rich and famous. To settle scores. For attention. For money. But this isn't some online spat. It's on the BBC website, with an interview.

Mike re-tunes the radio, moving from all-talk to music. The warm notes of Joni Mitchell's 'Big Yellow Taxi' fill the car; guitar chords are picked out in clusters of three, like soft rain on a tin roof. She sings about fading optimism and life consumed by the city. A prayer that everything would one day be as it was, of taking what is good and leaving behind what is bad.

"Best thing ever written," he says as our luck changes, hitting green light after green light. "I got a live version from the Fillmore. It made me decide to learn how to play a five-string."

We don't speak for a while, but his eyes meet mine in the mirror.

"You think Judah Eisenhart is lying?" I say. "Wouldn't that screw up his career?"

Mike snorts. "My brother used to drive the kid around too. Nice as pie one minute, but he turned on a dime."

We slow to a crawl outside a massive building with mirrored walls hung on monolithic concrete blocks. Expensive sports cars and black SUVs gather in a tree-lined car park. Uniformed guards wave people past.

Mike pulls over and ambles around to let me out, standing back, both hands shoved in his greasy grey jeans pockets, and gazing up at the hospital building.

"Mr Biedermeier is in the best place right now."

I mumble agreement, though I've no idea why.

He pats my shoulder. "There's a whole bunch of people helping him. Let them do their jobs."

Biting my lip, I head inside.

———

Whether run on a shoestring or funded by new money, hospitals always stink of the same cleaning products. The Cedars Sinai is vast and airy and painted an inoffensive shade of taupe. Joyful water bubbles from a fountain surrounded by actual trees in terracotta pots. Fluorescent lights hum. Voices and footsteps echo.

When I tell the woman at the Welcome Desk who I'm here to see, her expression darkens, and she indicates a row of empty seats, promising a doctor will come find me.

The hospital is busy, with people coming and going,

phones ringing, and medics hurrying to their next call. I should have brought a book to read or headphones for music.

"Kyle?"

I look up.

"Kyle Macdonald?"

I shake hands with a small man, perhaps a year or two younger than my dad. He's wearing a starched white lab coat over pale blue scrubs, and his brown hair, speckled grey, like his thin moustache, pokes out from under a paper cap.

"Dr Gupta. I'm in charge of Aaron Biedermeier's care."

He steers me through a maze of corridors and into an anonymous room with a long pine table surrounded by grey office chairs. Empty paper cups and scattered pastry flakes suggest a recent meeting took place. Official-looking papers sit in two piles. One stack of uniform, crisp sheets of A4. The other is an assortment of photo-copies and handwritten notes, with creased corners and dates circled in red ink.

"Make yourself comfortable," Gupta says. "I under-stand you've had quite the journey."

He seems kind. Crows' feet crinkle shining eyes, and I'm about to ask about Aaron's progress when there's a knock at the door. It's Dupree, his jaw set in a hard line. Gone is the solicitous guy who paid for dinner last night. The guy who made it his job to help me get home fast. Today, he barely registers my presence.

"Good morning," the doctor says. "I wasn't aware you'd be joining us."

Dupree grunts, pulls out a chair, and starts tapping his phone, a thundercloud brewing in his eyes.

"I was about to provide an update on Mr Biedermeier. So your timing couldn't be better."

He might as well be talking to a brick wall. Dupree doesn't answer. The doctor glances at me, and I signal to continue.

"So it's been six days, and we haven't seen any significant improvement," Gupta says, "but neither has there been a deterioration."

Dupree places his phone on the table. He looks at me. "Do you have your passport?"

Colour rises in my cheeks. "I didn't think we were doing that here."

He casts a skyward glance. "You said you wanted to go home."

"I didn't talk to my lawyer yet."

He stares. Unblinking. "So you got money to burn?"

I'm not sure what point he's trying to make, and I shake my head. "I just thought..."

He cuts me off. "When was the last time you saw an attorney behind the wheel of a low-end Toyota? They leave the clock running when they take a piss. You pay while they use the bathroom."

"Bryn is a friend."

"The guy's working for free? You got that in writing?"

My insides are tense. Bryn said this was all pro-bono. A favour to his girlfriend...as a favour to Milly. But what if there are limits?

"Kyle, let me give you something gratis. A bit of advice. There is no charge whatsoever. You ever hear the expression, '*There's no such thing as a free lunch?*'" I nod. "Corny as Kellogg's, right? But people say it. Because it's true."

I glance at the doctor, wanting him to step in and say how hospitals aren't the place to talk money. Except this is America, and hospitals thrive on money. Right now, Gupta stares past me through a window, looking out onto the street and a billboard advertising great rates for car finance.

"Perhaps we can head to your office after I visit with Aaron?" I say, playing for time. If I can call Bryn and run him through what's happening, he'll tell me what to do. And while I'm on, double-check that there won't be any unexpected bills.

Gupta clears his throat. "We should talk about Mr Biedermeier's ongoing treatment."

Dupree doesn't bother stifling a yawn. "Strikes me, there's nothing to discuss. Biedermeier is a vegetable until further notice, and I need this gold-digging faggot to let me do my job."

The room falls silent. Hear a pin drop silent. Last night, Carlton Dupree was a gracious host, at pains to suggest ways to make my life easier. Now I'm a *gold-digging faggot*?

Gupta forces his best professional smile. "Mr Biedermeier was placed on antibiotics, but we discontinued them this morning. Any infection has cleared."

Dupree pushes back his chair, causing it to smack up against a glass wall. He pokes a bony finger at Gupta. "Am I correct in thinking you head this hospital's committee overseeing charitable grants? And that

Biedermeier Pictures is one of the more generous donors?"

Doors open on the other side of the glass wall, and a bunch of guys with cameras and recording equipment start setting up equipment.

"The press," Dupree says as his phone dings. "I figured we should issue a statement about the crap Judah Eisenhart is sharing with every low-rent website."

I'm stunned. Nobody said anything about me talking to reporters.

"You want me to say something?" I'm stunned.

Dupree's look is withering. "We already ran something through Legal. You get why we need to do this?"

When I say nothing, he continues.

"They're calling your husband *Har-Gay Weinstein*, and all because some talentless cocksucker wants five more minutes of fame." He takes a sheet of paper from one of the piles on the table and slides it my way. "You just need to read this out. Stick to the script. Anyone who asks questions, let me speak."

I scan the page. "Why am I talking about Tim Larson?"

Dupree's fingers tap an irregular rhythm on the table, his gaze darting. "Just read the words as written."

A cold shiver settles like an uneasy knot in my stomach. My hands tremble, and I catch Gupta's gaze, sharp and probing, as he slides a carafe of cucumber water my way.

"There's no way I can say any of this."

Dupree groans in frustration. "Jesus Christ. We paid Eisenhart to shut his mouth. And now, the cops are talking about reopening the Larson case. Do you remember what happened there? You remember when? You remember where? Of course, you do. You were there too."

I jump to my feet. Trying to breathe. Air isn't getting through.

"I got wasted in Vegas and married a stranger."

He nods and smiles. "Spot on dude. It's Romeo and Juliet. Stick to your story, and everything stays hunky dory."

"It's not a story," I say. "It's true."

I stare at the statement. *'Tim Larson was not in Aaron's suite at Caesar's Palace. I've never met the guy, although I extend my sympathies to his family. To have his name dragged through the mud by Judah Eisenhart is disgraceful.'*

The press conference area is already rammed.

"There was a kid," I say. "In some other room."

Dupree glances at the doctor, who sighs and gets to his feet, going to wait in the corridor, pulling the door shut behind him.

Only when he's sure we can't be heard does Dupree lean in, his face against mine.

"You need me," he says. "You need my help to dig you out of this shit pit. The cops have CCTV footage. They have Larson arriving at Caesars right before you and Aaron."

"What does that prove?"

"It proves you were in the wrong place at the wrong time. I have to say, you look kind of wasted in the footage I watched. Like you took something. You acted edgy."

Heat rises through me.

"Eisenhart is out to extort money. He called last night and named his price. You get how Aaron is in no position to defend himself or you."

I stare down at the statement. "Was Larson in that hotel room?"

Dupree fidgets and tugs at the collar of his shirt. "It was CinemaCon. Half of Hollywood was in Vegas. Aaron liked to invite people in the industry to his suite for drinks. He had the best room in the house. Of course, he wanted to show off. Maybe Larson...I don't know. Perhaps he tagged along."

He shrugs like this is explanation enough, but I'm not done. "Were you there?"

Dupree sighs. "Look, Kyle, right now, I'm offering you a way to get out of whatever shitstorm Eisenhart plans on launching. Go out there. Read these words. Walk away."

Gupta taps and opens the door. "Gentlemen. I'm a busy man. Mr Biedermeier is only one of my patients. Please agree among yourselves who wants to see him. And for the love of all that is holy...I want all those press people out of my hospital."

Dupree fixes me with a stare. "Did you bring your passport?"

As I reach into my bag, I hear Milly screaming, no. But she's not miles from home in a weird ass meeting with a guy warning me the cops are studying CCTV. She wasn't in the wrong place at the wrong time.

"Tim was in that hotel room," I say as I hand over my passport. "I'm right, aren't I?"

Dupree smiles. "Your faith in me means a great deal."

After he's gone, I turn to Dr Gupta. "Did I just do the most stupid thing ever?"

———

Gupta leans in to squint as he punches numbers into a keypad outside an anonymous, pale pine door. It clicks open, and he steps aside. The curtains near the bed are drawn, and a diffuser sprays orange blossom as if trying to fool my brain into forgetting this is a hospital room. A state-of-the-art entertainment system sits unused next to a well-stocked fridge. There's a plush couch, armchairs, and a glass coffee table with an untouched fruit bowl.

And the constant rhythmic click of machines keeping Aaron alive.

My nan died when I was six, and my grandad insisted on an open coffin. Mum said I didn't have to see her, but something made me go into the sitting room. I wanted to know if she still looked like my Nan. She was wearing a blue dress I remembered seeing at Christmas, and they'd done her make-up and combed her hair. I touched her ice-cold hand and yelped.

Aaron has the same not-really-there thing going on. His cheekbones jut out sharp and high, and his skin appears dewy and tanned. I lean in closer. This man is my husband.

Gupta mumbles something about privacy and steps out.

I pull over a chair, setting it next to the bed.

"Hey there." My voice is shaky. "I guess Siri forgot to

remind you about the annulment?" I check for the slightest flicker he might have heard. "I came here thinking your name was worth dropping to jump the line at auditions. Can you believe that? I'm that shallow. That deluded."

I get up and pull back the curtains. His room faces the hills.

"You have a lovely view. Shame you're not making the most of the facilities."

I go over to a fridge stocked with vintage Champagne, primed for impromptu drinks should his eyes open around wine o'clock.

"You couldn't keep a simple promise. I've been dragged into whatever you stirred up, and I don't deserve any of this. All I did was get drunk in a casino on a stag weekend. People do stupid shit like that in Vegas."

Did one of Aaron's eyebrows twitch? I'm not close enough to be sure.

"Guess who's meeting me after this?" I sit beside his bed, leaning close so the machine regulating his breathing can't drown me out. He needs to hear this. "Noah Winters. Your Noah. We're having coffee and getting to know each other."

I swear his lips turn down.

And now I'm angry.

"Did you do what Eisenhart claims?" I rub my temples. "Are you the sick pervert they're all saying?"

The room stays silent except for the rhythmic beeps, clicks, and laboured breathing. I shift in my seat and signal to Gupta that I've said what I came to say, and he opens the door, pulling his best professional, concerned face.

"Medical opinion is divided on whether patients in a coma can hear when we speak," he says.

I nod as I get to my feet. "What's your opinion?"

He cocks his head, his eyes narrowing. "As per findings published in the 'Journal of Clinical Nursing', there is evidence to suggest patients may have varying levels of awareness and can sometimes hear and respond to external stimuli. Brain-imaging technologies have revealed signs of responsiveness to auditory stimuli."

"So that's a yes?"

He sighs. "It's a matter of believing what you need to believe if it makes this any easier."

————

Dupree hasn't left the building. When I return to the boardroom to collect my things, he's playing with his phone in a way meant to suggest casualness, but a pulsing vein on his forehead says otherwise.

"I sorted the press," he says. "We'll issue the statement online. In your name."

A guy in a crisp grey suit sits at the table, flipping through new paperwork. Now and then, plucking a tissue from a pocket to dab at his eyes.

"How was your visit with Har-Gay?" Dupree says. "I haven't been able to face the sick bastard for days. The sound of that mother-fucking breathing machine makes me want to hurl."

I check nothing is missing from my bag. "You should have that printed on a get-well card."

He introduces me to Tissue Guy, also known as *Larry from Legal*. We shake hands, and his grip is firm. Over-compensating. The handshake insecure men use to signal dominance.

He speaks without eye contact. "It's a pleasure to meet you. I wish it could have been under better circumstances."

I don't wait for either man to suggest sitting and pull out a chair.

"Unless I'm mistaken," I say, "this is where you tell me you both have my best interests at heart."

Larry sniffs and dabs at his eyes once more. "Mr Dupree has asked me to explain ways to speed things along." He sounds apologetic. "The Beverly Hills Hotel is a nice place to visit, but who wants to live there? Am I right?"

I don't bother answering, not that it stops him from droning on about how the divorce process works in this country, spelling out long words like I'm stupid. Dupree stands with his rigid back to the window the whole time.

"This was fun," I say, pushing back my chair. "But I'm going online and booking a flight home, so I need my passport back."

Larry looks pained. "The issue we have, Mr Macdonald, is that any divorce petition needs both parties' signatures. Even when neither contends with ending the marriage."

Jesus, when did life get this grim? I remember the day David Cameron made same-sex marriage legal. I was in the Pink Flamingo when the first gay couple celebrated. I squeezed a guy's hand and told him we'd be like them one day.

"Fine," I say. "Hand over my passport and show me where to sign."

Larry's face changes. "It's complicated, Mr Macdonald. You file the petition and serve a copy to the respondent. In this case, Mr Biedermeier...and he gets 30 days to file a response."

I sit back in my chair, having already heard this from Bryn.

Larry glances up at Dupree, who nods for him to go on.

"The court takes extra care in these situations to protect the incapacitated spouse's rights and interests. This might involve additional hearings and a more thorough review process."

Dupree intervenes. "You had to be living under a rock not to know Aaron Biedermeier got attacked. Who's to say that wasn't your doing?"

My eyes widen. "I didn't even know I had a husband until your phone call."

Dupree's smile radiates an almost saccharine sweetness. "OK, and you need to understand that wasn't me talking. I'm just playing Devil's Advocate. Asking the kind of thing any judge might."

He's enjoying this. Watching me squirm.

"What are my options?"

"Stay in LA and wait for Aaron to regain consciousness or go home, and Larry here acts as your proxy, signing each document the court sends our way."

"When you get my passport certified?"

"Exactly." Dupree is back to his smiling reptile self. "I knew you'd see things our way. And look, I get how complex this all sounds, but trust me, we do this shit all the time."

Larry straightens his pile of already neat and tidy papers, and I stare at Dupree, searching for the slightest hint of deception.

"Fine," I say. "Call your friend at the embassy."

Dupree nods. "Dude is on vacation, so...it might take a few more days."

My brain feels overloaded. "Define 'a few'."

"I can have your passport back by Monday afternoon. Until then, kick back. Enjoy your weekend. See some sights. It's a pretty town, especially at night."

A text pings to remind me I have a coffee date with Noah Winters.

"OK," I say, feeling like I let a snake talk me into eating an apple. "But if I'm not booked onto a flight Monday evening."

He holds up his hands. "Trust me, Kyle. I'll make sure it happens."

---

The relentless Los Angeles sun blazes from a cloudless sky, casting sharp shadows on the bustling pavement. The air is thick with heat. Palm trees, standing like sentinels, offer scant shade, their leaves rustling in the scorching breeze. Birds fly, feathers splayed, caw-cawing.

I raise my arm, scanning for a taxi. On my phone, Starbucks on Sunset is a ten-minute drive. Fifteen minutes into the journey, my cab driver groans as the brake lights ahead stay red. Ambulance sirens sound. An angry horn blasts. We've gone five blocks. Should I text and rearrange?

My phone has no service.

"I think I should walk," I tell the driver.

He grunts and gives a dismissive wave. "Stick to the shady side of the street. You Brits burn easy."

Even slathered in Factor 50, I feel the back of my neck crackle like pork ribs as the sun cooks the pavement. I didn't reckon with how humid it gets here or how heavy the air hangs with exhaust fumes. My legs turn to rubber, and I'm soaked through in seconds.

When a familiar coffee shop logo looms through a shimmer of heat haze, I wonder if my mind is playing tricks. I'd expected something more glitzy. This is Sunset, not the Birmingham Bullring Shopping Centre. Starbucks squats at the end of a row of pizza parlours and burger joints.

Inside, I could be in any coffee shop in any city. It's all dark timber piles pretending to support the ceiling and high-set windows hung with fake foliage. Shiny machines hiss. The walls are a collage of local art.

But they have air-conditioning.

A barista wearing a green visor asks how my day has been.

Even though I must look like I walked through a car wash, I tell her I'm good while scanning tables for Noah Winters. Everyone here is dressed the same, in regulation off-duty-celebrity dark glasses and wide-brimmed base-ball caps.

"I'm meeting someone," I say, order a skinny latte, and then spot him, letting myself down with a whimpering sigh.

Noah Winters is the typical all-American jock. Tall, lean, and athletic, with broad shoulders and a chiselled jaw. He's 22. At least, that's what his official bio claims. Worn jeans sit low on his hips. His t-shirt is faded to look retro. His dirty blonde hair is cut short, and even from a distance, he exudes sexy.

"I'll be over there," I say. "By the window."

Our eyes meet, and he raises a hand.

"Hey there," I say, twisting with self-conscious shyness.

"It's a warm one today, huh?"

I shiver. Not because we're under an air-conditioning vent, but because my body doesn't know what else to do. He's Noah Winters.

The barista brings my coffee. "You found your guy."

"We're not together," I say, and my face burns. "We just met. I'm married to the man he's going to marry."

"O...K..." She stretches out her answer, backing away. "If you need anything more, be sure to come find me."

Noah nods at the empty chair opposite. "You should sit before you stick that other foot in your mouth."

The guy is super famous, super gorgeous, and super here in front of me. Unlike most everyone else, he isn't hiding behind sunglasses.

"This is a cool place," I say. I never use the word cool. I'm not ten. "Do you come here often?" Kill me now.

"Aaron has a house in the hills." He waves his hand towards the window. As if I'm going to understand what that means. "It's great when I don't have to deal with an uninvited guest."

I bob my head like those dogs you sometimes see on the parcel shelf of battered Volvos. Like I have any idea who his uninvited house guest might be. A nightmare soon-to-be mother-in-law, perhaps? Someone from the studio is on 24/7 call to coach him on what to say, to who, and when.

Noah's eyes connect with mine. "You already met Dupree."

He says it like he's waiting to hear my take on the guy. And even if he strikes me as a reptile, it's not the right thing to lead with. I've no idea if Noah loves or loathes Aaron's PA.

"Carlton arranged my room at the Beverly Hills," I say.

He makes a dismissive humph noise. "That sure does sound like Dupree. He spends half his life complaining he can't cover wages, the other half spending money that don't belong to him."

My face is on fire. "It's a lovely room, though. But you know, I get how it isn't cheap, so if you'd rather, I made some calls and found some places cheaper. I guess it never crossed my mind to ask who authorised my room. I'm sorry."

Noah studies me, half smiling. "It's true then about English guys...you spend half your lives apologising."

My back straightens. "I'm actually trying to be polite."

His eyes scan mine in a way that leaves me feeling exposed. But in a good way. "Ignore me, Kyle. Today is what my buddies call one of my asshole phases. You're not the only one dealing with Dupree. He invited himself to stay at Aaron's place because his wife threw him out. I got the whole *Aaron and I go way back* guilt card."

My mouth falls open. "Carlton Dupree is straight."

It's Noah's turn to laugh. "I prefer not to think of him as having sex with anyone or anything. Animal, vegetable, or mineral."

I take a deep breath. "Dupree is what I wanted to talk about."

He pulls a face. "You wanted to ask about his sex life?"

My shudder is involuntary. "I need to know...can I trust the guy?"

Noah squints. "If you ever shake his hand, be sure to count your fingers."

My mouth is dry. "So...you wouldn't give him your passport?"

He leans back in his chair, his expression dour. "I'm guessing this isn't a hypothetical?"

"There was a lawyer. I figured he'd be my witness."

Noah groans. "Tall guy, always sniffing, and you have to bite your tongue rather than scream at the fucker to blow his goddamn nose?"

I hang my head in shame.

"You want my two cents, phone Dupree. Tell him you're on your way over. See how it lands. Maybe I've got him all wrong. Occasionally, the creep surprises you just when you think you have him figured out." Noah gulps his coffee and fixes me with an awkward grin. "My momma often said I try too damn hard to find light in the darkest rooms."

I force a smile. "And is it OK for me to stay at the Beverly Hills Hotel?"

He pulls a face. "Why do you think I give a damn?" His watch beeps. "Kyle, I know this will make me sound like a total jerk, but I have to be somewhere. My agent fixed up a table read. Not that I want to sign for a sitcom, but streaming is the future, and Aaron isn't likely to cast me in anything new anytime soon."

He gets to his feet, and I do the same. For a minute, it's like we might hug, and I go to lean in, pulling back when he reaches to shake my hand. If he noticed, he said nothing, instead fixing me with the most perfect smile.

"Perhaps we could meet for dinner?" he says. "That's if you can stand more of my company."

Did Noah Winters ask me out? For dinner. Like on a date. He brushes my arm, and my heart leaps. It's all I can do not to curtsey.

"Sure," I say, using my best nonchalant hetero-guy voice. "That would be ace."

Ace? Cool? Who the hell am I?

Noah pulls a pair of dark glasses from his shirt pocket. "Call Dupree and tell him you need your property back. It's not like he can refuse."

A car draws up outside, as if on demand. This guy's life is timed to the minute.

He's about to climb in but stops and, for a moment, looks troubled, as if wrestling with something for which

he has no words. Then his smile slots back into place. He
waves and is gone.

My fingers dial the Biedermeier Pictures number.
Noah is right. Dupree can't refuse. A testy receptionist
machine-guns questions, and I stumble over answers
before being put on hold.

"Yo." Dupree's voice interrupts bland rock muzak.
"What can I do for you? Studio tour, perhaps?"

"Not exactly." I start light and airy, like this is one of
those calls I didn't want to make, but what the heck, here
we are. "I hate being a pain, but I'm in a store right now,
trying to buy something with my credit card, and they
insist on seeing ID. And, well..."

I leave the question hanging, hoping he doesn't ask
to speak to a non-existent checkout assistant.

Dupree's sigh scratches down the line. "Dude, I told
you I needed the weekend. If you're short on cash, I will
courier something over. How much do you want...a
grand, two?"

This isn't right. Nobody pays for a fancy hotel room
and showers strangers with cash.

I clear my throat. "I understand how everyone is
busy. And you're being super helpful, but...I've changed
my mind about the whole passport thing. I want it back.
Now."

Dupree goes silent for a moment. "Okay, dude, let me
call Larry."

"Fuck Larry," I snap, determined to stop being so
British.

There's a click, and he's gone. Anger flares, white-hot
and sudden. I'm not being left on hold by some jumped-

up social secretary. I call him right back, sail through the receptionist's interrogation, and when he picks up, don't wait for him to speak.

"I'm getting into a taxi, and I expect my passport to be waiting."

Dupree stays silent.

"I'm not bluffing," I say, although a telltale hiccough in my voice makes it clear that I am.

He yawns. "You didn't get all that stuff back at the hospital? I had you down for someone more intelligent. There's a process to follow. Would spending a few more nights in a great hotel be so awful?"

"I don't trust you."

There's a silence. Like he's working out how best to respond. I hear a lift door pinging.

"Dude, I'm on my way out of the office right now to meet with the underwriters. Your husband is getting his fag ass kicked, and the studio is being screwed over."

The line goes dead, and I stand there, my heart pounding.

What now?

# 5

I'm knee-deep in tourists on a street corner near the Chinese Theatre, with my phone pressed against my ear, when Bryn answers.

"Dupree has my only form of ID," I say, not waiting for any friendly hello. "His legal team was supposed to make a copy, but now..."

"Hey, there." Bryn's voice is soothing. He's used to talking anxious clients down from self-imposed high ledges. "Take a minute, Kyle. Breathe."

"Is there nothing you can do? Like issue a writ, a cease and desist...anything?" Words tumble out. "Should I contact the British Embassy?"

There's a pause.

"What would you tell the British Embassy? It's not like Dupree tricked or forced you into doing anything. When they ask, you're going to have to explain how you willingly handed the passport over to your husband's legal team."

In my head, I'm replaying what Milly said about identity theft and fraud. Although, who in their right mind would want to steal the identity of a bit-part actor who plays morning assembly piano at a failing inner-city school?

"Tell you what," Bryn says, "if you don't have it back by tomorrow lunchtime, I'll make some calls and arrange a temporary travel document. That way, you still get to fly home at the weekend, and I'll deal direct with Biedermeier Pictures."

"A temporary travel document?" I say, surprised.

"It takes a few hours and like a billion forms, and we'd need to file a police report."

I pace the crowded pavement, dodging tourists posing for selfies. Despite the blazing sunshine, a chill runs through me. Bryn is here to do me a favour. Probono. He doesn't need to hear what's lurking in the darker corners of my head. But who else is there to tell?

"I keep getting flashbacks to that weekend in Vegas. That kid in the hotel room. What if I was the last person to see Tim Larson alive? Dupree is already talking about how the police might re-open the case."

Bryn goes quiet for a moment. "I'm checking something."

It doesn't stop me from spiralling. "I was off my face, and I can't even be sure I saw a kid. I mean, shit like that happens, right? Your mind makes stuff up."

"Even if you did see a guy, how would you or anyone prove it? Your memories are hazy at best."

I know he's right, but can't let go of the unease.

"I just checked a news report," Bryn says. "Larson

had been dead for at least eight hours when they found the body. What time did you get to the hotel room?"

I try my best to remember. "After midnight. I can't say for sure when exactly. 2 a.m. Perhaps later. It was still dark outside."

He's tapping on his computer keyboard. "Sunrise in April is around six in the morning. They found the Larson body at half-four. If any kid was in that room, it wasn't him."

The tightness in my chest loosens. "You're sure about that?"

"I know it's tough when memories get fuzzy, but the facts don't line up for you to have seen Tim Larson. And as for the cops, they won't re-open a six-year-old investigation just because some has-been reality star is shooting his mouth off."

The panic that took root in my gut subsides. All I did wrong was marry a monster. That I can handle. I can sign my way out of it. Whatever dark secrets lurk in Biedermeier's past, I played no part.

"I'm still kind of on edge about my passport," I say. "Why would Dupree even need it?"

Bryn leaves a beat. "I mean, sure, you get how a certified passport might help speed things along for me, but there's nothing for you to sign apart from divorce papers."

My heart jumps back into my throat. "Can you call him?"

"Sure. I'm on it, but Kyle. I need to check one thing. And don't think I'm accusing you of anything. Truly, you know I'm one hundred per cent on your side here, but..."

I swallow. This already sounds bad.

"You read all that crap Eisenhart said. These parties happened all the time, and if you did happen to see some kid in that hotel room, who's to say it wasn't someone else Biedermeier was abusing?"

Bryn's words land like a blow. I'd fixated on Larson. The possibility of my running into some other victim hadn't crossed my mind.

"You think Dupree would pin something on me?" I say, trying and failing to keep the panic from rising in my voice.

"I mean, probably not, but it makes me think we should aim to get your passport back sooner rather than later. And refuse to sign anything he sends your way."

I clench my fist, partly scared, partly furious. "I'll call him."

Bryn hesitates. "Be careful. Don't let him rile you, and ping me right after."

We end the call.

Tourists bustle, oblivious, as a reckless plan takes shape in my addled brain. Dupree is staying at Aaron's house. My passport is likely there too. Noah won't be home. He's at a read-through. And Dupree was heading out for meetings.

———

I zigzag through groups being led from one set of handprints to another. The pavement is wide, and the inlaid stars are big and shiny. A taxi would take me to the Biedermeier front door, but any driver would ask questions like why some pasty-faced English tourist is asking to be dropped outside the home of a Hollywood director whose name is splashed across the front page of every newspaper in town.

Right then, a kid hands me a flyer for a *Hollywood Hills Star Spotting Tour* and points to where a line of older people in gleaming white trainers and chain-store jeans board a double-decker bus. A woman in a faded red cap and *Star Tours* polo chats with Asian tourists, her teeth gleaming white against tanned skin.

I wander over, determined to act as casually as possible and not like a crazy person who just hatched a plot to get his stuff back from within the security-guarded home of a Hollywood director.

I pull a crumpled bill from my pocket. "One ticket for the tour."

She takes my money without question, handing over a fluorescent wristband.

On the bus, shutter clicks and beeps from digital cameras punctuate excited chatter. I'm the only guy not wearing a Hawaiian shirt. Kids bounce on laps, their faces pressed to the windows.

There's one empty seat, and I nod a greeting to a middle-aged woman fanning herself with a tour brochure. Her eyes are glassy and unfocused. Perspiration beads on her forehead. I ask if she's OK, and she musters a smile, insisting she'll be fine when the air-con kicks in.

On cue, the engine rumbles into life, and fans roar.

"At last," she says, looking less like someone about to

die of heat exhaustion. "Who are you here to see, sweetheart?"

I can't tell her the truth. "A Kardashian, perhaps..."

An older man leans across the aisle. "I'm here to see the Biedermeier house. You hear what they've been saying about him?"

The woman next to me shudders. "He's like all the Dems. Like Hillary Clinton. Can you believe they still didn't lock her up?"

A girl behind joins the conversation. "Are you people for real?"

The older man extends his neck to fix her with a swivel-eyed stare. "Pardon me, young lady, but it sounds like you're one of those snowflakes who need to learn to think for themselves."

The woman beside me shuffles in her seat, takes a slug of water, and then shuts her eyes. Her breathing still sounds ragged.

"Are you sure you're OK?" I ask again. "Should I tell the driver? Maybe they have handheld fans."

She waves away my concern. "I'm at *that* time when the hot flashes just happen."

The onboard chatter becomes a constant backdrop to our cheesy tour guide's narration.

"Ladies and gentlemen, welcome aboard the fabulous Star Tours bus. I'm your host, the one and only Chase Sterling. Most of you probably remember me from *Hollywood Squares*. Well, buckle up, folks, because we're about to embark on an adventure filled with glitz, glamour, and more celebrity sightings than you can shake a selfie stick at."

I haven't thought this through. How do I get *the one and only* Chase Sterling to pull over and let me off when we reach Aaron's house?

"As we cruise along the iconic Sunset Boulevard, keep your eyes peeled for the stars on the sidewalks," Chase says. "This is Tinseltown, baby. Speaking of stars, if you look to your left, you'll see the legendary Hollywood Walk of Fame, where our favourite actors, musicians, and talk show hosts have left their permanent mark. You know you've made it when your name is etched in gold on the sidewalk."

There are whoops of delight.

"Now, let's swing by the famous Hollywood sign, the colossal symbol of this magical city. And hey, who knows? Maybe you'll catch sight of a daring actor or actress posing for that perfect Instagram shot with the sign in the background. Hashtag goals, people."

The bus labours into the hills, past manicured gardens.

"Ladies and gentlemen, be ready to glimpse the glamorous world of the rich and famous, where dreams become a reality and luxury knows no bounds. If you look to your left, you'll see the home of Mr Neil Diamond."

A three-story white stucco mansion overlooks the city, its driveway lined with expensive cars. The woman in the next seat grips my arm. She's turned a nasty shade of green, and I wave to catch Chase's attention, but he's too busy doing his job.

"And on your right, we have the infamous Bieder-meier mansion." His voice turns whisper-thin. "As you may be aware, this director is making all the wrong kinds of headlines."

Chase leaves the sentence hanging as we stare at a pale yellow palace with manicured lawns dotted with shapely topiaries. Groomed hedges line a winding brick driveway leading to a grand entrance framed by soaring columns.

This is where Noah lives with his temporary house guest, Carlton Dupree.

"Mr Biedermeier isn't around, and that's for the best," Chase says. "We have kids on board."

The guy across the aisle laughs. The snowflake girl gives him a sour look. There's a thud as my seatmate's head slams against the window.

I'm on my feet. "Excuse me. I think this lady needs help."

The engine judders to a halt along with the air-conditioning, and, within seconds, the bus becomes a sweatbox.

"Be jabbers, I'm melting," a woman cries. "Why do things like this always happen to me?"

There's a mass exodus, and Chase takes charge, helping the sick woman down the bus steps. Her eyes have rolled into the back of her head, and I ought to hang back and make sure she's OK, but we're parked across the road from where I need to be.

I duck into a thicket of trees, and Chase doesn't bother with a headcount as he helps the sick woman back onboard. If this were a school trip, he'd be fired on the spot. Once, I found myself two kids short on an educational visit to a Roman museum, and all hell broke loose.

The bus coughs back to life. Hidden behind a tree, I hold my breath.

Brakes squeal. Someone must have noticed my empty seat.

The hillside drops away beneath me, and if I scramble to hide, I might never get back. And then what? I bake to death in the California sun until a dog walker finds my bleached bones picked clean by birds.

The engine starts back up, and the bus rumbles out of sight.

————

Leaves rustle in a gentle breeze. The soft scent of roses drifts on the breeze, and the whirring motors of sprinklers and chirping birds punctuate the tranquillity.A solitary car passes as I walk the perimeter of Aaron's mansion, taking in the lay of the land. Breaking and entering has never been my thing. I much prefer the thought of finding a spare key left under a flower pot. The only way in and out appears to be through intercom-managed metal gates.

A sidewinder of sweat snakes down the back of my neck. The dryness in my mouth intensifies.

Two women emerge, speaking rapid-fire Spanish, from a smaller gate hidden by trees. One is younger, with a ponytail. The older woman has grey hair in a neat bun. The older woman stops, mutters something, and hurries back in just as a bus pulls up. The younger woman calls something after her and climbs on board.

The gate is still half-open.

I sidle along the wall. One last check, and duck through.

A huge pea-gravel courtyard opens onto the back of the house. Moss grows in patches between stone flags, and I climb steep steps to an open door that leads into an empty kitchen, slipping past and into a well-lit hallway, where framed movie posters cover sun-dappled walls and an intricately carved staircase swirls upwards to a landing lined by doors. Behind one of those doors, Dupree squats—an unwelcome cuckoo in a *Vogue Interiors* nest.

I take the steps two at a time. Door after door opens onto enormous beds with crisp, matching linen and half-drawn blinds.

"Focus, Kyle," I tell myself. "You can do this."

There's one room left. Of course, he'd pick the one furthest away from prying eyes and ears. I wipe sweaty palms on my trousers before turning the handle. It creaks, and I freeze.

Light seeps through unopened curtains, casting shadows on the walls. A large bed dominates, its sheets rumpled as if tossed aside in haste. My eyes scan around, searching for anything that might work as a hiding place. I start with the bedside table, rifling through drawers, finding sunglasses, keys, and a half-empty bottle of whisky.

"Come on," I mutter in frustration and move to the

closet, where three matching blue suits hang next to three white shirts.

Pressure mounts as I open and slam shut cupboards. Dupree could be back any minute.

There's no sign of my passport. What was I thinking? It's with Larry from Legal or tucked away in Dupree's pocket.

Gravel crunches from outside, and I peer around the heavy lace curtains to see a black car making its way up the drive. Doors open below, and footsteps climb the stairs.

There's a knock. "Carlton?" It's Noah. How do I explain why I'm here? "Are you home?"

Please go away. Please don't find me.

The handle turns.

"I don't care if you took a sleeping pill. I'm coming in. We need to talk."

I scramble across the floor and dive under the bed, but not quickly enough.

"Who's that?" There's fear in Noah's voice. "We have security. One button, and the cops will be here."

What choice is there? I shuffle into view, trying not to look mortified at being found snooping in a stranger's bedroom.

"Kyle?" His mouth drops open. "What the hell?"

"I was just..."

Noah's face flushes with a mix of disbelief and anger. He crosses his arms over his chest, taking one step closer.

"I tried calling Dupree," I say, "and when you said he was staying with you..."

"You figured you might as well break into my home?"

I half stand, my hands still in the air, like someone surrendering. "I get how this all looks, and I'm truly sorry."

Noah shakes his head and half-smiles. "There it is again. You're always gonna find some way of telling me you're sorry. Dude, I get it. You need to get home." He sits on the edge of an unmade bed. "What makes you think he brought it here?"

"I called him. Like you said. He told me he wasn't at the office, said he was at home, about to head out for meetings."

His expression softens. "OK, but why would he leave it here?"

I sit too. Noah's right. My head is in pieces. I'm not thinking straight.

He lays his palm against the back of my hand. "Seeing how you're here, let's search. And then, you let me call Larry from freakin' Legal and get this sorted once and for all."

"Thanks," I say, my voice a whisper.

We start searching, moving to a desk in the corner. It's antique, heavy, and ornate, with a locked drawer.

"Do you have a key for this?" I ask, tugging at the stubborn drawer.

Noah's brow furrows. "I've never needed to open it. Aaron must have the key."

"We could force it."

I find a letter opener on the desk and poke at the lock. The drawer creaks open, revealing a cluster of letters and a leather-bound journal. Noah rummages, finding a formal-looking document, yellowed with age. A wedding certificate, stamped San Francisco City Hall. The names on the certificate are Aaron Biedermeier and Bo Hyson.

Noah sits. "I mean, when I found out about you, that was a shock, but Aaron was married before?"

It's tempting to ask if they talked much before an attack placed his husband-to-be in a coma, but their wedding is a business arrangement, so maybe not.

Noah snaps back from staring at the paper. "Any sign of your passport?"

I rummage some, but everything in the drawer looks old, yellowed, and official.

"You're right. I should try calling that Larry guy."

———

In a downstairs room, floor-to-ceiling windows line one wall overlooking a cobalt-blue swimming pool. It's a style supplement mix of Persian rugs, battered leather couches, and crushed velvet chairs. Framed stills from Biedermeier's biggest movies cover the walls, and a baby grand piano sits in one corner below a shelf of awards. I spot an Oscar.

"You've really never heard of this Hyson guy?" I say, staring at the pool. A huge inflatable yellow duck floats at one end.

He pulls out his phone, patting the sofa for me to sit. "You ever heard of Spokeo?" I shake my head. "When you hang around the writers' room on cop shows, you learn a lot of crap. Spokeo is like a way of tracking down people who might not want to be found." He calls up a site on his phone. "So, there are 1.3 million results for Bo Hyson."

He types some more, scrolls through screens, clicks filters, and then a smile lights up his face.

"Would you look at this? I got an Estelle Hyson, who sold a bungalow in Culver City and moved to Georgia."

"Should that mean anything to me?"

"Culver is a movie town. Sony had a lot down there. Six years ago, Estelle Hyson bought a property in River Valley with Bo and Dwayne Hyson."

I glance at the dates on the wedding certificate.

"Looks like Aaron and this Hyson guy had a *business arrangement*." I surround the word with air quotes. "They got hitched in January 2016."

Even as I say the date out loud, I hear how it sounds. Four months later, he married me in Vegas.

Noah takes back his phone. Three minutes later, he looks up.

"You want the good news or the bad?"

"Good. Always good first. That's the law."

"OK, so the weather tomorrow looks good. 82 degrees. Light breezes. Humidity is down."

"And the bad?"

Noah sighs. "There's no record of any divorce."

The room tilts. The walls close in. This is all too much information. "I need to go home," I say. "I shouldn't even be here." I get to my feet and start pacing. This isn't good. This is very bad indeed. I married a man who was already married, drunk or not. I'm a bigamist. People go to prison for that. I wouldn't last five minutes in a rough American jail. I'm too pretty.

Noah grabs my arm, shaking me free of day terrors. He is dialling a number.

"We need to confront Dupree." Now into the phone. "Carlton. I'm with Kyle. I accidentally broke open the lock on the dresser in your room. We need to talk."

---

A limo journey across town passes in a blur. My gaze is unfocused. As a kid, I dreamed about Hollywood, watching movies, and telling myself that one day my name would appear in the titles of a film. Los Angeles became my Emerald City—a beacon. The reality I now see through the back window of a Prius is soulless skyscrapers that tower over tent towns. No yellow brick road. And a wicked witch hides around each corner.

With my fingers clenched around the crumpled marriage certificate, I'm not sure Noah's plan to front up to Dupree holds water. I'd rather call Bryn and ask him to report my passport missing.

Noah's phone pings.

"It's him," he says. "Wants to meet at the studios."

I swallow. "Can you do this without me?"

Noah tells the driver to pull over and turns to face me. "I thought you were on board with all of this. Why the change of heart?"

I stare through the smoke-glass window at people passing by. What would they do if they knew Noah Winters was parked in this huge black limo?

"Don't you see?" I say. "I didn't need to be here. I was never married to Aaron. Not legally."

Noah nods. "So Dupree has nothing on you."

"Why fly me over here? Why put me up in a hotel?

Why take away my passport?" I shift in the seat to face him. "That night in Vegas. I heard voices from some other room, and there was a guy. A kid. Younger than me. I needed the loo, and I saw him. He saw me and looked, I don't know, terrified."

Noah's face turns red. I've pretty much told him the rumours being spread around town by Judah Eisenhart are likely true. The man he plans on marrying is almost certainly a paedophile.

"You're sure about that. Six years is a long time. You'd been drinking, I guess?"

At first, I nod and then shake my head.

Noah groans. "So, yes, you're sure, or no, you're not?"

"I saw the guy. He had a scar under his eye. And yeah, I was drunk, but not so far gone that I blacked out."

He shakes his head. "And this kid...you think he was alone?"

I take a breath. Long and slow. "There were voices, but...I don't know. Could be he was watching TV."

Noah's eyes stay locked on mine for a long minute.

"Who remembers what they were doing six years ago?" he says. "I forget what I ate for dinner yesterday. There has to be some kind of explanation. Maybe the kid was a relative. That happens. Aaron has six brothers. They're always calling up, begging for favours. Studio tours. Concert tickets..."

Our eyes connect. "Weekends in Vegas?"

Noah's chest deflates, and disappointment radiates like heat from a fire. He taps on the screen, separating us from the driver. "This thing with Dupree—it's my battle. I should drop you back at your hotel."

We don't speak much until the car reaches the entrance.

"Once again, I am sorry about the whole invading your personal space thing," I say. "I'll call Biedermeier Pictures and talk to Larry. It's not like they need me to sign any divorce papers. It was cool meeting you."

Noah grins. "I enjoyed spending time with someone more crazy than me."

He pecks my cheek, and a shiver runs down my spine. I've let too many good men go, and while I know I'm hardly likely to sail off into any sunset with Noah Winters, what harm would it do to suggest we get dinner?

"I figure I'll be here a few more nights," I say. "So, if you want to...maybe hang out?"

"Sure, that sounds good." Noah's reply is soaked in forced brightness. He must get this all the time. "Call me tomorrow, and we'll figure something out."

I'll go back to my room, drain the minibar, and text everyone on Grindr.

———

I take a long shower, washing away the dirt, grime, and shame of a day I wish I could take back. As I'm drying off, my phone rings.

I answer. It's Noah.

"You don't think it's weird how Bo Hyson moved to the other side of the country the week after you married Aaron in Vegas?"

"Fake married," I correct him.

"People don't sell houses in seven days. The legal shit alone drags on for months. Someone had to have helped him out."

"You think Aaron paid him to disappear?"

"OK," Noah says. "You know how you said we should hang out. I booked air tickets to Atlanta. You've got to admit that it's weird that the guy upped and left town like his ass was on fire. Pack a bag, and I'll send a driver."

Part of me is thrilled. I bet we get VIP treatment at the airport. And then a thought hits. "Don't airports ask for some form of ID, even on domestic flights? Dupree still has my passport."

"Shit." There's a pause. "Leave it with me."

The resolve in his voice calms my frayed nerves.

I pour myself an overpriced minibar drink and turn on the TV.

And freeze.

The scene is of an ambulance parked outside a seedy downtown motel. Two men look to be carrying a body wrapped in a blanket on a stretcher. Headlines scroll along the bottom of the screen.

**TRUMP DENIES RIVAL ASSASSINATION PLOT...
KARDASHIAN-JENNER FIGHT GOES PUBLIC...
JUDAH EISENHART DEAD AT 22**

# 6

The air-conditioning in my room is cranked up high. Even so, I struggle to breathe. My chest aches. My head is set to explode. I try lying down, but can't keep a limb still. On a muted TV screen, one woman shows another how to remove red wine stains from a raw silk blouse.

I need tough love.

The line rings three times before Milly's too-faraway voice answers.

"I'm still here," I say, aiming for breezy but missing by a mile. "There's been a development."

I give her one-sentence headlines: Still no passport. Noah is flying to Atlanta to track down Aaron's ex. Oh, and my Vegas husband's key witness turned up dead.

There's silence, and I picture Milly processing, her fingers tugging a strand of hair.

"When you screw up, you go big," she says, and I force a too-bright laugh. There's a weighty pause. "How are you holding up?"

Her question, posed with grace, undoes me, and bone-weariness hits like a truck. She's right about me messing up. And what was I thinking, handing over my passport to the kind of guy who looks like he'd dislocate his jaw to swallow kittens?

"I'm tired, but...OK," I say. "And Noah isn't some up-himself movie star. He's a cool guy."

She snorts. "A cool guy with an arse to die for?"

I allow myself to smile. "It does help."

"I get how this is like telling an addict not to take the bottle of pills left open on the counter, but did you stop to consider why he's so eager to help?"

I bristle, even though the question is fair. "He gets Dupree. And he was kind of rocked when he found out about this Hyson guy."

She leaves another beat. The line crackles.

"Just be careful, Kyle," she says. "Don't go swapping one complicated situation for another." I protest, but she continues, "You've only just met him, and you have a habit of leaping before looking. Did you run any of this past Bryn?"

"I keep getting voicemail."

Milly's superpower of calling out lies relies on eye contact.

Three sharp raps at the door cause my pulse to race.

"Are you running up a room service tab?" she says. "Tell Bryn you need it in writing Biedermeier Pictures plans on covering sundries."

More loud knocks.

I go to peer through the spyhole and see Dupree in one of his shiny blue suits, arms crossed, with a shiny,

angry face that looks like a bulldog licking piss off a nettle.

"It's him," I whisper. "Dupree."

"Great, let him in. Put him on. I'll be your UK representative, calling to make sure nobody is taking this piss out of my client."

He knocks again. "Come on, Macdonald. I know you're in there."

"Don't take this the wrong way, but I got this," I say.

She's still talking as I end the call, take a breath, and unlock the door. Dupree shoulders past without waiting for an invitation, trailing a wake of spicy cologne. His cold eyes rake over me, his lips curling at my gym shorts and faded t-shirt.

"To what do I owe the pleasure?" My question drips sarcasm.

"You heard the news?" His expression is unreadable. "Eisenhart was a pain in my butt, but nobody deserves to die. Not like that."

I nod for him to sit. "I only saw the headlines."

Dupree huffs. "Fucking junkie."

"Like Tim Larson?" I say, without thinking.

His eyes narrow. "Like almost every talentless hack who thinks he's better than anyone else. So, yeah. Like Larson." He spots my backpack open on the floor. "You plan on going someplace?"

I need to think fast. "I figured I might head down to San Francisco. See the sights."

"On your own?"

I try to swallow, but my throat is dry. "Unless you want to hang out."

He pulls an envelope from an inside pocket. "Larry needs me to get a signature."

I don't take it. "Wasn't this why you took my passport?"

"It's a non-disclosure agreement. Out here, they're pretty much standard. Most people can't take a piss without signing one."

"Sounds like something to run past my lawyer."

He snorts, like I said something funny, and takes a pen from his pocket. "The sooner you play the game, the sooner things move for everyone. Me included. Larry worked through his lunch to draft this, and you saw the guy. He loves lunch. You know things you shouldn't know about Vegas. About my employer and his proclivities."

"So, this is more of a gagging order?" I say. "Given some fancy lawyer name."

He sits, and his shoulders slump. "Listen, kid, I'm not the bad guy here. I'm trying to help. I made sure Larry took out all the bad stuff. All this says is that you don't plan on making claims on Aaron's estate now or at some point in the future. In exchange, you get ten grand and first-class tickets home. Trust me, even in this town, ten grand for one signature is a decent return."

His eyes glint.

"I still think..."

Dupree is on his feet. The good cop left the room. The bad cop took over. "Sign the NDA, or certain information gets leaked to parties interested in prosecuting certain indiscretions. You saw things that night you were too wasted to understand. But others will piece it together."

My chest tightens. "All I did was get drunk on a stag weekend."

He nods. Again, slowly. Again, it's like he's enjoying this.

"Yet here you are." Dupree picks at a manicured nail. "And failure to cooperate will drag you deeper. You mentioned Tim Larson. You don't think his folks are still grieving. Even now. They hired investigators. I still have some wet-behind-the-ears college kid calling and asking to meet up, wanting to check if I remember shit. And..." He glances my way. "Who knows just what I might recall if I put my mind to it."

He holds out the envelope again.

How could I let this happen? I'm not stupid. I have a degree in educational psychology. Do I sign and betray Noah by hiding the rot at the core of Biedermeier's glamorous empire? Do I join the ranks of dirty secrets buried to restore a tarnished brand?

Dupree taps his watch. "I'm on a schedule."

The walls close in. There are no good options—only less ruinous ones.

"I really do need to call my lawyer," I start to say, but Dupree raises a hand. And now he's smiling. A smile that looks almost real.

"I'm pushing you too hard, Kyle. Take a few hours. Read the NDA. Talk to your guy."

I peer at densely typed pages. Do I tell him I know about Bo Hyson? That the divorce is a farce? "What about my passport?"

Dupree looks down at the floor. "I'll make sure we send a courier."

My palms sweat. Every part of me aches. I've spent two days clenching my teeth, my arse, my everything. I should market this as a way to get shredded—the *bad decision* diet. Take one bad decision, multiply by three, and the pounds drop off.

———

Noah answers before the line rings, and traffic sounds suggest he's driving with open car windows.

"Dupree was here," I say, and despite chain-chugging minibar vodka, my voice shakes.

A car sounds its horn, and Noah yells to eat his dick.

"I got rid of him, but he's trying to make me sign an NDA."

"Breathe, OK? I'm twenty minutes away. Tops. Pack your things and take the emergency stairs. They exit into the parking lot."

It's like my whole body got squeezed into a vice. My heart hammers. "What emergency stairs?"

"How are you fixed for a road trip to Georgia? You can't fly, and I figured it might be fun to hang out for a while. And seriously, dude, I hear it in your voice. You need to get out of town."

I force steady breaths, focusing on Noah's calm confidence. He hasn't led me wrong yet. "When you say road trip?"

I'm already picturing a huge limo driven by a uniformed chauffeur. A fridge piled high with fine foods and expensive champagne. Overnight stays at top hotels. Rooms with hot tubs.

"Route 66," he says. "I haven't driven that road since I was eighteen."

I leave it a beat. "When you say *driven,* that's just an expression, right? I mean, there's going to be someone else in charge."

The line crackles and dies.

———

The emergency stairs lead to a pair of locked doors. A green box with a 'Smash glass to exit' sign is all that stands between me and the outdoors. Between me and a stretch limo.

I thump the box with my palm. Nothing happens. I try again and look around, spotting a metal hammer hanging on the wall. When I hit the glass, an alarm sounds as I charge through and into bright sunshine.

Noah calls out. "Over here."

Squinting in the afternoon sun, I spot him waving next to an out-of-place cherry-red VW Camper Van. The sort of breaker's yard reject you drive to Glastonbury. The kind of rust bucket you don't lose sleep over when it ends up stranded in the middle of a muddy field.

"Isn't this the coolest thing ever?" Noah says, as I weave between parked cars.

"Did you *buy* this?" I say. "With actual money?"

"Craig's List." He hops from one foot to another, like a kid who needs to pee. "The guy was heartbroken to part with it."

I peer through the window at the yellow walls decorated with cartoon characters. "Heartbroken, you say?"

"He said it's a decent runner. It'll get us to Georgia."

A voice pipes up inside. One I never heard before. And yet, it sounds a lot like Milly. What if Noah is working for Dupree? What if the plan is to lure you into this literal death trap by batting his pretty eyes and flexing his toned arms? It doesn't matter if this thing makes it any further than some pay-by-the-hour motel, where the cleaners will find my body.

"Jump in," Noah says. "The seats are super comfy."

I want to call Milly. I want to call Bryn. I want to call Mum.

"Have you heard the news today?" I say. "Or seen a newspaper?"

He shakes his head. "I try not to let too much crazy into my life."

How do you explain to someone that the guy badmouthing his fiancé was found dead in a sleazy motel? Answer: You don't.

He waves van keys in my face. "We should hit the road. Be good to make Barstow before nightfall."

"Barstow?"

Noah pulls a sheet of paper from his pocket. "I printed out an itinerary. Five days, and we'll be in River Valley."

"Five days of what?"

He looks at me like I'm slow.

"I told you. We're going on a road trip."

I take a step backwards and inspect his van. "You don't think we should find something more reliable?"

Noah ducks his eyes. "You hate it." He sounds like the six-year-old me trying to convince Mum and Dad to let him have a puppy. "I guess we could swing by a Mercedes dealership and have them take down all my details and keep a record of Noah Winters buying a reliable vehicle because he plans on heading out of town. Don't you see? This way, we vanish. Nobody tips off TMZ. Who's going to notice a van like this?"

"It's bright red," I say. "You could spot us from the moon."

His face suggests I'm raining too hard on his parade.

"If some dumb fuck hadn't let a stranger take their passport, we could be drinking cocktails in the American Airlines first-class lounge around about now before boarding a flight to Atlanta."

Harsh, but true.

"Did you just call me dumb?" I say.

His fingertips brush my cheek. I might never wash it again.

"I prefer to think of you as too trusting," he says.

Strange feelings rise through me. Hope and excitement. Fear and uncertainty.

"So, we should just hit the road?" I say.

Noah looks at me, his eyes earnest. "What's there to lose?"

Now is as good a time as any to point out that finding out his fiancé is married to some other guy is no reason to throw a party, but it puts me out of the game. After the weekend, I'll have my passport back. I'll fly home, and life will go back to normal. And what's one NDA between friends?

"I can't do this on my own," Noah says. "This is me asking you to help a buddy out."

"You can charter a private jet. You can have someone drive you to River Valley."

He stops and stares up into the bright blue sky. "I have to know what happened to Tim Larson. Nobody else seems to give a shit."

"And you think this Hyson guy can tell you?"

"He was married to Aaron. He had to have been there. In Vegas."

I want to argue that all the signs point to him not being there. Aaron got drunk and married me.

"OK," he says. "So, I asked around. I know for sure he was there."

His phone pings, and he stares at the screen and then at me. And then he falls back against the van, sliding down and onto the floor. His face drains of colour. And he looks up at me. "Judah is dead."

I stay quiet.

Noah drops his phone like it's on fire, and when he looks up, his eyes glisten. "This was him. This was Dupree."

It's like the sun ducked behind clouds that weren't there. He's angry. Why wouldn't he be? And while I'm not signing up for the Carlton Dupree fan club, I just don't see him as the kind of guy who kills other guys. He's a pantomime villain at worst.

"Judah wasn't in a great place," I say.

Noah nods, staring at the ground. "We met for drinks a week ago. He was doing OK. I would have known if..." His lip trembles. "I'm not saying Dupree did it—not with his own hands. But he made sure this happened."

I kneel and want to put my arms around him and

make things right. Except he's a famous movie star, and I'm a supply teacher from Birmingham. Our relationship hasn't reached the *hug-it-better* stage.

On his phone, I stare at photos of Judah. Something makes me zoom in on his face. On his eyes. On a tiny scar.

"I've seen this guy before," I say.

Noah doesn't look up. "He did a reality show."

"No, I mean. I saw him in real life." My chest constricts. "He was in the hotel room. In Vegas. The night I met Aaron."

Now, Noah meets my eyes, sorrow etched into his face. "I was there too."

# 7

P alm trees cast long shadows over the far side of the hotel car park as we climb into the battered van. Noah rubs his face, eyes red-rimmed, and movements jerky as he turns the key. It's been a long afternoon.

"We can still go to the cops," I say.

His jaw clenches. "And tell them what? Dupree will find a way to wriggle free. It's what he does."

"There must be something."

Noah looks tired. Like he's been all the way to hell and back. "You think this is the first body linked to Biedermeier Pictures?" His tone turns biting. "Judah pissed off the wrong people. Just like..."

He looks away, blinking hard.

"Like who?" My pulse quickens. Was he going to mention Tim Larson? Again.

Noah shakes his head, and we sit in silence, staring at the beautiful people swanning in and out of enormous cars.

"Why *are* you marrying him?" I say. "And please. I don't need any more bullshit about business arrangements."

He doesn't answer right away, and I see how he argues the case for and the case against in his head. The sun dips lower in the sky, casting an orange hue. Our little piece of the world seems to hold its breath. His fingers tighten on the steering wheel, his knuckles whitening. His jaw works silently, and the muscles in his neck tense and relax.

When I finally get my answer, it's delivered in a whisper.

"It's about facing him every day and reminding him of what he took from me. Let him see that he didn't break me."

A chill runs down my spine.

"Can't you talk to the police?"

The idea of any man binding himself to someone so monstrous, not out of love or necessity but in the name of revenge, is a life laid to waste. I've held grudges. I still do. But this feels huge. Life-destroying huge.

"He abused you?" I say.

Noah nods sharply. "But that's not why I need him to see me each time he wakes up."

Do I dig deeper? Ask what he means.

"Will you come with me?" he says, without eye contact. "Help me find Hyson."

I hesitate, torn between fear of Dupree's reach and the unwillingness to abandon a new friend. One who needs me.

"Why does finding some stranger matter so much?"

Noah swallows thickly. "I've been lying to you. Back when you found that marriage certificate. I already knew about Bo Hyson. I've *always* known about Bo Hyson." He takes a breath. "You've met him too."

I stare, confused. "How? Did he spend time in Birmingham hanging around shitty backstreet gay bars?"

Noah sighs. "That night in Vegas. He was serving drinks when you came back to the hotel. Dupree made him dress up like a bartender."

It's like we're playing pass-the-parcel, and something even stranger is revealed with each layer of paper.

"You've lost me," I say. "He was married to Aaron, and yet he was OK with me. With the whole Elvis wedding thing? He just stood there and poured champagne."

"Hyson knows things. Dark, ugly secrets. Things Dupree needs to keep hidden." He punches the steering wheel. "Secrets people get killed over to protect."

My breath catches as the implication lands. "You think Dupree had Judah murdered?"

Our eyes lock, a shadow passes over Noah's face, and I shiver despite the afternoon heat. He reaches over, his grip tentative yet firm on my hand. "I can't do this on my own. If you want to walk, I get it."

My breaths come shorter. "Hyson most likely hates the sight of me."

Noah shakes his head. "Bo left town right after that weekend for a reason. I wanted to talk to him and make him see sense, but Aaron saw to it that I went out of town for location shots on my first big movie."

The weight of Noah's secrets threatens to pull me

under. But his quiet desperation reels me back. And
Dupree has my passport. I know stuff. What if I'm the
next guy stretchered out of a downtown motel?

I meet Noah's gaze. "Let's get the hell out of here."

————

Noah catches me staring. To be more precise, he sees me
making dreamy eyes and wondering what I did right to
find myself on a road trip with a Hollywood heartthrob
with an obvious daily gym habit. We'll share a room
tonight, and there's every chance I'll catch sight of his
bare bum. He might be an uninhibited guy who wanders
around in his boxers all the time.

"What gives?" He raises a questioning eyebrow.

"I guess I never thought of you as a driver," I say, and
I hear at once how stupid this sounds. "You're a huge
star, so I thought you'd be ferried from one lavish party
to the next by someone on the payroll."

Noah exhales audibly. "You do get how I wasn't born
in LA? I learned how to drive a pickup truck. At weekends, I played the guitar outside Costco in my home
town to make beer money."

"Sorry," I say, blushing. "I shouldn't believe everything I read online, right?"

He stares at the road ahead. "I only ever drove stick
the one time."

I tell myself to stay calm and that this is no big deal.
Driving is driving. "You do know how a clutch works,
though?"

His look verges on a glower. "You want to drive?"

I *would* prefer to be in the driving seat because I'm the worst passenger. Ever. Dave often refused to take us anywhere unless I agreed to a vow of silence.

"My driving licence is back home," I say. "I never thought to bring it."

"I'm fairly certain you can still drive without it being physically in the vehicle."

"In every TV show or movie I've seen, the police always ask for licence and registration."

Noah nods sharply, admitting defeat. "I guess. You take over when we hit the open road."

The lights ahead change, and he crunches the gear-box, filling the cabin with the stench of burning oil. Anxious fingers bunch into fists, but I go to my happy place.

We pass upscale boutiques and trendy cafés, palm trees lined up like saluting soldiers, and people dressed to impress. The gnarl of traffic gives way to open roads, modest houses, humble storefronts, and anonymous storage depots. A battered billboard welcomes us to San Bernardino—the town time forgot.

The air here is different. Cleaner.

I spot my first Route 66 road sign, and it's all I can do not to squeal. It looks exactly like those in movies. Shielded in shape, eye-catching white with bold, black lettering. The number "66" takes centre stage.

Noah grins at my excitement. "Living the dream."

I shift in my seat to look around into the back of the van and see a roll of blue tarp and oily rope. No luxury tent, portable generator, or solar-powered fridge.

"Is there some secret celebrity-only hotel in

Barstow?" I say. "Hotel breakfasts are the best. At the Beverly Hills, they do eggs six different ways." I count them off. "Boiled, fried, poached..."

Noah gives me a *what-the-hell* look. "I figured we'd camp out."

I sneak another glance at the van's contents. "Would that not necessitate a tent?"

"Trust me. We've got everything we need."

I spent one night 'under canvas' and vowed 'never again'. Dave lured me to the Gower Coast in Wales, promising modern campsites with shops, shower blocks, and heated swimming pools. We parked in a field with one cold tap and pitched our borrowed tent next to a couple who had a loud and spiteful fight and even louder make-up sex.

"What about food?" I say.

"There's a camping stove, and diners serve burgers."

I reach for my bag. "We could find a cheap motel."

"The last thing we need is Dupree tracking your cards." Noah pulls a box from down the side of his seat. "I have burners."

The pack contains two flip phones—the kind sold cheaply in charity shops.

"These were props from my last film, 'Zero Trace'. It seemed appropriate for our situation, y'know—lying low and all."

My eyes perform an involuntary roll. "Right, and we're trying to blend in by driving a cherry-red Camper Van straight out of a 1970s sitcom?"

His expression changes. "Beware anyone who tries to

blend in. Who's going to come looking for two guys driving this rust bucket?"

I examine one scratched and grimy phone with an exaggerated grimace, flipping it open and shut as though it might bite. I'd trade a kidney for an antiseptic wipe.

Noah holds out one hand. "Give me your cell. I'll snap the SIM and toss it."

Is the guy mad? My beautifully sleek iPhone is part of my life. I saved and saved and *saved* to buy top-of-the-range.

"Tell me you're not so out of touch with the real world that nobody ever mentioned flight mode," I say. "Or location services?"

He avoids eye contact.

"When you board a plane," I continue, "they always announce about switching your phone into flight mode so it doesn't interfere with the navigation system. Some settings also make us untraceable."

Noah's face is best described as blank. "Nobody ever said that to me."

A huge penny drops. "You never fly commercial."

He blushes. "It's not like I'm alone on the plane. The crew sometimes comes too. And we transport props."

I take his ultra-fancy phone, navigating settings to show him how to stop us from being found.

My life as a fugitive begins.

———

Noah sings along to Billy Joel, playing one or other of his hits no matter which station we tune in. We duet on 'Just the Way You Are', begging each other not to change, and hand jive to 'The Longest Time', laughing at each new move. I reach for the dial when the announcer cuts to the news, not wanting to risk hearing more Judah Eisenhart headlines.

The evening sky turns inky black and huge, and traffic thins to a point where we're pretty much alone on a desert road.

"We should stock up on food and water," Noah says. "There's a general store in Barstow."

"And a motel?" I say, hopefully.

He laughs. "You'll love sleeping under the stars. Have faith."

"Is there a particular reason for stopping in Barstow?" I say, peering into the darkness. "It's kind of isolated."

He grins. "*Every* town on Route 66 is isolated."

We leave the road, rattling down a potholed lane, kicking up dust and gravel. The van rumbles as we pull into a dusty petrol station. My stomach knots as Noah cuts the engine and turns to me. Is this where he cackles and calls me a fool for trusting him? Is this where he says he's working for Dupree?

"I need to be real with you about something," he says. "It's eating me up inside."

"Shoot."

"I kinda get the hots for guys with an English accent."

My face is on fire. What exactly do I say to that? I get the hots for super-in-shape American jock actors with eyes that could melt ice.

He nods, his lips pursed. "That's all. I just wanted you to know in case anything happens."

My whole body tenses. "Like what?"

"I'm a messy drunk," he says, laughing now. "If we end up drinking in a bar on this trip and I come onto you, just remember, it's the accent. Not you. Slap my hand and tell me to behave."

Well, isn't that just the biggest kicker going? Big gold star for the guy in the van who just made it 100% clear he doesn't fancy me now and might only fancy me when drunk.

Noah looks at me, his eyes still searching mine, like there's more he wants to say, but then he pushes open the van door and jumps down. I get out, too, and walk around.

Barstow is an authentic desert town with barely any people and a single streetlamp, like a half-built movie set. We're parked in front of a run-down store with a flickering neon sign that reads 'Gas and Convenience'.

The fuel pump pings to signal the van is good to go, and I follow Noah into the store and stare at rows of cans and packets. There's no fresh fruit or anything approaching a vegetable.

"First, we take care of the basics." He grabs a box of spaghetti. "You ever had one-pot mac and cheese?"

"Is that your signature dish?"

"I'm an excellent cook. But we're talking road food. It has to fill you up and stay put for the whole day. If you get my point."

He reaches down a tin of beans, tall cans of tuna and

corn, and cheese spread in a bright blue tube. I pick out a
bottle of water and soft loo paper.

As Noah pays, he leans over the counter to pet a
kitten, causing his shirt to ride up, treating me to bare
flesh. His phone peeps from a back pocket, flashing one
missed call.

From Carlton Dupree.

Hope drains. Of course, they're in touch.

"See these?" Noah points to a display of key chains.
"We should buy one for every town we visit."

"Yeah, sure. Whatever." I show how I get that he's
joking, but I'm tired, and keeping up this act is too much
like hard work. Chances are, this is the only town we'll
visit together. I wonder how he plans to end my life. Add
the drugs to the one-pot macaroni and cheese.

How could I be so stupid?

I know the rules. Never follow a stranger to a second
place. And certainly, don't let that stranger drive you
deep into the desert.

There's a postcard rack by the door. Dog-eared black
and white photos of Marilyn Monroe and James Dean;
overexposed shots of Rodeo Drive and Venice Beach; the
Hollywood sign set into a too-green hillside beneath a
too-blue sky. That sign got me onto a plane. That sign
lied about how dreams could come true.

I pick out a retro-styled image of the sun setting
behind the iconic white block letters. The colours are
faded, one corner is creased, and the pre-printed text is
smudged with an old coffee ring, but Milly will love it. I
pay, stamp included, and borrow a pen. I sign it 'Love

Kyle', scrawl her address, and drop it into a box marked *weekly collection*.

———————

"Time to put up the tent," Noah says as we return to where we parked the van, its insides still exuding the smell of well-worn fabrics and stale road trip snacks.

The rusty door handle feels coarse beneath my hand.

He unloads a greasy stove and a burnt-bottomed pan, fills it with my precious bottled water, and sets it to boil.

"We should have music."

He opens the driver's door and plugs his fancy phone into a socket wired to speakers. The opening chords of my favourite band play.

"Wait...no! How did you know?" I am genuinely surprised.

He grins. "You talk a lot. I pay attention."

Two songs in, and a beep signals low battery.

"Sorry," Noah shrugs and turns on the radio.

The airwaves crackle with preachers calling out to God for salvation. He twists the dial, and we catch the end of a song as a voice cues up the news.

"Toxicity tests carried out on the body of onetime Hollywood actor Judah Eisenhart have revealed high levels of an undisclosed narcotic, according to a report released today by the Los Angeles County Coroner's Office. Eisenhart, once a prominent figure in Hollywood, was found deceased in a seedy motel in downtown Los Angeles, a stark contrast to his former glamorous life."

Noah clasps his hands together and bows his head. A stranger on the radio is talking about someone he knows. Sandwiching Judah's demise between '*a message from our sponsor*' and the weather forecast.

"The coroner's statement indicates levels of the drug found in Eisenhart's system were well above therapeutic or recreational amounts, pointing towards a potential overdose. The Los Angeles Police Department has not ruled out foul play and is continuing its investigation into the circumstances of Eisenhart's death."

Words fade in and out of focus. Noah mutters something, his lips barely moving.

"It's going to be OK." I rub slow circles into his back. "Everything will be OK."

Noah's eyes are red-rimmed. "How do you figure that out?"

He's got a point. OK is one of those mean-nothing things we say when the world goes to shit. OK is never enough. My phone beeps with a call from Bryn, and I duck around the side of the van, leaving Noah staring blankly ahead.

"I guess you didn't get your passport back?" he says. "First thing tomorrow, we'll file a police report. Start things moving. What time is good for you?"

Do I tell him I'm in a van in a desert town trying to comfort a guy mourning his friend?

"Would you be mad if I asked for time to think things through, Bryn? Perhaps I got Dupree wrong, and we should cut him some slack."

There's an awkward pause.

"You're going to trust that creep?"

"Judah Eisenhart died. I thought...maybe we should show some respect."

Another pause.

"Respect won't run both ways."

"Two more days," I say. "Three at the most, I promise."

I hang up and walk back to Noah, seated on a rock. The pan of water bubbles away. His face has become a mask of pain and anger.

———

One-pot mac and cheese is the closest thing to hell I have ever tasted. Tube cheese like leather, overcooked spaghetti, and chunks of dry tuna. Given that he lost a friend, I force myself to eat at least half of what I'm served.

Noah gathers logs and stokes the fire. My mind drifts back to when he was paying for gas.

"I saw you had a missed call from Dupree," I say. "Perhaps he wanted to tell you about Judah."

His shoulders heave. "Probably couldn't wait to break the good news."

"Why would you say that?"

"Judah was causing trouble for Aaron. Now he isn't."

I leave it for a few seconds. "Are you saying Dupree might have had a hand in what happened?"

Noah's eyes flicker in irritation. "Can we talk about something else?"

"Sure." I nod. "But you know, if you need comforting with my hot English accent..."

The look he gives me is one of disgust. I do this a lot. Say the wrong thing at the wrong time to the wrong people.

I shiver, not because the night air is cold and my T-shirt is too thin, but because I feel like crap.

Noah offers me his shirt. "You look cold."

"Dupree is going to keep calling," I say. "What do you plan on telling him?"

He brushes my arm with his hand. "I already fed him some lines about needing space to clear my head after what happened to Aaron. I said I was renting a car to drive to Napa."

"Napa?"

"Wine country. I'm a movie star, remember? We're known for doing crazy, self-obsessed shit. What's he going to do? Send me to the naughty step."

Noah glances at the sky, and my heart wants to believe him, but nothing adds up.

"What if we go back?" I say.

He stares like I'm mad. "Why would we do that?"

"Judah will have a funeral. Shouldn't you be there?"

He shuts his eyes tight and screws up his face. "What about you?"

"My lawyer will call Dupree's lawyer and tell him to make sure my passport is waiting at LAX along with a first-class ticket home."

He half-smiles, half-sighs, and pokes a stick into burning embers. "So, I do the rest of this drive on my own?"

Finding Hyson is Noah's thing. Not mine. But there's

something I need to know. "Did Dupree want me out of town?"

He doesn't answer. And that's when it hits me. I'm such an idiot. I came here believing I'd scored some golden ticket, and look at me now. Am I really that dumb? Did it take nothing more than a handsome guy turning up at my hotel in a funky van?

*Hey, let's go on a road trip, man. It'll be fun. And we can solve a bunch of mysteries. Fix up the world. Make things good again for everyone.*

Like something out of a book by Nancy Drew.

And much as I dread Noah's answer, I have to ask.

"Those tears for Eisenhart," I say. "Was it all some kind of act?"

He stares like I slapped him. Hard. And then he jumps to his feet, rattling with rage.

"You don't get how someone killed a buddy of mine? You seriously want to know if those tears were real? Of course, they were real, man. Get a grip." He storms away, then stops and turns, rounding back on me and pushing his face up close. "This is about more than your shitty fucking passport, dude."

I force myself to stay calm. "Give me one good reason to believe you."

Our eyes meet. I want to believe him. Of course, I do.

He steps back and nods over at a rock.

We sit. For the longest time in silence.

"I want to tell you everything," he says in a voice that sounds like it just woke up. "But now isn't the time."

"Try me."

The night drapes itself over Barstow, a blanket of

stillness punctuated only by the crackling whispers of the fire. Flames dance and flicker. Shadows play in the dust. Above us, the sky is clearer than any sky I've ever seen. Stars twinkle like lanterns, a tapestry of light wrapped around a silver moon.

"What happened to Jonah...it got me thinking about Tim Larson," Noah says. "Dude was a friend of mine."

I say nothing.

"Tim was different. Not like the rest of us. Desperate to make it big, no matter what. He...I guess he didn't fit in. He wasn't a party guy. It was just the one time."

I swallow before speaking. "The one time...what?"

"I swore nothing bad was going to happen."

Noah's words hang between us. Angry in the night air. Every tree around us moves closer, blocking out the light.

"Dupree took charge. Said there was no way we could call an ambulance. The press would be on us like white on rice."

"An ambulance?"

He stares up into the stars. "I was in Vegas. With Tim. With Judah. We were kids, and we just wanted downtime. We got sick of the fucking chaperones."

"You were there when Tim died."

No answer.

"They found his body in some alleyway."

Noah doesn't speak for the longest time. I'm not even sure he's breathing.

"We took him there," he says. "Me and Judah. Dupree took care of everything. Said not to worry and that he'd find some way to cover up what happened. If anyone asked, we needed to remember Aaron was never there."

A whole pile of pennies drop. "Tim overdosed. In that hotel room."

Noah hangs his head.

"And that's where I came in?"

———————

It's quieter out here than any place I've ever been. We're on the edge of a town, yet there's no one around. No sounds. Nobody has their TV set turned up loud. No cars prowl the single street. We're still sitting together on the same rock, watching fireflies.

"Should we set about getting some sleep?" I hear myself say.

Noah shrugs. "I guess."

He ties the oily rope between trees while I unfold the tarp, setting loose a billion spiders. Some are the size of small puppies.

"I suppose you expected better of me," he says.

I hold my tongue.

Our dying fire snaps and pops. Cold air descends.

"It's not so bad when you wrap yourself," he says, handing me a blanket.

I lie on the ground, wrapping myself up, turning away, still not sure quite what to say. Noah's breathing slows, then he gasps, sitting up and looking around.

"Kyle...are you awake still?"

I grunt to signal yes.

"What I told you before. You won't tell your attorney?"

He sounds like a little boy. "Why would I do that? How does it bring Judah back?"

There's a long pause. "Or Tim."

I roll onto my side. In the half-light, his eyes shine. "Are you sure about tracking down Hyson? What if we re-open some horrible can of worms?"

He sighs to himself. "Back in Texas, I lived for acting. It's all I ever wanted to do. So, when I got a lead on an audition. For Aaron Biedermeier. I jumped at it." He takes a long breath. "I may have lied a little about my age. Afterward, he invited me to dinner. At fucking Spago. I wanted to believe it was because he saw potential in me. And maybe he did. Just not the potential I hoped for."

I reach for his hand, and his fingers are icy in mine.

"Then came the parties at Chateau Marmont. The drugs. The men." His voice turns shaky. "Aaron passed me around like a puppy on a leash. A plaything."

"You don't have to tell me any of this," I say.

"Tim and me...we kind of bonded in our misery. Judah too. We were being used as toys at those parties until we got too old to be the kind of kids Aaron liked to have around." He turns to me then, his eyes glistening. "I left everything too late."

"You were young. He manipulated you."

"I had a brain in my head, Kyle. Money enough to buy a ticket and get out of town."

We lay there in heavy silence.

"I'm sorry," I say finally. "No one should have to go through something like that."

Noah squeezes my hand. "It was a long time ago. But I want you to understand why I stayed quiet. Why I was trapped."

I still want to ask how he's now marrying the guy who ruined lives. An owl hoots, its call echoing through the night. Now isn't the time.

Noah shifts closer, resting his head on my shoulder.

"About Bo Hyson," I say. "You think Dupree made him sign an NDA?"

"It's kinda his thing."

"What if that means he can't talk to anyone about what happened back then?'

There's a long pause, and when Noah next speaks, it's with less assurance. "Bo will come through for me."

I'm about to close my eyes when I hear what sounds like heavy boots on dead leaves. Footsteps moving closer.

"What's that?" I pull my knees close to my chest.

"A coyote?" Noah says. "Though they usually don't come this close to where folks live, and anyway, I got a gun."

My body freezes. "You have a what?"

"It's in the constitution, dude. The right of the people to keep and bear arms shall not be infringed."

"Noah, please say you don't mean a *real* gun—something that can kill people. We're not in the Wild West. Guns are dangerous."

He pulls it from under his makeshift pillow. "It's a starter's pistol, dummy."

It looks and feels real. Cold. Heavy.

"Did you get it, especially for this trip?"

"I found it in a closet at home. It makes noise enough to scare off any critter looking for dinner."

Under thin blankets, Noah wriggles deeper for warmth, and I brace, listening for another rustle. The night air seeps into my bones, and I stare through holes above us into the vast, star-lit sky.

A howl echoes, and Noah's hand finds mine once more. In complete darkness, the warmth of a body next to mine becomes a comforting presence, and as my eyes close, he whispers as if talking to himself.

"I wish we could stay like this, always. Life is so complicated." His voice seems to be weighed down by longing and resignation.

I pretend to be asleep.

# 8

The sun shines through holes in the tarp. I awaken and see Noah's phone, just lying there. On the ground. Within easy reach. I could hold it up to his face, unlock the screen, go through his recent calls and texts, and work out just how true what he told me last night might be.

I leave it be.

Noah still smells so good, despite a day on the road with no place to shower. His body against mine is incredible. It's been too long since I shared a bed. Not that itchy blankets on damp soil count.

Of course, I have an erection, which will become obvious if I shift even slightly. Pins and needles spread to my thighs, and my back spasms.

"You awake?" I whisper.

He shifts a little. "Figuring out where we might find decent coffee. You up for that?"

Every man gets morning wood. It's natural, but any attempt to ignore the intense throbbing in my groin only makes things worse. Noah shuffles away, yawning, and I give thanks to the gods of inappropriate erections.

"So, this tent?" he says. "Do I know how to build one or what?"

"It wasn't as bad as I expected," I admit. "Though I didn't sleep much."

"Each time I looked, you were dead to the world."

Did he watch me sleep? Is that creepy or sexy? Was I snoring or lying on my back with my mouth wide open, showing off both chins? Did I drool?

He gets to his feet, and I check his groin. The bastard slept in baggy joggers. He grabs his phone, stares at the screen, sighs, and drops it. Unlocked. "There's a washroom at the general store. You want to head over?"

"Give me ten minutes to feel human." I stretch my arms. "I'll catch you up."

"I don't mind waiting."

Just go, I plead silently.

"I'm not a morning person, Noah. Never have been."

He pulls on a vest. His is not the body of a man who goes to fruitless auditions for daytime soaps and gets told to stay in touch in case something different ever comes up. They'd hire him on the spot.

"Take your time." He grabs his phone. "I'll ask if there's anywhere around here for breakfast."

———

I've been away from home for four days. My parents think the Manchester training course lasts a week. By now, they'll wonder why I've not called with updates.

"Kyle, at last." Mum sounds relieved—like she's been both waiting for and dreading my calling. "Is everything OK? Gloria from next door heard on the radio that someone was shot outside Boots on Piccadilly, and we all wondered if it was you."

I look around at the sparse, unfamiliar surroundings. "Everything's fine, Mum. Manchester is a big city."

"It's just...well, you know how much I worry, dear. You get yourself into some awful pickles."

The worry in her voice is unmistakable. I'm thousands of miles from home, and my current situation could indeed be termed 'an awful pickle'.

"The course is running longer than they expected," I say. "The organisers need me to stay a few more days."

She inhales in a way that tells me she knows I'm lying, but she isn't going to push it. Mum will assume it's something to do with a man. It's always something to do with a man.

"I'll be back soon enough," I say, crossing my fingers to make the lie good.

The sound from her end muffles. She'll have covered the receiver to relay my news to Dad.

"Your father wants to know if you've spotted anyone from Coronation Street."

I manage to laugh. "Not yet, but I'm in a training room all day, and they make us stay in the hotel at night."

"Like a jury?" Her voice wavers.

"It's a bonding exercise," I say, hating myself for the speed at which lies land fully formed in my mouth. "We have to spend as much time together as possible."

"A letter came." Mum changes the subject. "From the school."

My mind races. It's likely to be the head seeking an update on my mystery illness. She's not the sort to email or text.

"Shall I open it?" Mum sounds hopeful. "It might be important. Perhaps a promotion, thanks to this course you're on."

"No," I say, and it comes out sharp. "I mean, yes, you're right about the letter. It is to do with the course. They said we'd all get one, but it's super confidential."

She goes quiet, wrestling with doubt and a longing to believe me.

"The lecturer is calling me to join the others for breakfast," I say.

"Breakfast?" Mum sounds surprised. "It's the middle of the afternoon."

"We're running late, and it's been a long morning. It's more a sort of brunch."

I tell her again how much I love her and make her promise to say the same to Dad. The line clicks, and she's gone.

I need to do better.

———

Noah and I leave town after a breakfast of stale pastries and lukewarm coffee, starting slow and giving the engine time to wake up. Before long, an already too familiar stench of burning oil signals we've hit 50 mph. Small towns pass by in clouds of dust. He turns on the radio and sings along. Like last night never happened. I want to join in, but can only think about Judah Eisenhart.

"I called home," I say, as the radio crackles and we lose reception.

"How are your folks?"

"Good, I guess. But I hate lying to them."

His gaze flickers. "You didn't mention me?"

"I didn't tell them I was coming here full-stop. As far as they're concerned, I'm on a training course in Manchester. It's a city in the north of England."

"Believe it or not, we do geography in American schools. I know where Manchester is."

I nod. "Sorry."

"It's just next to Paris, right?"

The desert skies stay blue and endless, with barren land stretching for miles. Part of me wishes this was my life—that I could spend the rest of my days on an empty road in a battered van with Noah Winters. Except, life isn't like that.

When I ask if he thinks Dupree bought the whole Napa Valley wine tour story, Noah shrugs. "I told you, movie stars go batshit all the time. I figured I might text and say I'm joining a cult and getting my head shaved, so he freaks about casting me in any upcoming movies."

He fiddles with the radio dial, finding more Billy Joel. 'Say Goodbye to Hollywood'.

Occasional trucks rumble past, heading in the opposite direction, and tumbleweed rolls like a scene from a movie. All that's missing is the whistling soundtrack to

'The Good, The Bad and The Ugly.' Noah keeps glancing my way.

"Is everything OK between us?" I say.

"About last night..."

"What happens in Barstow..." I start to say, and realise how near the mark that sounds. "What you told me goes no further. You have my word."

This seems to settle his jitters. "What say we go a little crazy tonight and find a motel?"

I could kiss him. "With running water, fluffy towels, and electricity?"

He pulls a face. "Have to be honest with you. None of that is a given in this part of the world."

———

Nestled against a backdrop of pine forests and juniper trees, the Desert Mirage Hotel has rooms available, and judging by the almost empty car park, plenty of them. A neon sign, flickering with a nostalgic glow, buzzes, offering a welcome.

We fill out forms with fake names and pay cash. The woman in charge never looks away from a telenovela.

I flop onto a lumpy bed, but Noah doesn't rest. He's at the window one minute, over by a chunky wooden table the next, studying a local magazine. He's in the bathroom, cleaning his teeth, then back at the window.

"You trying to get your steps in?" I say.

He looks at me like he forgot I was in the room. "Sorry, did you need to sleep? Am I driving you crazy? I can go out. Take a walk around the neighbourhood. Maybe find someplace to eat."

I pile pillows behind me, moving my legs so he can sit on the bed. "Look, if this is still about last night..."

He hasn't moved from the spot. "You think I'm a monster, right?"

"You were fifteen. You watched your friend get sick." I pick each word with care. "I can't begin to imagine how hard that had to have been for you."

His laughter is sharp and cold. "I could have insisted on calling down for medical assistance. I could have saved Tim's life."

I get up and go over to where he stands, glued to the bobbled grey carpet. "You were manipulated and abused by someone with all the power."

A dark shadow crosses his face. "And now Judah's dead because I didn't speak up sooner. How can you even look at me?"

My throat tightens. "You don't know for sure what happened with Judah had any connection with that night in Vegas. The guy was a loose cannon." I pull a low stool from under the table and sit. "All that matters now is that we find Bo Hyson and talk him into speaking out. The world needs to hear what kind of guy Aaron Biedermeier is."

He stops me from talking. "What if it's like you said? What if he can't help?"

I swallow. "Is this your way of suggesting we head back to LA?"

Something inside Noah seems to break. His body shudders, and I jump up to hold him as his tears soak my shirt. When his breathing steadies, Noah lifts his head. His eyes are bloodshot but resolute.

"There will be moments like this," he says.

I force a smile. "What? Moments where you let me see the real Noah Winters."

He shudders. "My publicist would have a nervous breakdown." He grabs a towel from the back of a chair. "I should shower. Then let's find someplace to eat. Somewhere with cutlery and plates. All those things they talk about in fancy magazines."

As the bathroom door clicks shut, I let out a breath I've been holding since Barstow. I can trust him.

———

We find a small place to eat on a street corner. One step up from a roadside diner, the curvy font on the menu suggests they're aiming for a European feel. The waiter finds us a table near the window.

"Are you OK with being so exposed?" I say. "What if you get mobbed by fans demanding selfies?"

Noah grins. "This isn't LA."

The walls are painted pale yellow, and the floor is bare concrete. A dim light casts shadows, and we order beers from a different waiter who reels off the specials like he couldn't care less if we stay or go.

Soon enough, it's obvious the pair of us have nothing in common. Nothing to talk about. I try telling him what it's like to stand in front of 36 eight-year-olds who sort of hero-worship me and also wish me dead. He nods and grins in all the right places, just like this is a TV chat show, and it's some other guest's turn to shine.

"What's it like being famous?" I say. Out of the blue, and mostly because I'm sick of avoiding the subject of Aaron Biedermeier.

Noah shifts in his seat, folding and refolding a paper napkin. "Honestly? Exhausting."

Outside, storm clouds roll in, deep grey tinged with green, and the first fat raindrops spatter the pavement.

"Most days, I feel like a performing monkey." Noah doesn't lift his gaze. "I smile on command and say the right things. Kiss the right asses."

Across the small dining room, cutlery clatters loudly. I lean closer, unsure what to say.

He shuts his eyes and sighs. "This—right here, being nobody in a nowhere town—this is good for me."

Dinner is served, and despite all the curly, swirly words on the menu, it's bog-standard roadside diner fare. Meatloaf with potatoes and bottled sauces.

"Being a nobody is overrated," I say. "You have to love how you get to eat at all the best places, walk red carpets, and have people act like they care what you think about global warming."

Now he's laughing. "Mr Winters, if you could play any role in a movie about climate change, what would that be? And who are you wearing?"

The rain turns torrential, washing dust from the pavements, clattering off buildings, and hammering on the windows. A third waiter swoops in to ask if we might like to move somewhere quieter.

"Here is good," Noah says. "I'm nobody special."

I push away my plate. "I think I preferred your mac and cheese. This meatloaf is awful."

Noah grins. "I think we accidentally got something intended for the dog."

It's still raining.

"You want to make a run for the hotel?" I say. "Get an early night?"

Noah stands abruptly, pulls money from his wallet, and heads for the door.

———

As Noah showers, I peel off my sodden shirt, wringing water onto cracked bathroom tiles. I wipe a hand across the steamed-up mirror. My eyes appear tired. An early night is the right thing to do.

We came back from dinner to find someone had been in the room, and pushed together the two single beds. Housekeeping has marked us down as one of them there gay couples you read so much about these days.

Noah walks past, buck naked, grabbing a towel.

In the shower, hot water cascades. This is all perfectly normal, I tell myself. Even though he told me all that stuff about Tim Larson. Even though he confessed he was marrying a paedophile to further his career. All of this is fine.

When the water shuts off, I hear Noah humming a tune.

A Billy Joel song that found its way into our collective consciousness.

When I emerge, wearing a t-shirt and boxers, he's in

the bed nearest the wall, possibly naked, possibly not. I peer through the window. Above the chemical glow of street lights, a full moon shines radiantly through tattered clouds.

"That's so beautiful," I say. "Back home, you never really get to see the sky. It's all light pollution."

He laughs. "LA is all about the smog."

Safely under thin covers, I stare at water-stained plaster. My mind drifts to Dave, my last failed romance —the painful end is still an open wound.

"Have you ever really trusted someone?" I say, unsure if Noah is still awake. "Enough for an actual relationship?"

He leaves my question hanging for a while.

"There was someone. It just wasn't meant to be." His words are careful, and his tone is unreadable. "We don't always get to pick our future."

I turn onto my side to study his silhouette in the darkened room. "Being famous must make it harder to meet guys. Everyone wants something from Noah, the movie star."

A long sigh. "You have no idea."

Through the open window, insects hum and twigs snap as unseen creatures traverse the rain-drenched undergrowth. Noah's breathing steadies with sleep. My mind spins, trying to make sense of everything. I came here on a whim, intoxicated by celebrity sparkle. I wish that tomorrow morning I was teaching double maths.

# 9

The van wheels kick up clouds of red dust as we trundle along the track leading out of town. A cooling breeze cuts through an already blistering morning. The sun creeps from behind mountains.

Breakfast was porridge and toast, served with acidic orange juice. The hotel owner hovered, sharing winks and nods and asking how we slept.

Noah put his foot down, and tiny town after tiny town passes by in the dust of the van's wheels: diners, gun shops, liquor stores. The desert skies are blue and endless. The beautiful, barren landscape goes on for miles. Part of me wishes this was my life—that I could spend the rest of my days on an empty road in a battered van with Noah Winters. But life isn't like that.

We pass another Route 66 sign. They no longer feel so special.

Noah goes to put on the radio, but I stop him.

"Can we do some talking...sort of...stuff?" I say.

"Sure. You want to go first or..."

I breathe in and go for it. "What exactly does Bo Hyson have on Dupree and Biedermeier?"

Noah chews his lip. "Photos, phone calls. Documents."

"Stuff to prove Aaron was abusing kids?"

Noah looks uneasy. "Do we have to do this now?"

It would be so easy to nod and shut the fuck up. Agree to avoid anything ugly. Because asking makes someone uncomfortable.

"I'd feel better if I knew."

Noah's eyes turn distant. "The first time it happened, I was fifteen, and I only agreed because Aaron told me I was his special boy."

"Did you know he was married?"

There's a long silence. "I was fifteen. Fresh off the Greyhound. I didn't even know two men could get married."

I shift to look at Noah. His face glows red.

"One night, there was a party. Shit got weird. It was late, and a group of us were in the backyard. Hyson was there. Not part of anything, just there. Watching us. Keeping an eye. Music was still playing, but Aaron had passed out in his bedroom. I don't know what drugs he took, but he was gone."

He stops for a minute, swallows, then continues.

"All at once, there he was. Yelling about how everyone had to fuck off. Leave his house. He was going to call the cops. He grabbed hold of one guy and threw him against a wall before he started punching. I talked Aaron down and got him back inside, but he was just so... I don't know. Just so wild. I'd never seen him that way."

"Did that happen a lot?"

"Not especially. I told him to sleep it off, and now it was my turn. He grabbed hold of me in the bathroom, put his hands around my neck, and told me if I ever tried to leave, he was going to kill me." Noah wipes a hand across his face. "And he meant it."

He takes a breath and reaches for a bottle of water.

"The next day, Hyson took me to one side. He said to run the hell away and put as much space between me and Aaron as possible. Said he kept begging Aaron to book into rehab for sex addiction."

I weigh a question, one that could sound stupid. "Why the hell didn't you just listen?"

He glances my way, then back at the road. "Tim asked me not to go."

"You stayed because some other guy asked you?"

Noah flinches. "You don't walk away from one studio and go next door and ask if they're hiring. Aaron could fix it, so neither of us ever worked again. Leaving wasn't an option."

"So, you kept on doing what he told you?"

"We agreed between us. At some point, it would end. Tim got invited to dinner with a guy who worked at another studio, and they wanted him to ditch Biedermeier. He said yes, but only if they took me as part of the deal."

I wrinkle my nose. "You had a ticket out?"

"CinemaCon was supposed to be our last hurrah. We agreed to go because Aaron laid down the law. We had a meeting booked for the Monday after Vegas."

I rub my temples, struggling to process Noah's story.

"If you and Tim had an escape plan, how come he overdosed?"

Noah's knuckles pale on the steering wheel. He's no longer a polished actor in a rented suit, smiling for the cameras and thanking Jesus for some award. He's a man who's carried around unbearable guilt for six long years. "You think it was that simple?"

"Well, yeah, actually. I sort of do."

He doesn't look at me. "There's a saying in Hollywood. Trust nobody. Secrets never stay secret for long. Dupree found out about the deal, and I guess he had to decide. Which one of us was worth more to the studio?"

Now I'm stunned. My mind reels. "Tim was murdered?"

Noah doesn't need to say anything. He just needs to say nothing.

"You told me Tim got sick, and Dupree took charge. You helped move the body. But that wasn't what happened at all, was it?"

Noah signals to pull over.

We sit a while with the engine clicking over, the sun bearing down, and the van growing ever hotter inside. But neither of us goes to open a window or move.

"You asked me last night if I'd ever been in love," he says.

I hold my breath. I don't need air. Not right now.

"I was kinda close to that with Tim," he says. "Right up until they did what they did."

———

Up ahead, a ramshackle gas station beckons. Neither of us has spoken since Noah poured out every scrap of his heart as crows circled overhead, weeds tumbled, and a truck rumbled by, rocking our little red van. How Judah got back in touch because the night terrors still wouldn't quit after six years. How Noah met up with him for drinks, and Eisenhart was in a bad way. Jumpy. On edge. Convinced he was being watched. He kept talking about Tim Larson. Speaking as though he were still alive. Noah didn't know what to say or do, so he told Dupree.

We're parked next to rusty petrol pumps at 'Bud's Gas & Go.' A radio chatters faintly as the attendant, a gaunt man, lumbers from a tumbledown shack. Dirt cakes under his cracked fingernails, and he speaks in rapid, clipped Spanish, caring not a jot whether we understand.

My phone pings with a news alert. I scan the headline, and my stomach drops.

"The police have reopened their investigation into Tim Larson's death," I say.

Noah stares, stricken. "Why now?"

I read on. "Judah left a note."

He grabs my precious phone and hurls it through an open window, across cracked concrete. The guy in charge of the gas station holds out his hand for money. I pay and get out to retrieve my phone.

The screen is cracked, and the case is buckled.

When I climb in beside him, I say nothing at first. And then I show him the shattered screen. "You think my travel insurance will cover this?"

At first, he glares. Then he laughs. He laughs so hard

that he chokes. He chokes so hard that he starts to sob. And then I can't stop him. He's falling apart in front of me, turning into a pool of tears.

The 'Bud's Gas & Go' guy is staring.

"You want me to drive?" I say.

Noah nods, opens the door, and jumps down. I shuffle over.

When he gets back in, his hand finds mine and squeezes. "We need to find Bo Hyson. Before Dupree comes looking for me."

My heart aches for the boy who still lives in fear of a predator who stole his youth.

"It's not going to come to that," I say. "For one thing, you've got me. I have a yellow belt in judo. Which is pretty much what they give you just for turning up to class, but, you know...Dupree would need to come through me."

Our eyes meet, and a silent agreement passes. Noah leans in, his lips meeting mine in a tender and hesitant kiss—one moment that lasts an eternity, charged with fear and longing.

He tastes salty. His hand slides into my hair.

And then we spring apart, stunned. A vulnerability shines in his eyes. Nerve endings tingle as I turn the key, and the engine splutters.

"I didn't mean to do that," he says. "I'm sorry."

I only sort of nod. Because I'm not sorry at all.

Not one bit.

# 10

High above, the midday sun blazes in a cobalt sky as we roll into the desolate parking lot of *Maggie's Diner*. Its weathered sign half-heartedly announces its presence in chipped blue lettering.

Our eyes adjust to the chaos inside. Children scamper among tables, and parents yell for them to stay put. Waitresses in mustard uniforms scuttle past, weighed down by trays.

"Nothing like a kid's party to help you relax," I say as Noah bags the last free booth and slides onto its vinyl seat.

He leans back and shares a small smile. "It's refreshing to see people again after all this time on the road."

A TV mounted in the corner plays the news on mute. An exhausted waitress takes our order—a chicken fried steak for Noah and a plain green salad for me. I'll pick at it and set it aside. The last thing I want is food. The

Hollywood Hills sign appears on the screen under another *Breaking News* banner.

"I need to ask you something," I say, and despite the loud family celebrating a birthday at the next booth, keep my voice low. "Hyson was a part of what happened in Vegas. He was there that night. Serving drinks. That makes him complicit. You seriously think he's going to hold up his hands and tell all?"

Noah's eyes dart around the crowded diner. "Hyson isn't Dupree."

I press further, refusing to back down. "You think Judah saw it that way?"

Noah slams a hand on the table. "Hyson is one of the good guys." Realising he's attracting stares, he continues in an urgent whisper. "Dude was as trapped as any of us."

I shake my head, struggling to reconcile this new version of events. "Are you telling me Aaron was abusing him too?"

Noah leans in closer, his voice low and intense. "Bo owed money to the kind of people who don't discuss repayment plans. Aaron kept them at bay in exchange for his silence."

"How much money?"

Noah looks away. "Dude liked to bet on horses. Liked it a lot."

"What changed?"

"After Tim died, Hyson went off on one at Aaron. Told Dupree to go fuck himself. They cut him a deal."

"Vanish and the slate gets wiped clean?"

Our food arrives, and as the server refills our drinks, I

gather my thoughts.

"Why exactly are we driving across America?" I say, doing my best to sound supportive. "Can't *you* hire a lawyer to go to River Valley and get Hyson to talk?"

Noah stares at his untouched plate. "Bo wouldn't trust a stranger."

On the TV screen, a reporter in a dark blazer poses outside the hospital where Aaron lies unconscious.

"Please, Kyle," he says. "Just trust me on this one. It's best if I talk to Hyson. Man to man."

I inhale. Noah is putting way too much faith in someone who, by all accounts, he hasn't seen or spoken to in years. A man who took the money and ran.

"Should you even be away from LA right now?" I say. "How's it going to look?"

He narrows his eyes. "Who the hell are you to judge me?"

I shrink back, my pulse racing. "I'm just saying how things might look."

He stares past me into nothingness. "I don't know if I'm strong enough to give up on the dreams I had growing up," he says. "I could go back to LA and talk to the cops. Tell them everything, and hope they understand that I was a kid and didn't know what I was doing. But I wasn't. I was fifteen. Tim had fixed up a meeting with another studio for the two of us. I was about to take control of my career. Does any of that sound like someone who didn't know what he was doing?"

I say nothing.

He sighs. "You wanted honesty. There it is."

Noah tosses cash on the table and slides out of the

booth.

———————

As we push through the diner's doors, lightning splits the sky, followed by an ear-splitting thunderclap. Fat raindrops immediately darken the sun-cracked earth.

Our moods change as he tips his face skyward, and his eyes dance with excitement.

"You in?"

I hesitate, uncertainty gnawing. He's gone from being furious and fragile to playful and free.

"Race you," I say, taking off with Noah hot on my heels.

The deluge plasters our clothes to our skin, and we whoop triumphantly, arms spread wide, tumbling into the van, soaked through and exhilarated. Steam rises from our bodies, and I run my hands through drenched hair, sneaking a sideways glance at Noah. Raindrops cling to his long lashes.

"What happened between you and me yesterday?" I start to say.

Shutters come down. "It didn't mean anything. I was stressed out and wasn't thinking." He turns on the ignition. "Sorry if I gave you the wrong idea."

My cheeks burn. The cheek of the man. God's gift! Count to ten, Kyle, don't say any of this out loud. You're in the middle of nowhere. It's not like you can book an Uber or jump on a bus and be in the Pink Flamingo telling Milly what an entitled tit Noah Winters turned out to be.

"You didn't." I force a casual laugh. "I wanted to check if we're both on the same page. Imagine if we got together. We'd spend all our time arguing over who used whose retinol serum."

Noah chuckles half-heartedly.

"Total disaster. Non-stop drama."

Strained laughter.

The air grows thick with tension.

Noah's eyes connect with mine, and for one suspended moment, I'm sure he's going to kiss me again. Instead, he throws the van into gear.

Disappointment curdles my stomach as we rumble back onto a potholed trail.

———

We've been on the road for hours, trading only small talk. Recent days hang heavy, a weight neither of us knows how to lift. A sign indicates 40 miles to Albuquerque.

"Should we stop for the night?" I say, unable to take the hush any longer.

The sky shifts from brilliant blue to deep orange and red as the sun dips behind a mountain range, leaving a trail of pink and purple hues. My legs are stiff from disuse, and my stomach is rumbling. I get a text from Milly and hold it up to show Noah.

"Meet my BFF. Total hag."

He wrinkles his nose. "Can we even say that word these days?"

"Milly has it on a t-shirt. She wore it to Pride."

Noah smiles. "I was on a float at San Francisco Pride. I wanted Aaron to come along, but he made excuses about needing to be on some conference call. I figured he was just shy. Didn't like that he was so much older than the rest of us in tight shorts and leather harnesses."

It's the first time he's made Aaron sound even halfway human, and I pick up on the pain and hurt of what they could have been. Should have been. I place a hand on his shoulder, and he leans into it, the tension in his body dissipating.

"OK, so it wasn't all bad with Aaron," I say. "Tell me your favourite memory."

"He took me to a Cubs game." Noah's voice cracks. "My first ever baseball game, and even though I figured I'd hate it, the whole thing was amazing. We had so much fun together."

I dare myself to brush a hand against his leg. Not in any way sexy. A friendly hand. One that says I'm here for you.

"It's OK to have some good memories," I hear my sensible self say. "You're going through a lot. This is all so...overwhelming."

He looks both at me and through me. "Kyle, I need to tell you something more."

———

We roll into the outskirts of Albuquerque as the last rays of sun dip below distant hills. Noah follows signs to a highway rest area and pulls into a space. Other travellers move around their vehicles in the waning light, stretching road-weary limbs.

I jump down from the van to walk off the knots in my lower back. He joins me, bearing energy bars and bottled water, and we chew in silence, watching headlights flicker on the nearby freeway. The air carries the hint of creosote mixed with sage.

It's talking time.

"The day before Aaron was attacked, I heard him on the phone with Dupree," he says. "Aaron never uses the handset. He always puts people on speaker, so he gets to walk around the room as he talks. He says it's the only proper exercise he gets."

Noah allows himself to grin at the memory.

"They were planning something dramatic to win public sympathy." He puts down his beer. "Like having someone attack Aaron. Something they could label as homophobia."

"They staged the attack on Aaron." The pieces start falling into place.

Noah's eyes turn haunted. "Things went too far. And with Aaron out of action, there was nobody to sign cheques."

I replay the phone call in my head from when Dupree dropped into my life. He said something about me being Aaron's next of kin.

"And the hospital? They believed I was Aaron's husband."

Noah glances away. "Dupree orchestrated that. He knew your marriage certificate wasn't worth the paper it was printed on."

"Nobody checked?"

"Why would they? Dupree was Aaron's right-hand man—head of Biedermeier Pictures. Aaron could wake up any minute. They took him at his word."

"But he knew where Hyson was, all the same?"

Noah shrugs. "Bo has changed his life. You'll see when we get to River Valley. He's not the man he used to be, and Dupree knew there was no way he could get him to fly back to LA and play nice."

"Enter the dumbass English guy," I say.

Noah's hand brushes against mine, a silent comfort. "Cute but dumb."

———

The heat of the day still clings to asphalt and gravel. We're in what a sign claims to be a rest area with full facilities. It's more like a slither of wasteland, fenced in by low-rise buildings and lined by trash boxes over-flowing with rancid waste.

We sit on the ground with our backs against a low wall, cradling lukewarm cans of beer. With each sip, I taste grit on my lips. From somewhere nearby, the faint strumming of a guitar and the chitter-chatter of people and laughter reverberate.

Noah tilts his head. "Wanna go check that out?"

We've been so engrossed in our mission and focused on finding Hyson that the idea of doing some-thing completely normal seems wrong, but there's a hunger in his expression, a yearning for some brief respite.

"Why not?" I stand and hold out a hand to pull him up.

We meander down a bustling avenue lined with stores, peddling everything from intricate pieces of jewellery to aromatic spices and textiles. Hunger sets in, gnawing at my stomach, egged on by the intoxicating smells of sizzling meat, sautéed onions, and peppers.

Above a bustling bar, I spot a comical cartoon of a cone-nosed donkey sporting a sombrero. A spry young waiter with trimmed brown hair and dark, attentive eyes greets us, and I see how Noah checks him out. Then again, so do I. I'm human.

"We need more beer," I say. "Cold this time."

We're led to stools at the bar and handed menus.

The burrito I order is unlike any I've tasted before. It's wrapped in a creamy-coloured tortilla, and the insides burst with the tang of green peppers, the salty crunch of jet-black olives, the sweet earthiness of cumin, and a subtle hint of sour cream. We toast each other with chilled beers, exchanging stories of places we've been.

Noah admits he's never left the country. "I get how that must sound. Me being this big movie star and all. But these days, they do everything on green screens. It's all about the budget."

One beer follows another, and my head starts to spin. Whenever I speak, Noah leans in, focused. He wants to hear what I have to say.

I point out how a guy along the bar is staring. "You might have been recognised."

He follows my gaze and laughs. "I should have packed a bunch of signed headshots."

The guy catches us looking and raises his bottle in a toast.

"You should go talk to him," I say.

"I'm off-duty. We're on a date."

I put down my beer. Did he say what I think he said? When our eyes meet, his face is red.

"You know what I mean," Noah says. "We agreed to hang out."

I boop his nose; God knows why. I never boop noses. It's gross. I'm drunk.

The guy from across the bar jumps down from his stool and heads over. He's older, with thinning hair and a chiselled chin.

"I think I recognise you," he says, not to Noah but to me. His voice is rich and deep, soothing yet commanding.

"No," I say. "This is the famous actor. I'm a nobody."

Noah's face falls, and I wonder if he's irritated that this stranger didn't recognise him. He's GQ Cover Star Noah Winters, after all.

"You mind if I sit?" The guy holds out a hand. "My name is Charlie."

He's wearing expensive cologne that smells of burning leaves and pepper.

"So, what's the deal here?" His eyes lock onto mine. "You guys on vacation?"

"We work for the government," I say, and again, God knows why. "We're here to spy on the locals."

He double-takes. "You're a Brit?"

"I prefer international man of mystery."

He laughs—a deep-throaty sound—and I glance at

Noah, whose brow furrows. The barman serves up Jaeger bombs, and Charlie shuffles his chair closer. His arm brushes mine, sending an unwelcome tingle up my spine.

"Tell me about your friend," he says. "Another man of mystery?"

I snort—probably because of the beers. "He's as boring as hell. Works as a school teacher."

Noah's expression tightens. "Teaching isn't boring. You meet so many people and change young lives."

His voice is smooth as honey, and I imagine him mentoring a classroom of eager students who are patient and kind.

A faint blush rises on my cheeks.

"Bullshit," I say, all at once realising how out of it I am and how one more round of drinks might not be such a good idea.

Too late. Beers and chasers arrive.

As Charlie pulls his chair closer, his thigh presses against mine, and I shift away. Noah's eyes grow stormy, and when Charlie brushes my arm, he tosses cash on the bar and stands abruptly.

"We should get going," he says, his voice taut.

———

Outside, the night air is crisp and sobering. I hurry after Noah, grabbing his arm. His bicep firm beneath my fingers.

"Slow down," I call after him. "We can't all afford a personal trainer."

He stops and turns around. "You sure you don't want to go back inside and hang out with Charlie?"

I catch my breath. "Give me a break, Noah. Don't you get it? I was trying to make you jealous."

He looks at me like I'm crazy. He's probably right, because I might well be.

"Jealous?"

My voice comes out in wobbles. "Ever since that *moment* we had, I can't stop thinking about you."

Noah takes a step closer, and his eyes dart to my lips. He wets his own with the tip of his tongue. My pulse quickens. Slowly, he lifts his hand to cradle my face, and I revel in his warm and electric touch. Unable to resist any longer, I close the distance between us. Our lips meet, soft and seeking at first. Noah tastes of beer, and his stubble scratches my skin. The kiss deepens, our tongues entangling, and he pulls me tighter with a low, vibrating groan. When we finally break for air, he manages a shaky laugh.

"Wow. So, that happened."

Dizzy with desire, I lean in for more, but he steps back.

"We should take this slowly." His voice is thick and low. "I don't want either of us rushing into something we'll regret."

Though longing throbs through every fibre of my being, his tenderness and care mean everything. I nod, exhaling the breath I'd been holding.

"Yeah, you're right. It's been a long day."

As we walk back to the van, Noah slips his hand in mine. Our fingers intertwine, fitting perfectly together.

———

Somehow, we manage to put up the tent, avoiding contact, avoiding words, and avoiding eyes.

In the dim light, I study Noah's beautiful sleeping form, his chest rising and falling with each breath. The air is sticky. Heavy. Suffocating. My heart is weighed down as the raw reality of that second kiss sinks in. The lingering taste of his lips stays fresh in my mouth.

"Damn it, Noah," I say aloud, running a hand through my hair. "Why do you have to be so...perfect?" He's unconscious, but I need the words out of my head. Set free.

Noah grunts a meaningless sleep mumble.

I lean in closer, drinking in each feature of his face. That tiny scar you never see in photographs. A mole, a mere freckle, really, above his right eye.

"You probably can't hear me," I say, "but I need to tell you. These feelings—they're real. And we could be more than friends. I could give up my job. I'm sick of teaching at that school. The kids are all wankers who hate me."

He grunts again. This time, the sound trails off into soft snores, and I reach over for his shirt, burying my head in the fabric, breathing him in.

I'm falling for someone unreachable, drowning in his own world of pain. I shuffle free from my blanket, pull his shirt around me, and wander over to the van, climbing into the driver's seat and closing my eyes.

"I think I want to love you, Noah," I tell the almost silent night. "Even if you'll never know it."

# 11

My eyes open, but I can't work out where I am. Everything seems familiar, but wrong. I slept in the van—the whole night—and now, a cardboard thermometer taped to the dashboard reads 95 degrees. Noah is already up and about, crouched by the camping stove, shirtless, as if posing for Esquire. He drank as much as me, so how come he looks fabulous while only the blood of a newborn stands any chance of reanimating my broken body?

I didn't dream it, did I?

We kissed. Again.

This time, properly.

It's becoming our thing. Kiss the living hell out of each other, and then act like nothing happened.

He's heading this way, but the good morning smile lighting up his face doesn't hint at some *deep and meaningful* chat, where he explains it's not me, it's him, and he's not ready for a relationship. Mainly because he's engaged. To the man I thought was my current husband.

Until we discovered he's still married to a man who went into hiding rather than be implicated in a paedo sex ring. Not complicated at all. Why I don't get invited to more 'Never Have I Ever' challenge parties remains a mystery.

Noah reaches through the open driver's window and hands me a bottle of water and two pills. "Did you sleep OK?"

I nod but say nothing. Having studied Debrett's from cover to cover, I get how much etiquette matters. Even in a beaten-up van by the side of the road, it's not the done thing to vomit in the face of your travelling companion.

"Take both of these and drink all the water. Dehydration is a killer," he says, and I hold out a hand.

Mostly because the act of actually nodding hurts.

"What are these?" My voice is husky. "My stomach can't handle aspirin."

"Tylenol. And drink plenty of water."

"Do you have nothing stronger? Like whatever Michael Jackson used when he couldn't sleep."

Noah grunts, turning to return to his camping stove. "Take the tablets and quit with the drama queen act. I'm trying to be nice, asshole."

"Can we talk?" I croak after his retreating form. "About last night..."

His shoulders tense as he shifts to face me. "Now?"

I fake a laugh and wave away the moment. "God, no. I mean, last night was yesterday and all that."

His eyes stay locked on mine before he lets loose a heavy sigh and climbs into the van, taking his rightful place behind the wheel. I still haven't taken the tablets.

He grabs a bottle of what I hope is water—I have a habit of peeing into containers when half asleep.

"Thing is..." I start to say and pause, searching for the right words. "I don't want you to assume I took advantage of you because of being drunk and stuff."

His gaze flickers to meet mine. "Is that what you think happened? *You* took advantage of *me*?"

I hang my head, shamed by how arrogant that sounded. "It's just...I felt something, and I thought you did, too, and I don't know. It was impulsive, and you know...I did drink a lot, and I'm not a drinker."

Jesus, now I'm openly telling industrial-size porkies. Milly reckons I have a gene that makes me immune to the effects of beer until after two in the morning, when I invariably insist on gatecrashing karaoke parties.

"Don't stress," he says. "It's been a strange few days, and we were tired. And, like you say, wasted."

I watch a big-beaked bird hop around a row of overflowing bins behind a car parked up on bricks. Noah's trying to let me down easily, but I hit the ground hard. What's stopping me from admitting how I *totally meant* to kiss him? And my only regret is that the moment passed too quickly. Even now, with a sandpaper tongue and someone playing bongos in my brain, I'd do it again. And again. And again. But cut me through, and I bleed cowardly custard yellow, so I fake a relieved face and let out a relaxed sigh.

"Thank God for that, because it would have made the next few days super awkward. And I was counting on wrangling a wedding invite. I mean. When you guys set a date and everything. Because I'm sure it won't be long now."

He nods but doesn't smile.

I can't stop babbling.

"Have you decided on the dress code? I was thinking that if I manage to get home between then and now, I'll get the suit I wore to my friend's wedding last year. It just needs dry cleaning. And Mum has a friend who works at the laundrette near Tesco. She's always getting the curtains done at half-price. Otherwise, I don't know. When we get back to LA, do you think Aaron might let me go wild on Rodeo Drive? Like Julia Roberts in 'Pretty Woman'. Did you see that film? You must have. It's a classic. That bit where she turns on the sales assistant and says 'big mistake'. I mean, come on."

Noah lifts a finger and places it on my lips.

"I've been trying to boil water," he says. "It's taking forever. You up for exploring the neighbourhood?"

Way to change the subject.

———

After piling our few belongings into the back of the van, we drive in silence through run-down streets, scanning for anywhere that might sell halfway decent coffee. This part of town is home to bail bondsmen and pawn shops.

Noah points to a café. The frontage doesn't scream artisanal cold brew and freshly baked cronuts, but a sign says they're open.

Inside, the air is warm and greasy and smells of bacon. A handful of patrons slump over tables or line up on stools at the counter. A woman with frizzy hair scoops scrambled eggs onto bright blue plates. We slide into a booth by the window. The seats are the ubiquitous cracked red vinyl, this time deftly patched with silver duct tape. A younger woman pours coffee into chipped white mugs, and Noah takes a sip, waiting until she's gone to pull a face.

"So," I say. "You've seen me at my worst. I'm a messy drunk."

I follow this with an awkward laugh. Like a teenage girl, and at least two men at the counter shift around to stare. With his shoulders hunched and eyebrows knitted, Noah peers through the grimy window. Is he having second thoughts about this road trip? I rack my brain for something—anything—to make things right.

"Cards on the table time," I say. "I like you."

Way to go, Kyle. I sound like one of the girls in the class I teach, play-punching a boy's arm and declaring *everlasting like*.

Noah chews his lower lip. "You're pretty cool, too."

Is he deliberately misunderstanding? Or offering me an easy out?

"I mean...I *really* like you," I say, and this time, he nods. "But we both know this can't become a thing. Not with how life is and why we're even on this trip."

Noah shoves away his coffee. Frizzy Hair watches from her scrambled egg station, like she thinks we might steal dishwasher-stained cutlery.

"In another place and time," he says vaguely, and I wonder if that's a line from one of his films, a play, or something he read in a book. Or a Donna Summer album title. Either way, it's not like he's leaving room for me to argue.

When the silence gets too much, I swig what's left of my sour coffee, put down the cup, and sit back, stretching my arms with an exaggerated yawn.

"We should hit the road," I say. "The sooner we find Hyson, the sooner we get back to everyday life."

He reaches across the table to squeeze my hand. "I care about you too, dummy. But yeah. We don't always get everything we want."

My face is on fire. He wants me. That is what he said, right? We don't always get what we want. He means me.

"Probably for the best," I say, and it comes out a little high-pitched. "I'm incredibly competitive, and I'd get weird every time you did a love scene. I'd be like...'*Did you feel anything when you kissed that guy?*' Or girl. Or, you know, whatever. I mean, there are all kinds of people, right? You can be them or they or..."

He squeezes my hand once more, like he's searching for my babble mode off-switch.

———

The engine hums as it crosses an invisible threshold, marked by sun-faded signs declaring, "Welcome to the Lone Star State." On either side of the road, the arid plains unfurl like aged parchment, sun-kissed and time-less. Mesquite trees stand like ancient sentinels, their twisted limbs reaching for the sky. Clusters of cacti punc-tuate the tableau. They don't look real. More like some-thing the kids in my class would draw.

"Home sweet home for you," I say, more to break yet another lengthy silence than to make conversation about how Noah hails from Texas.

He pulls an enquiring face. "How do you figure?"

"You're a Texpat, right?"

This time, he nods. Amiably. "Fredericksburg born and bred."

This state is so huge. More than twice the size of the UK. I know this because, last term, Year Six did a '*Fourth of July*' school assembly where each kid stood up to recite facts about different American states. It was the most bum-numbing thirty minutes of my professional life.

"You think it might be fun to call in on your mother?" I say, and catch a warning flicker in his eyes, a tensing of the shoulders as he tugs at his shirt like it got even hotter in here.

"Fun?" he says, in the sort of voice that my aunt Pat uses when her cat drags a dead bird into the house.

I ought to know better, but press on. "We could take a little detour."

Noah's knuckles whiten, but his voice stays even. "I'd love to show you where I grew up and introduce you to my mom's famous pecan pie. But it's complicated."

"Complicated how?"

An uneasy quiet fills the van, interrupted only by the occasional cough from the engine.

"You're right," I say. "My mum would totally freak out if I turned up unannounced. It's rude to visit without a gift, and all we have is two sticks of chewing gum and a can of Tang. Maybe we could have found a gift shop back in Albuquerque. We still have that key fob from Barstow, right?"

Noah exhales. "My mom is an amazing woman. She worked three jobs to keep food on the table. She's the reason I believe in love and goodness. But after I left home..."

"All I meant is..." I try to find the right words. "How long has it been since you last saw her?"

His fingernails dig into the steering wheel's worn leather cover. "You think growing up queer in Fredericksburg was fun?" The atmosphere in the van grows heavy. "Mom did what she could to protect me, but she couldn't be there 24/7."

"Hey, look." I hold up surrender hands. "It's no big deal. Just a suggestion. Sorry if I pushed the wrong button."

He glances over and then back at the road. "She was a woman trying to bring up a kid on her own, and she needed all the friends she could find. When she let me get on that bus." He breaks off and wipes his hand across his eyes. "It's not a good idea, OK?"

Part of me wants to dig deeper. The stupid part of me.

"Sorry," I say. "And yeah. We're on a tight schedule. It's not like we allowed for detours. And I...I didn't mean to hit a nerve."

"A nerve?" He all but splutters. "You want to talk to me about hitting a nerve? This trip was a shitty idea, dude. A really shitty idea."

For a long minute, I'm stunned into silence, and when I next speak, my voice comes out weird. Twisted and broken. "What are you saying?"

"When we get to Amarillo, I'll pay to put you on a bus back to LA."

The silence that follows is deafening.

"Is that what you want?" I say, but Noah doesn't answer. Much as I know this is more about what happened last night, I refuse to roll over and let him win. "Gee, thanks, Mr Big-Shot-Movie-Star. But I don't need *you* to buy my bus ticket. I have money of my own."

As proclamations go, it's shaky at best. My credit card is on the brink of destruction, and my wallet is empty. It's payday soon, but not today. I'm going to end up stranded in Amarillo, virtually penniless. All because I suggested we visit his mother.

Noah slams his fist against the steering wheel. "Fine, your Lordship. Buy your own ticket."

I'm about to answer back, but he holds up a hand.

"Until you board a Greyhound, we don't talk, and you put a lid on acting like a total douche."

———

The Amarillo Greyhound bus station is a hulking relic of days past—a weathered monument shadowed by skyscrapers. A faded brown and yellow paint job does little to hide the wear and tear. Travellers huddle in groups. Vending machines thump and whir with each punch from a frustrated hand.

It's a sixteen-hour journey to LA, with one change in Phoenix. Despite what I said in the heat of a still unexplained moment, Noah insisted on paying for my ticket. And then he walked away.

"Good luck with the wedding," I called after him in my best sarcastic voice. "May all your troubles be little ones. But old enough for your husband to screw."

He paused, like he wanted to turn around and tell me to *fuck the hell off*. Instead, he carried on. Walking away, turning a corner, and leaving my life.

And now I need Milly. She picks up after two rings.

"Where have you been?" she says. "I must have left you like a billion messages. You need to come home. Now. Forget about tracking down this other husband."

"It's all gone wrong," I say, biting my lip and swallowing the urge to sob. "Me and Noah had a huge bust-up, and he dumped me at a bus station."

"Woah. Slow down. Back up. You're in a bus station?"

I relay edited highlights of the out-of-nowhere fight. In fits and starts. Half crying, half gasping, but leaving out both kisses. Milly stays quiet.

"And now I don't know what to do." I clutch the phone closer to my ear. "What if he's right, and Dupree *is* trying to set me up for Larson overdosing? The Hyson guy was my only hope."

"Babe." Milly's voice turns soft with worry. "You need to come home. Call Bryn when you get back to LA. They have a spare room. I'll pay for an air ticket."

"And how long before there's an international arrest warrant out for the murder of Tim Larson? Mum would never live down the police kicking in her front door while she's watching *Emmerdale*. Imagine having to explain to her choral group that her son is sitting on death row."

Milly's laughter rings out, a familiar and comforting sound that chips away at the edge of my worry. "Your mind goes to dark places fast, Kyle. That Hyson guy isn't your *only* witness. The hotel security cameras will have footage."

"It was six years ago," I say. "I auditioned to play a desk constable in EastEnders and had to tell Pat Butcher the police wipe CCTV tapes every twenty-eight days."

"Trust me, Kyle, if there's any way those tapes could be linked to a murder case, they'll be bagged up and sitting in a police lock-up."

Could she be right? Noah mentioned the cops coming to the hotel to take prints.

"I'll book us in for a mani-pedi the day after you land," she says, and a massive, happy, Milly-shaped lump forms in my throat. She's always there for me, no matter how deep a hole I dig.

"*You* know I didn't kill anyone," I say. "I panic when spiders get washed down plug holes in case they're the sort that can't swim."

She's laughing again. "Remember that time you found a fly lying on its back, in the throes of death, and spoon-fed it with water?"

"It still drowned."

"The defence rests. Kyle Macdonald literally wouldn't knowingly harm a fly."

After hanging up, a hollow loneliness creeps back in. What exactly did I do to deserve any of this? Is it so strange to suggest dropping in to see someone's mother? I look up from my phone, scanning the waiting area. Everybody here is tired and acting like they wish they were already on a germ-filled bus going someplace other than Amarillo.

And then I spot Noah.

Standing at the end of a row of blue plastic chairs.

Watching me.

My vision floods as he makes his way over. Is he here to make sure I leave town?

He picks his way between bags and cases, nodding apologies at people who throw dirty looks. I want to tell them to quit being so mean. This is Noah Winters, and he's famous.

And now he's in front of me.

"I didn't miss you, then." His hand brushes my arm.

I muster a grin. The look I'm going for is warm and welcoming. "They just announced a delay. God knows what happens when I change in Phoenix."

More than anything, I want him to gather me in his arms and tell me we should be together. I want to hear swirling strings. I want to see a film of waves crashing over rocks—trains bolting in and out of tunnels.

He nods to sit, and I wipe two chairs with a wet wipe from the only open kiosk.

"I once went to Phoenix," he says. "It's not the greatest place to change buses."

My smile hides the fact that he didn't already shatter my heart. "I've walked through Digbeth at midnight and survived. They make us hard in Birmingham."

He reaches for my hand. Is it any wonder I'm confused? Did he take some sort of course on how to put out confusing signals?

"I was so mad at Mom. She let me get on that bus. I

was only fifteen." His focus moves to the worn-out station floor. "But how could you know that?"

I figure it's best not to speak. Just in case he lets go of my hand.

"All she cared about was the money I might get. She kept on telling me I had it in me to do more. She meant I had it in me to make more money and send more money home. I had it in me to pay for her to drive a better car. To get her hair fixed at a fancy salon. Pay someone to fix the leaky John. And sure. I get it. Nobody wants to work three jobs. But why didn't she leave all that stuff behind and come with me? What kind of mother lets her kid move to LA?"

I make sure he's looking at me when I speak and cross my fingers that I'm not about to ruin everything again. "The kind of mother who couldn't stop you from going, even if she tried."

At first, he falls silent. And then he bobs his head. "She didn't stand a chance of changing my mind."

There's another question I need to ask that could backfire. "Did you ever tell her anything about what happened with Aaron?"

The world buzzes with life, but Noah lingers, caught in thought. Deep furrows on his brow signal some storm raging in his mind.

"The day I called and said I got cast in my first speaking role, she sounded so happy. We talked about the premiere, and I wired cash. Told her to buy a new dress. I said if she came to LA, I could make sure the studio paid for a hotel room."

A bored voice announces my bus is boarding.

"I called her right after Aaron asked me to marry him," he says. "She screamed out loud. Like every one of her dreams was coming true. She told me to make sure he knew he'd have to answer to her if he did me wrong." He stops and huffs to himself. "Like that would matter to him."

He leans forward, and his fingers tighten around mine.

"Do you get how, if I turned up unannounced and said I was heading to Georgia with a man who drunk-married my fiancé in Vegas...that might have set off alarm bells?"

He releases my hand, but I snatch it back.

"We'll find Bo Hyson," I say, staring up at the yellowing bus station ceiling. "For Tim. For Judah."

Noah takes a deep breath. "I called one of those *no-win, no-fee* phone lines. The woman I spoke to explained everything. If I stick to my story, I could be charged with perjury. Accessory after the fact. Obstruction of justice. I'm looking at a ten-year stretch, minimum."

Noah looks like he's done pretending to be the hero in this action movie. Then it hits me—this is the moment where I need to step up.

"No," I say, my voice firm. "I'm not going back to LA. We're not letting anybody sweep what happened to Tim under some rug."

Noah looks at me, surprised.

"No buts," I say. "You're talking about doing the right thing, about facing the consequences, and I admire that. But you don't have to do any of that alone."

He stares as if seeing me for the first time. "What are you saying?"

"You're Noah Winters. You can afford to lawyer up even if they make you collect litter by the highway for a year. What's the alternative? Let everyone think the boy you loved was a junkie who overdosed and died in some alleyway. We find Hyson, and he makes this right. For Tim and his family."

Noah's eyes search mine as if looking for signs that I might be like every other let-you-down loser in his life. "You'd really do that?"

———

Shadows cling to the crumbling facades of buildings, rats scurry, and the occasional stranger staggers past as we navigate a maze of alleyways and dimly lit streets. As dawn breaks, the sky shifts from deep, dark, inky blue to milky grey. And there it is. Our little red van. A solitary street light casts a warm halo.

Noah fiddles with keys and climbs in, but I stay rooted to the pavement.

"Why did you want to help me?" I say. "Back in LA. When you rocked up in this van at the hotel." I ask, not as an accusation but as a genuine question. "No matter what happens to me, you still get your big day. Your career carries on."

Noah turns to face me, his gaze steady and sincere. "I let everyone think Tim overdosed. Dupree told me to keep my mouth shut or risk screwing up my career." His voice wavers. "But something shifted when I saw what he was doing to you. It stopped being about the career, the fame, or what everyone else thought. It was about doing what's right and not letting another lie weigh down on my conscience."

The morning chill seeps into my bones. Pieces of a complex puzzle click into place.

"We're in this together now, you and me. Whatever comes next, whatever we face."

A look of relief washes over his face as he turns the ignition key, and the engine shudders into life.

"How about finding a place for breakfast?" he says. "Somewhere with decent coffee."

A weight lifts. Gone is the tension, replaced by unity and a shared mission. I reach for the radio, but he stops me.

"No more Billy Joel. Let's just talk."

# 12

Noah Winters lingered near balcony doors, pressing himself against damask-papered walls. Cigar smoke tangled with the smells of whisky and cologne, making the air heavy. He loosened the tie he bought special that morning, knowing tonight was a big deal.

Men in hand-tailored suits laughed too loudly while young actors arranged themselves artfully on velvet chaise longues. How did they know how to do that? Noah tried but felt dumb, like a girl. Like someone playing the part of a girl. He shifted his weight from one foot to the other, wanting to disappear. He just did not belong here.

There was some other guy he sort of thought he knew. A guy he'd seen at auditions. About his age. Or maybe just a few years older. He strutted around like he already cracked the code.

A hand gripped his arm. "First time?" The guy was 30, easy, and his alcoholic breath was hot on Noah's face. "Don't worry, you'll get used to these parties. Biedermeier throws a good one."

Noah shook him off politely. He needed to leave. Now. Catch the next Greyhound home to Fredericksburg and forget he ever thought Hollywood was any kind of dream worth having.

"You look like you're waiting outside the principal's office."

Noah turned to see a guy leaning against the wall, his pale blue eyes glinting with amusement as he took in the scene. About his age with a lean, rangy build and rust-coloured hair that brushed his shoulders. His faded Ramones t-shirt and scuffed leather jacket stood out among the designer suits.

"I'm Tim." He extended his hand.

"Noah."

"The guys here are something else, huh? Don't let them intimidate you." Tim shared a roguish wink. "Half of them are too wasted to remember their own names. The rest are trying to recall where they told their wives and mistresses they were going."

Noah shifted his weight. "I shouldn't be here. Got in over my head."

"Maybe. But you're here now." Tim cocked his head towards the crowd. "It's not like you have to let them touch you."

Noah's stomach churned. Tim was right, and he couldn't run back home with his tail between his legs. If he wanted to make it in LA, he had to stop acting like a dumb virgin. He knew what was expected.

He'd been here already. Twice.

"C'mon." Tim tilted his chin towards the balcony. "Let's get some air."

And then they were alone, out on a balcony overlooking LA. The city sprawled in a glittering panorama.

———

"Trust me, you'll die if you don't try the breakfast burritos at this place," Tim said as he led the way down a bustling LA street. Noah hurried to keep up, dodging locals, heads buried in their phones.

Palm trees silhouetted the cloudless blue sky. LA was nothing like Texas.

Inside a side-street café, the air was rich with cinnamon and sizzling bacon. Tim grinned, clearly in his element, and chatted with the waiter as they grabbed a table.

"Tell me about Fredericksburg," he said, dunking a chip in salsa.

Noah felt his face burn. "There's not much to tell. It's a small town outside Austin."

"And you're what...fifteen?"

"Back in March."

"Well, happy late birthday then." Tim blew him a kiss. "I'm a New Yorker born and bred. Moved out here when I was thirteen after my agent got me cast in a Disney sitcom."

Noah's eyes widened as Tim shrugged like having an agent and being a TV regular was nothing special.

"The show got cancelled, but I made enough money to rent a place out here."

"With your folks?"

Tim snorted. "We're not close. On account of me being a fag. Happy enough to take whatever cash this fag sends home, mind. You met Carlton Dupree?"

Noah had met many men since Aaron Biedermeier told him he had something special.

"Dude fixed me up with a rental unit. Kinda fancy. He'll do the same for you."

Their food arrived, and Noah took a tentative bite of the giant burrito.

"I grew up eating these babies," he says. "But this is amazing."

———————

Noah stared at the invitation, a knot forming in his stomach. Another party. Again, at the Biedermeier mansion.

"You kind of have to show." Tim sprawled on the bed in a rental unit that was anything but fancy. "If you're serious about making it in this town."

"What do you mean?"

"I mean, if you want a break in the business, you have to play ball. That means going to parties, making nice with the right people, and not asking questions. It's not like any of this is forever. Two years from now, you'll be tending bar, watching some other kids take their first steps."

Anger flared in Noah. "I'm not here to tend bar."

Tim grinned. "I know. So, let's go buy you something to wear."

————

"They didn't even ask to see my invitation," Noah said as security guards waved them past.

Tim laughed. "Your face fits, dude."

When they reached the main salon, Aaron greeted them with over-enthusiastic hugs before slipping away to talk to a group of men trading box-office numbers.

Noah grabbed Tim's arm. "Let's get something to drink."

Tim shook his head. "I have to talk to some dude about a part in a movie." He nodded over to where a much older man stood, waiting. Short, stout, with thinning hair.

The music grew louder, pulsing through the walls and rattling Noah's bones. The walls closed in, making him feel like he was being watched. His heart started to race. His palms grew clammy.

"There you are." He turned to see Aaron Biedermeier. "I want to introduce you to one of my friends."

————

Noah leaned against the balcony railing, gazing out at the hazy neon cityscape. Another weekend, more men with grabby hands and predatory eyes. The sliding door opened, and Tim stepped out, holding two glasses of champagne.

"We have to stop meeting like this," he said. "Thought you could use a drink."

Noah accepted it with a weak smile. "Thanks."

Tim eyed him. "You okay? You seem off your game tonight."

"I'm tired of this." Noah's voice cracked. "All of it. The parties, the drugs, these guys..."

He shook his head, ashamed of the dull resignation in his tone.

Tim went quiet for a moment. "Yeah. It's not the dream, is it?"

Noah swirled his champagne, watching the bubbles fizz.

"We could just leave," Tim said. "Forget LA. Fuck the whole fucking lot of them. Just you and me. I don't have an ego. We can wait tables somewhere new, somewhere better."

Noah met his intense gaze, a spark of hope flickering. "You really think we could take off and make a fresh start? We're under contract, surely."

Tim gripped his shoulder. "We also know stuff that can make those contracts go away." He pulled his phone from his pocket. "I call this my insurance policy."

Noah scrolls through photographs of men whose names the world knows, doing things with boys whose names the world doesn't.

"I'd rather flip burgers in bum-crack nowhere than die more each day. We deserve better."

Emotion clogged Noah's throat, and he managed a jerky nod, blinking back tears, then pulled Tim into a fierce hug. They held each other tight as the party raged on inside.

When they finally pulled back, Noah rested his forehead against Tim's. Their breaths mingled, hearts hammering in sync.

Tim squeezed Noah's shoulder, his eyes filled with empathy. "When we get out of here, things will be different. I promise."

Noah answered by closing the space between them.

The kiss tasted of champagne and new beginnings.

———

Noah double-checked the bus tickets as Tim finished packing. They'd climb on a plane in Vegas in three days and head east.

"One last party," Tim said, zipping his duffel bag.

Noah tucked tickets into his wallet. "Why can't we just forget about Vegas and go now?"

"Dupree is up my ass about CinemaCon." He held up his phone, scrolling through call after call and text after text. "I'm going to be the Belle of the Ball."

Noah hated what was happening to the guy he loved.

Tim touched his shoulder. "We've got this. Four days from now, we'll be stretched out on a beach somewhere, just you and me."

The voices in Noah's head started laughing. 'Who the hell do you think you are? Some jerk from Fredericksburg with an oversized ego.'

"Hey." Tim had a hold of his arm. "We're doing the right thing."

"What if we're not?"

Tim kissed him. "I'd sooner be dirt poor with you than in this vipers' nest."

———

As they stepped off the plane into Vegas's dry heat, unease coiled Noah's guts in knots. As a little kid, he often played with a boy who lived two streets away. Joey. Most everyone called Joey's mother a witch because she set herself up as a fortune teller. One afternoon, drinking lemonade, Noah asked what his future held, and she shook her head sadly. And so he went through life, waiting for the other shoe to drop.

"Boys." Aaron greeted them when they stepped out of the elevator into his suite. "I'm so glad you're here. Go on in and enjoy yourselves. It's party time."

The suite was packed with industry players, marking the end of CinemaCon. That young guy was there again. The one he saw before. And this time, they got to talking.

"I'm Judah," he said. "Aaron just cast me in his next picture."

"Noah. And like...wow. Good for you, dude."

Up close, the guy looked even younger. He acted less like he had his shit together.

Noah stuck to soda, determined not to mess up, when his future felt so close within reach. Tim was his usual party-animal self, chatting to producers and working the room. Noah's chest ached each time their eyes met. Just one shared glance conveyed their hopes, complicity, and bone-deep understanding.

When it happened, Noah knew. He just knew. He had felt it coming—an ill wind blowing.

———

Noah wasn't green. He'd been around drugs. Aaron's parties always featured rooms set aside, but this was different. His chest tightened when he saw Tim talking to an older guy, and he watched as Tim followed him down a narrow hallway into a bedroom, closing the door.

"Mix," Dupree hissed in his ear. "Do what you're here to do."

Later, when Tim joined Noah on the balcony, Noah knew something was wrong. People like him don't get a happy-ever-after. Not even a happy-just-for-now.

Tim's eyes looked glassy and fixed. His laughter was too loud. He was slurring and acting like he wasn't even sure where he was. Or who he was.

"I know our flight isn't for another few hours, but what if we get a cab to the airport?" Noah said, determined to act normal. "You can sober up."

Tim mumbled something before heading back inside.

It all happened so fast. One minute, Tim was talking to some older guy over by the bar and laughing like he just heard the best joke ever. The next, he was on the floor. Eyes lidded. A trail of drool hangs from parted lips.

Someone yelled to get help.

They kept on talking, but Noah couldn't make out words. All he heard was the sound of the other shoe falling.

# 13

M y stomach screams, 'Feed me!' when the first signs for Oklahoma City appear. The skyline looms like a distant mirage, the setting sun painting buildings in hues of pink and orange. We've hardly spoken since Noah spilled his story, pouring out his heart and choking back tears. Even Billy Joel kept his distance, letting Ed Sheeran take over.

Skyscrapers rise in silhouette, modern towers juxtaposed against a domed capitol building. Neon signs advertise diners and motels in mid-century fonts. The Oklahoma River winds through the heart of the city, glinting blood-orange as wide brick-built streets give way to towering glass facades. Street lights flicker as the last hints of the sun fade.

Noah parks outside The Grand Hotel, and I peer at the tall art-deco towers of what is almost certainly one of the finest places in town.

"We don't need a room," I say. "I'm down with camping out in a rest area."

"We're neither of us much use to anyone in this state. Tell me you wouldn't kill for a shower and clean clothes. Dinner and wine that don't come from a cardboard carton. Eight uninterrupted hours of sleep."

Everything about this sounds like heaven.

He puts on his baseball cap and shades to check us into the hotel as I wait in a red leather wing-back chair, watching this part of the world wander past while trying to find words that come close to explaining how sorry I am.

"You ready?" Noah hands me a room key card.

I haul my backpack onto my shoulder, and he calls the lift.

The doors ping open on floor six, and when I step out, he doesn't follow, and I ask if he maybe pushed the wrong button.

He blushes. "I'm three floors up—964. I wanted rooms closer, but nothing doing. I figured we could meet for dinner at eight."

I don't have it in me to do anything more than tell him that's a fabulous idea.

———

Separate rooms. The notion strikes me as ludicrous. Prissy. Passive-aggressive. Mine is a generic beige box with way too many table lamps. A window looks out over the sprawling city skyline.

I sink onto the perfectly made bed, the starched sheets cool against my skin, run my hands over the soft duvet, and then ball it in my fists.

My breath comes faster as I look around at the bland art, the polished furniture, and the plush towels. It's so clean, so impersonal. I grab a stiff pillow and crush it to my chest, then fling it across the room. It hits the wall with a soft thud.

Tears prickle hot behind my eyes, but I blink them back, staring at the ceiling as the hollow in my chest expands, picturing Noah three floors above, lying on his own smooth, crisp sheets.

A chasm opens between us.

The tears fall now, burning down my cheeks as I gasp for air and bury my face to muffle the sobs, thrashing on the bed, clawing at the duvet, kicking, and punching until feathers burst from ripped seams. I want to tear this room apart until it looks as destroyed as I feel.

And then I fall back, chest heaving, face wet. Loneliness crushes me more than I've ever known. The yearning for Noah becomes a physical ache, like someone severed part of me.

My phone pings with a text from Noah...

Dinner?

I text back that I need sleep. That I have a headache.

He can eat alone. Separate rooms. Separate tables.

I splash cold water on swollen eyes and blow my running nose. I'm not hungry any more. I need a drink. I need noise, crowds, and distractions from the gaping hole inside me. Grabbing my least rumpled shirt, I head out alone.

———

The night air is humid as I set off, waving away the offer of a taxi, needing space to clear my head.

My phone dictates directions, and up ahead, neon lights flash. I head towards the sound of music and laughter, along a busy street lined with bars sporting rainbow flags.

More than anything, I need a drink. I want to perch myself on a bar stool and wave down a man with access to beer and tell him to keep them coming.

I push my way inside what looks like the busiest bar. It's small and packed wall-to-wall. The guy serving is tall and muscular, with a thick beard and tattoos. Not my type. Not normally, but tonight, he could be. He nods, pulling a bottle from a cooler and popping the top. I take a long swig.

From there, I move next door to the lively club, where music throbs and strobe lights wash the crowd in techni-colour. A guy smiles my way, but I want to lose myself in the noise.

On the dance floor, my eyes close, and I let go of everything holding me down.

And he's just there.

A dark-haired, bright-eyed stranger. Cocky as hell. Built like a brick shithouse.

He leans in. "Want to get out of here?"

I follow him through the crowd.

His apartment is a mess. A student share, I guess, with clothes strewn. Pizza boxes, beer bottle candle sticks.

We're on his bed, kissing. His hands explore my body, and his touch is gentle, almost reverent. Do more, I want to yell in his face.

I moan, arching my back as he reaches for a condom.

"You good with this?" he asks.

I need him.

————

Hunger overwhelms me as I join a downtown queue at a food truck run by drag queens. Their infectious laughter lifts my shame-filled spirits, and I watch as they toss eggs onto griddles, flip burgers, and dole out portions of 'fries'. I order the biggest burger on the menu, and the queen behind the window winks knowingly.

"For the road," she says with a smile. "You look like you partied hard."

A black SUV whips past, and the guy driving yells abuse. An empty bottle hurtles from the snarling crowd, and flashing blue lights send us scattering.

I shrink into shadows as men in uniform line the abused, not the abusers, against a wall, cuffing them amid cries of protest.

Shame burns as I slink away, unseen.

Exhausted and disgusted with everything about myself, I return to the fluorescence of the hotel's empty lobby. My body aches. My shirt clings. A guy sitting behind the reception desk looks up from reading a book and nods good evening. It's more like good morning.

————

My hotel room is a mess. How do I explain what happened? I sink onto the edge of the bed, head in my hands.

Noah trusted me with his darkest secrets and his deepest pain, and I repaid that trust by getting wasted and hooking up with some random guy. He wasn't even hot. Not really. Not when my beer goggles slipped.

Bile rises at the thought of fumbling fingers and sloppy kisses. It meant nothing—just a pathetic attempt to numb my hurt. The worst kind of betrayal. Will Noah forgive me? Or have I lost his friendship for good just when we were starting to truly connect?

Disgust and disappointment will cloud his kind eyes when he learns what I've done. And he has to learn it because I can't not tell him. How could I be so careless with something so precious as his trust?

Except, despite everything, a small, dark part of me doesn't regret anything at all. I wanted to escape the pain and forget myself for a few hours in a stranger's arms. I wanted to be the guy who drinks happy hour cocktails at the Pink Flamingo and flirts with the bar staff. The guy who fucks a different stranger each weekend.

And, so, that's what I became.

The relief was temporary, sure, and now the hollowness returns. Tenfold.

# 14

The smell of pancakes turns my stomach. I need black coffee, not stodge. My throat is dry, and my head is pounding. Last night comes back in flashes. Strobe lights and gyrating bodies. Hands grabbing, lips crushing together. A penis that felt larger than it looked.

Other hotel guests chat and laugh, loading plates with breakfast bounty. Families, couples, and friends.

Noah has already laid claim to a quiet corner table and is playing *pick-up sticks* with strips of crispy bacon. How come he still has access to box-fresh sweaters when I'm down to a chewing-gum-grey t-shirt, rinsed in the bathroom sink, and drip-dried on the shower rail?

Our eyes meet, and his smile is both genuine and inviting. He gets up, like a gentleman might, to pull out a chair and wave to a waiter for coffee. "Did your headache get better?"

"Yeah," I say, and sort of want to say more but can't be bothered.

"You look like crap."

"Yeah, cheers. None taken."

I stare down at the table. How could I let myself be the kind of guy who picks up strangers, fucks on a futon, and lies about needing to get home as he's booked on an early shift?

"I think you serve yourself," Noah says.

"Coffee will do."

"You should fill up. We have a long day of driving. I totally recommend the blueberry pancakes."

My stomach flips.

"You OK, Kyle?" he says. "You're kind of sweaty. You didn't get a bug or something?"

I push back my chair. "Is the bathroom through there?"

Out of sight, I pour myself two enormous glasses of orange juice and glug them down like they're my dying wish.

A small girl stares.

"You're not supposed to do that," she says. "It's rude to drink standing up."

I pull my best *go-screw-yourself-little-girl* face.

There's a newsstand near the breakfast bar, loaded with the morning papers, and I scan headlines, taking in little, until I spot a familiar face.

Aaron.

And then the headline.

**ABUSE ALLEGATIONS DIRECTOR WAKES FROM COMA.**

———

How do you rain on someone's parade when they're acting like they don't care about a single thing in the world?

Noah is demolishing a second stack of blueberry pancakes. Does the guy have some fat-eating gene that lets him eat whatever he wants? Mac and cheese. Burgers dripping grease. Coffee topped with enough whipped cream, sprinkles, and marshmallows to put anyone else into a diabetic coma. His six-pack stays put while I'm already hiding the strained top button of my jeans behind a heavy-duty leather belt.

"Hey," I say, forcing my voice to stay steady. "Did you catch the news this morning?"

He cuts a pancake in half and rams it into his mouth. Butter dribbles down his chin. "Did I miss anything?"

"It's just...I think perhaps you ought to..."

He's not listening and has taken out his phone to tap at the screen. I hold my breath, waiting for whatever reaction the news of Aaron waking from his coma will bring. And then he holds up the screen to show me a photograph of a street lined with neon signs.

"Beale Street," he says. "You are going to love Memphis, dude. It has such a vibe."

A waiter comes to clear plates, and Noah engages him in mundane conversation before returning to me. "What did you say about the news?"

I make a decision, and it's probably not my shining moment. I decide not to tell him about Aaron. Not that I plan on actively stopping him from finding out, but why accelerate what will almost certainly be his speedy return to LA?

Noah extols the virtues of Graceland and Shelby Farms Park and how we *have* to go line dancing.

Memphis sounds like hell.

He grabs his phone again. "I should call the hospital. They expect me to call this time most mornings."

Damn it.

"He's awake." I blurt. "Aaron. I saw a newspaper headline. I wasn't going to tell you...but now you know."

Noah stares as my cheeks turn red. For a moment, the only sound is the scraping of plates.

Eventually, he speaks. "We should hit the road. Aaron's waking adds pressure. We can take turns and drive the night through."

"You could ask at reception," I say. "They can probably arrange a flight. I'll get a bus. Whatever."

He wrinkles his nose. "I mean, we need to crack on to River Valley. At some point, I'm going to get pressured into going back to LA to be photographed at Aaron's bedside."

I baulk at this rare glimpse into just how little love there is between the two men.

"Let me at least ask about flights," I say. "Just in case."

Noah pushes away his plate. "Aaron will be fine. Shit floats."

---

Noah fiddles with his wallet, flirting with the receptionist, and she keeps glancing back at her colleague to signal she's assisting someone famous. I loiter near a wall-mounted TV screen, half listening to feel-good stories and cheerful banter from upbeat daytime presenters.

*Coming up...a scatter cushion that could change your life. Jay's been out and about finding the perfect avocado. And understanding the psychology of socks. Why do they disappear in the dryer?*

Then, Aaron's face fills the screen, and a 'Breaking News' banner scrolls: *'Director at the centre of abuse allegations out of coma'.*

They've used a still from some movie premiere, his usually confident grin replaced with an expression that's all too human. Noah has to have seen, but he acts like he doesn't care while posing for a selfie with the reception staff and high-fiving a porter.

As he walks over and grabs his bag, our hands brush.

"We should hit the road. Darlene, on reception, reckons today will be *hotter than a two-dollar pistol.*"

I follow him outside, blinking in the morning sunshine. Is he playing things cool until we're alone, making out this is nothing, just in case someone already tracked him down and there's a long-lens camera trained on us? I see how his hands tremble as he fumbles with a key chain.

"You mind driving today?" he says. "If we're stopped, I'll charm our way out of a ticket."

"You don't think it might be better to head for the airport?"

He holds up a hand, like this isn't up for discussion. "I know how you're the expert on driving stick, but I should let you know, first is sticky, but she drives like a dream after that."

We get in. I turn the key, crunch the gearbox, and kangaroo out of the hotel car park, following signs for the I-40.

––––––––

Noah doesn't reach for the radio today. The only sound comes from the engine and the rumbling road. Green fields meet the clear blue sky, trees pepper the landscape, and I take in huge lungfuls of fresh, earthy air to calm my rattled nerves.

"Noah," I say, my gaze steady on the endless road. "I'm sorry about dinner last night."

He sniffs. "You missed a great lobster."

I want to say more and explain everything, but shame sticks the words in my throat.

He holds up a creased map. "Did we just pass Stillwater?"

Another sign blurs by.

"How about Shawnee?" I say.

"That could work." He squints at the map and purses his lips. "There's a good chance we're lost."

My stomach knots. Part of me hopes we never find our way from this nowhere space.

"Want me to pull over?" I say.

He shakes his head. "We'll get where we're going."

I hear how he's forcing himself to sound upbeat, and yet his hands refuse to stop shaking. His face stays clammy and pale.

"Are you...OK?" I say. "You want to talk about Aaron?"

I steal a glance. His jaw is clenched, lost in thought. And that's when I realise. Everything he said back at the hotel was a lie. Noah Winters was playing a part. Acting. He wants to be with the man he's due to marry. Not me.

I break the tense silence. "If you're having second thoughts, that's fine. I mean, fly back to LA."

He doesn't speak.

"I'm pretty sure if I take the next exit, we'd be on the right road for the airport."

Noah heaves a sigh laden with frustration. "What's waiting for me there? A bunch of fawning reporters wanting to hear how happy I am that the fucker woke up."

I give it a heartbeat. "And are you?"

Noah turns to me. "Am I what?"

"Happy."

The silence between us grows deafening.

"You don't have to pretend with me," I say, picking each word with care. "I know this is complicated."

He stares through the side window. "You don't know me. You don't know anything."

I sense this cruelty is a defence mechanism and refuse to bite back.

"We all have to do stuff we don't like," I say, trying to be upbeat. "And it's not like you're marrying him 'til death do you part. It's six years. Five, really, if you think about it. You're bound to spend time apart before announcing the divorce. And there's going to be location filming."

Noah's jaw tightens. "When you put it like that, who can resist?"

"This whole road trip thing," I continue. "Maybe you needed a distraction."

"Shut the hell up," he snaps. "You're not my fucking therapist."

I fall silent, and the tension in the van grows stifling.

His voice comes out strained. "I just...I don't know what I want any more."

It's the most honest he's been, and I realise how much he's struggling between loyalty to the past and yearning for something new. I ache for him and the pain this is causing. But now is not the time to push.

"It's going to be okay," I say. "The world keeps turning."

Noah stares ahead, tapping his fingers on the dashboard. "The thing is, Kyle, too many things have already happened. I need to see things through with him. Even if it destroys me."

I have never felt so powerless, and I reach across the space between us.

His body shakes with silent sobs.

# 15

Noah gazes through a half-open window, his eyes now hidden behind expensive sunglasses. I focus on the road ahead, hands gripped tight at ten and two. In my mind, I shuffle through all the things I could say to make any of this better. Except words can't work miracles. This won't get better.

A sign up ahead heralds the Checotah Lake Recreation Area, and on impulse, I take the exit. Noah shuffles in his seat as we pull into a sandy car park dotted with faded picnic tables.

"I thought we should take a break," I say. "Stretch our legs. Clear our heads."

Noah surveys the lake, calm and blue under the blazing sun. Maybe I did something wrong, breaking the trip, but I can only take so much sulking in silence. A breeze rustles through pine boughs, and a wisp of a smile makes it to his face as he points to a yellow and blue sign.

"I would put money on you never having eaten at a Sonic Drive-In."

We join a slow-moving line of cars and vans, and when it's our turn, Noah leans across to bark a food order.

"Two Supersonic Double Cheeseburgers, extra onions, an order of cheddar peppers, and two Cherry Limeades."

"Now what?" I ask, as if navigating some unfamiliar ritual.

"You park up, dummy."

I steer the van under a canopy of trees, their leaves forming a dappled tapestry of light and shadow. The engine falls silent, and a profound stillness takes hold. Our tiny piece of the big, bad world holds its breath.

A gangly kid on roller skates weaves between parked cars and hammers on the side of the van.

"Dinner is served." Noah sounds happy for the first time since leaving the hotel. "This guy is our car hop."

The tang of cheese mingles with wood-smoked burgers. I've never tried cherry limeade. From now on, it's my drink of choice.

"This must be like a billion calories," I say. "Shouldn't it come with a side order of statins?"

"Road food." Noah winks. "Fills you up and stays put."

I lean back and shut my eyes. It's grown hot and humid, like another storm might have picked us out, but I'm too loaded up with meaty grease and cherry lime to care.

Noah nudges me. "Let's take a walk. Burn off those evil calories."

---

Our feet crunch on a gravel path. Under darkening skies, the water turns shades of deep green. The earth here is damp, and wildflowers flourish. As pretty as all of this is and as welcome as the fresh air tastes, I can't help but wonder if Noah is delaying telling me he's changed his mind about River Valley, and when at last he speaks, it's like he read my mind.

"You know there's always a chance of Hyson letting us down."

I swallow but try to sound upbeat. "Whatever happens happens."

Out-of-nowhere, he turns to me. "You make everything better, Kyle. You have no idea how much you mean to me."

I'm taken aback. "That's really sweet, Noah."

He crouches, picks out a flat pebble, and skims it over the water. It skips three times.

"One thing I do know for sure." He straightens up. "Dupree won't be waiting for us."

He turns to share a small smile before holding up his mobile, playing a press conference recorded on some shaky phone cam. Dupree has on a white shirt and yet another blue suit. He's sweaty and bug-eyed, trying to convince three rows of journalists that Aaron is awake but not yet up to talking.

"Where's Noah Winters?" The question from a woman with a black bob causes Dupree visible irritation.

"Noah is shooting on location and being kept informed of any change in Aaron's condition. We speak every few hours."

"The lying sod," I say, but Noah takes back the phone.

"Don't you see? This proves Dupree fell for the whole Napa Valley crap. Better yet, if he planned on fitting you up for what happened to Tim, he'd have made some kind of move by now."

I rub my eyes, frustrated and unsure how Noah has worked this out from one press conference.

"Has he been in touch?" I say.

Noah shows me six missed calls plus a string of increasingly abrupt text messages.

We stand together, staring at the water. A dam bursts inside, and my eyes prickle. Soon enough, I'm sobbing, bent double, and choking back tears. I've tried so hard to deal with every bit of madness the past week has tossed in my path. Each new hand grenade chucked my way. Eating junk food in a car park next to a lake has been the first thing that came close to being real.

Noah cocks his head to one side. "I'm still here for you."

I force my mouth to smile. "This is just...I don't know...sleep deprivation."

The first cold drop of rain hits the back of my head. Lightning spikes, and thunder moves closer. He grabs my hand, and we run together, tumbling into the van, panting. Him in the driver's seat, and me pulling a towel from a bag.

"Had your fill of my driving?" I say.

He grins. "I was on '*The View*', and Whoopi Goldberg did this speech about how it's important to acknowledge that every single one of us has limits." He reaches down between the seats. "You're a brilliant map reader."

Torrential rain cascades, obliterating the lake as if some painter swiped a wet brush across a once-tranquil canvas. Still, the car hop skates past with food orders.

"Seriously?" I say. "People expect service in this?"

Noah pulls a face that sort of says sorry. "We built an entire nation on the idea that money changes everything. You pay, we play."

Almost as soon as it started, the storm blows itself out, and the pounding rain dwindles to a soft patter, leaving behind a surreal calm. The air smells fresh and rejuvenated. The earth has been scrubbed clean. The lake once again mirrors the perfect blue sky.

"I've decided." Noah switches on the radio and tunes to banjo-twanging country music. "Memphis, here we come."

———

As the sun descends, we get our first glimpse of the Memphis skyline and the mighty Mississippi River. Noah points out the neon lights on Beale Street.

"Mom brought me here when I was eleven." The city lights illuminate his profile, and there's a tenderness to his tone. "We had this beat-up Ford Taurus. More rust than car, and she hooked up a coat hanger to keep the exhaust from dragging on the road. But I always wanted to see Graceland, so we came."

I lean back in my seat. He's been so guarded about his family.

"It was mid-summer. Like now, hotter than hell, so we rolled down the windows and told the wind to do its work." He laughs to himself, and it sounds wistful. "I tasted the dust on my tongue and listened to the radio playing Elvis songs. Mom loved Elvis."

He pauses again.

"We didn't have much, but for a couple of days in this crazy city, we felt...special. It was Mom and me against the world, and I was so...happy."

There's a trace of longing on his face. He's the little boy who wanted nothing more than his mother's love, inside the man who still carries the wounds of walking into something terrible.

"We can go to all those same places," I say.

He considers it, then shakes his head, a gleam in his eye. "I can't remember the last time I was allowed out on my own to drink in a gay bar."

———

The Yellow Penny isn't what I'd pictured. Where are all the cowboy line dancers and the portraits of Dolly? This place is dark. And hot. And it stinks of sex and sweat. The bass pounds, reverberating through a sticky floor. Strobe lights slice through the darkness, revealing glistening skin and writhing bodies. They have a dark room. And a cage.

The barman slams down drinks, his fingers wet with spilled alcohol. After each beer, Noah downs shots. Doubles, not singles, waving for more each time. His grin grows loose. His laughter uncontrolled. He stumbles backwards into a guy trying to get served and slurs an apology, offering to pay for his beer and lurching for the bar to stay upright.

Noah points to the bottles lining the back counter. "Another shot. Tequila this time."

I shift uneasily. "Don't you think you've had enough?"

He acts like he's desperate to escape the pretty but poisonous little gift-wrapped world Biedermeier Pictures built for him. I wish I could say or do something to ease his pain, but a crowded, seedy leather bar is no place for a heart-to-heart.

One minute, he's waving his hands and singing to whatever tune blasts from overhead speakers. The next, he slumps onto a stool, propping up his head with his hand.

"If I go to pee, you'll be OK?" I say.

He blows a sloppy kiss. "I have all these hot dudes to keep me company."

I push through a crowded corridor to a bathroom that reeks of piss. The tiled floor is wet, and one flickering neon light illuminates a row of basins caked with grime. I choose the least disgusting stall, the floor littered with wads of wet toilet paper.

When I get back, Noah is gone.

I scan the dance floor, where shadows grind and grope. A big guy shoves past, the stench of sweat blending with the musky odour of sex baked into the walls, the floors, and the ceiling.

A hand grabs my crotch. Hot breath on my neck. "I got something you'd like, honey."

"Not tonight, honey."

Noah is sitting on a bar stool further up, but he isn't alone. A guy wearing a yellow rubber jockstrap whisper-yells something in his ear. Under strobe lighting, his tattooed arm looks enormous as he signals, bleary-eyed, towards the dark room.

I'm not about to let this happen. Noah's drunk and doesn't know what he's doing. Also, if anyone is going into a dark room with him, it's going to be me.

There's a hand on my thigh. A guy in leather chaps. "What are you into?"

"Not this," I say, looking back, but I'm too late. Noah's gone. And he has the van keys. What if he loses them? Or me?

A gloved hand grabs my wrist, but I yank it free.

Noah sways near a speaker, his eyes bulging and bloodshot.

———

A blast of night air causes all the beer and tequila chasers in his system to work their debilitating magic, and as we cross the street, his knees buckle. I catch his arm as laughter bubbles from within.

He throws back his head and roars. "It's been too long since I did this. Where now?"

I try to keep him upright. "Back to the van."

"Booooo."

I grit my teeth. He's doing what I do all the time back home. He sways and jabs a finger towards a line of men waiting to get into some other club.

"We should go dancing some more."

His chosen place to *go dancing* oozes little charm. A weather-worn rainbow flag hangs above the door, its colours muted by time. Noah's grin widens as he drinks in the scene.

"We have to drive tomorrow," I say. "It's already late."

He laughs and leans in, as if he's going to kiss me. "Why? We're looking for fun, right?"

I could let this happen. Just kiss him back. He's pissed as a fart, and this will be big, wet, and sloppy. Hands will find hands. We'll more than likely drag each other down some alleyway.

"Stop." I push him away. "Give me the van keys."

"Only if you kiss me."

I reach into his jacket pocket, jumping away as he swings to grab them back.

"That's not fair. You stole from me. That means you owe me *two* kisses."

"Nobody is kissing anyone. There will be no kissing," I say. "Just sleeping."

"Ah, come on." Noah juts out his lower lip. "I never dance these days."

"It's late, and you're wasted. Someone will have a

phone, and they'll film you, and it'll go viral. Noah Winters liquored up and dancing while the man he's going to marry recovers in a hospital bed. Dupree just told everyone you're on location, filming."

Noah stares like I slapped him sober. He staggers a little more, but then stands stock still.

"The world is a big old ball of dirt." He reaches for my arm. "I had three guys tell me they wanted to fuck me in there. That's good, right?"

I shift my weight to support him. "I'm sure your mother would be super proud."

And then he works free and skips ahead, swaying on the spot, spinning in circles, and looking up at the stars with a blissful smile. "For once, I got to be someone else. I didn't have to be Noah Winters, who makes movies. Noah Winters, who poses with his shirt off and talks about how much he lives for luuurve."

He strikes poses like Madonna doing 'Vogue', and then it's like the plug gets pulled, and he slumps down, squatting on the kerb. I sit, too, linking my fingers with his in a quiet show of support.

"You think I'm a pervert," he says. "I let Aaron make me do all that stuff just to get movie roles. Mom needed the money. It's not like he was ugly. You should see the guys who..." He meets my eyes. "How old were you, your first time?"

"Fifteen," I say. "Kind of. Me and a boy from school got to be friends. I went around his house most days. It wasn't serious or anything. He's married now. Got three kids. Drives a white van."

Noah belches. "Everyone moves on."

I hesitate, but then throw an arm around his shoulder. "I'm going nowhere."

"Kyle, you need to know. You're amazing, okay? You really are." His eyes turn intense even through the haze of alcohol. "I really care about you."

"You're drunk, Noah."

"Maybe. But that doesn't make it any less true." He leans in close, and we sit that way for a while. Three drag queens wander past and scream to get a room.

When they're gone, Noah lifts his head. "You're the first guy I ever told about what happened. And you didn't run away." I say nothing, sensing he isn't done. The tears start. "Back at that bar, I got to be someone else. I *want* to be that guy. I never got to grow up."

I cradle his head once more and let him cry himself out. When I'm sure he's done, we get to our feet and head for the rest area and our parked-up, battered van.

————

Sitting with the windows wound down, the only sound is the faint hum of the highway and a baseline from a distant bar.

"I need to pee," Noah says. "If I get dragged off by a trucker, remember me as a good guy."

I glance over my shoulder to make sure he's safe before pulling out my phone and calling Milly.

"Well, well, long time no chat, stranger. To what do I owe the pleasure?" Her playful tone hardens. "I'm assuming this isn't a social call. I saw the news. Your so-called husband is alive and kicking."

I pause, unsure what to say. Aaron is the least of my problems. "We're in Memphis, and somehow Noah talked me into going to some seedy bar. Jesus, it was bad. It made the Pink Flamingo look like the Savoy tearoom. I only agreed because I figured it might cheer him up. But he got crazy drunk, Milly. Like way over the top."

"Let me guess. He's away, throwing up in some hedge."

I glance around and see him taking a piss under a street light.

"We kissed the other night." I pinch the bridge of my nose. "And then tonight. It was like he wanted more."

She snorts. "I've been out with you enough times to understand that's what gay men do when they get hammered."

"When I saw all those guys touching him, I wanted to..." I trail off, unsure how to describe the possessive pang in my chest.

Milly groans to herself. "He's engaged. To Aaron Biedermeier."

I stare at a dark, star-scattered sky, more lost than ever.

"What if..." I begin. "What if it's not only because he was drunk? The more time we spend together, the more I..."

"Don't go down that road." Her voice softens. "At least one of you is going to end up hurt."

I comb fingers through my hair, watching Noah struggle to zip up his jeans before staggering into the road, causing a passing truck to honk.

"I should go," I say. "He's about to get himself killed."

She clears her throat. "One more question, Kyle. When do you plan on letting Noah know you're in love with him?"

———

Noah slumps onto the ground as I haul the tarp and rope from the van.

"You need help?" he calls. "You tie rope like a girl."

"I've got it," I say. "You rest up."

He tries to stand, stumbles, and then falls to his knees in a patch of damp grass. After several failed attempts, I toss the rope to the ground, swearing and cursing. A dog barks in a nearby yard.

"Noah." I nudge him with my foot. But he's out like a light, his soft snores blending with the distant hum of the highway. I wrestle him around and onto the tarp, on his side so he won't choke on vomit, and drape a blanket over his already comatose body. He seems content, wrapped in scratchy nylon, eyes closed, his chest rising and falling in a steady rhythm.

A part of me has guilt pangs at the sight of a big-time actor sleeping off a drunken night on the cold ground. Another part of me, a part I'm less proud of, can't wait for him to wake with a sore head and beg me to tell him he did nothing stupid.

"Goodnight," I say, and climb into the passenger seat, determined to get some sleep. Knowing already that tomorrow morning I'll ache like buggery.

I saw a different side of him tonight. Noah acted wild and unreserved, anonymous at last, seeking release.

Playing a role. That's what I'm doing too, if I'm honest. Playing the part of a friend when my heart wants so much more.

We almost kissed! Again.

His faint snores carry on the night air, and I stare through the windscreen, up at the stars. What if he doesn't feel the same? Or worse, what if he does but still won't leave Aaron? He can't abandon a 'fiancé' who spent the best part of a month in a coma.

At least, not for five years.

Can I wait that long? Probably.

I think about what Milly said. Telling him how I feel could go so wrong.

There's every chance he'll have no memory of what happened tonight, and I'll do what I do best and shove my feelings back down, ignoring the ache in my chest.

Exhaustion overrides, and restless dreams take over. Silhouettes of cacti and Joshua trees haunt the barren landscape.

Noah is there, but not there.

With me, then gone.

# 16

I'm jolted awake by knuckles rapping on the van window. My neck aches, and when I stretch, my right knee cracks. At first, I don't know where I am, and then I blink and see Noah holding two greasy paper bags and a cardboard tray of coffee.

"Rise and shine, sleeping beauty," he says with a grin as I blink away the grog of flashbacks. A dark nightclub. So many men. Carrying him back. The nearly kiss.

"What time is it?" I say, as he climbs into the driver's seat and hands me a coffee.

"Half after eight. Or eight-thirty, as you Brits like to say, to confuse the hell out of us dumb yanks."

We eat breakfast together in tired silence, with me masking schadenfreude each time he winces.

"How is the head?" I say.

"I've felt better." He glances over at the crumpled tarp on the ground. "Did I say or do anything I need to apologise for?"

I don't answer. Why open a can of worms? Instead, I

reach for the first-aid kit and dig out Tylenol. He swallows two with another glug of coffee.

"So, what's the plan for today?" I try to sound casual. "You think you're sober enough to drive, or am I back behind the wheel?"

Noah stares out across the empty rest area at a woman dressed in blue, wheeling a mop and bucket past a shed-like office building.

"We need to talk." He takes a deep breath, hesitating, and then looks at me. I repress a shiver. "You go first."

"I know what I said, and I get how this goes against everything, but I need to head back to LA."

I nod. Automatically. Like I knew this was borrowed time.

He runs a hand through his hair, a gesture of frustration. "Don't you want to call me a dumbass? A wanker?"

The word sounds weird coming from his mouth.

"I suppose I always knew this was coming," I say. "This whole road trip thing was only ever a way to fill time."

I'm trying to start a fight. It's what I do.

He stares ahead, his chin raised. "Aaron is awake, and sure, Dupree covered for me, but soon enough, someone will want to know where I am. They'll try tracking down whatever location I'm supposed to be shooting in. And when I'm not there..." There's a heaviness in his voice, a mix of duty and regret. "I wish things were different, Kyle. I really do."

The sincerity in his eyes is real. And that hurts the most.

"You've got to do what's best for your career." I make

it sound like he'd be mad to do anything else. "Whatever's best for your *business arrangement*."

I've picked each and every word to inflict pain.

"I need to talk to Aaron," he says. "About the wedding. About everything."

My face sets like stone. I smile, making sure nothing shows in my eyes. "You want me to drive to the airport? I'm no expert, but your breath alone tells me you're over the legal limit."

Noah's face tightens. "You know, Kyle, there's more to life than being a constant smartass. I'm dealing with actual issues here."

The words sting, but I scoff. "Oh, please. Spare me the sob story, Noah. You're running back to your perfect little life."

He folds his angry arms. "You think this is easy for me? You think I want to go back to all that shit? You're fucking impossible to talk to sometimes."

Anger boils inside me, mixed with sorrow. "So, that's it, then? Do we give up on finding Bo Hyson? Give up on maybe putting an end to all the bad things your beloved Aaron did to so many guys. Give up on Tim. On Judah. You go running back to keep your side of the deal."

Noah's eyes darken. "What's the alternative? Stick around with a guy who keeps pushing everyone away. How's that working out for you, huh?"

I want to hit back and hurt him more, but the words cut deep.

"It's better than faking a marriage," I say, but my voice lacks conviction.

He shakes his head, a bitter laugh escaping him. "You wouldn't know a real problem if it hit you in the face."

We've both crossed a line.

He starts the van, the engine breaking tense silence.

———

Noah manoeuvres towards the airport's long-term car park, where our bright red van sits out-of-place next to the luxury cars and sparkling SUVs—the embarrassing country cousin at a high church christening.

"I checked online. There's a flight in two hours." My voice is croaky from sitting in silence. "You change in Denver."

He nods and turns off the engine. It clicks as metal cools and contracts. Noah doesn't let go of the steering wheel. He's staring at a sign displaying details of how much it costs to park long- and short-term.

Finally, he speaks. "There's probably a British Consulate in Nashville. It's three hours away. But they'll help you get home. Don't worry about the van. Just text me where you leave it, and I'll have someone arrange collection."

I knew this moment was coming, but now I want more time.

"Couldn't Dupree tell the press there's a tropical storm or something wherever you're supposed to be? That you'll be with Aaron in a few days?"

He turns to face me, his eyes filled with regret and longing. "Even one more day, and this all gets harder."

I force an upbeat agreement, ignoring my heavy

heart. "Sure. And you're engaged to the guy. You need to be there. It's what everyone expects."

"If there was any other way..."

"Yeah." I swallow the lump rising into my throat. "We'll always have Memphis."

Noah hesitates, caught off guard. "Are you still pissed at me?"

Obviously, I am, but what good does it do to say anything out loud? He's still going to board the next flight. I'm still going to drive three hours to Nashville.

"We're so close to River Valley," I say. "Can't you see this through? Or all that stuff about getting Hyson to talk to the police and make things right—was that just words?"

I hear how I'm trying for a reaction.

He pulls the keys from the ignition and hands them to me.

"Sometimes," he says, "the things we want most are the things that scare us the most."

"So, what now?" My voice barely rises above a whisper.

"Now, we say goodbye."

He pulls me into a hug.

———

We stand together outside the terminal, watching as cars pull up. People get out, grab their bags, and hug farewell.

"I plan on talking to Dupree." Noah sounds less like my Noah. Now he's back to playing the role of Noah Winters, movie star. A man who tells people what they need to do to improve his life. "I'll make sure he keeps your name out of everything."

I can't help myself. "Good luck with that."

"Please, Kyle..." There's something new in his voice, and I realise I might be getting on his nerves by refusing to roll over and agree that flying to LA is the best thing for everyone. I count to ten in my head. Dave called me defensive, and I've worked hard to change, but, you know...leopards and spots.

"I hope you *can* find some sort of favour to trade that gets him to back off," I say, turning my voice down to cold. "But Hyson is the only witness still living. Apart from you. And Dupree. And the man you're about to marry. The odds seem kind of stacked."

"I could call Dupree. Tell him we need a private jet, and you get to come back with me. I'll make sure he returns your passport."

I stare, dumbfounded. Where was this idea ten minutes ago? Why was I supposed to drive to Nashville?

"Gee, thanks, buddy. I don't want to be no trouble or nothing."

"Kyle..."

I hold up a finger to stop him from talking because he's about to tell me again that he doesn't have a choice when he absolutely does. He wants my blessing. He's not getting it.

"Best go check in," I say. "When people recognise you, they'll insist on selfies."

Noah leans in to kiss my cheek, and I step back. He stares a moment longer, then turns and walks towards revolving doors.

My eyes feel gritty and dry. I'm exhausted. Days of driving in that ridiculous red rust bucket on a never-ending highway have made me want to curl up and sleep for a year.

A sign for the airport hotel offers rooms for 60 bucks.

———————

The hotel lobby is a sterile space—beige floor tiles and white walls with generic landscape paintings in chunky brown frames. A bored receptionist in a sky-blue polyester jacket glances up from her magazine long enough to slide a form across the fake wood reception desk.

"You got ID?"

I pat pockets, hoping to act my way out of this one. "I must have left my passport in the car." I turn around as if I plan on going to find it.

"No matter. Initial here and put your card in the machine."

I make my way down a hallway lit by humming fluorescent bulbs, the sludge brown carpet muffling any footsteps. The whole place stinks of industrial cleaner. Room doors in chipped white paint are marked with tarnished metal numbers.

This is not the Beverly Hills Hotel.

Inside room 108, two double beds sport covers with nondescript geometric patterns in murky greens and browns. Thin pillows flop against wood laminate headboards. A nightstand disfigured by coffee cup rings holds an ugly plastic lamp.

I kick off my trainers on the scratchy carpet and

collapse onto the bed furthest from the door. The sheets feel rough against my skin as I stare at the speckled popcorn ceiling.

At first, a single tear prickles, but soon I'm bawling like a baby into the covers. Crying until I can't breathe. Until my eyes are swollen shut.

This hurts more than when Dave took back the keys to our shared life. More than when a guy I kissed at the end-of-term school disco called me a cock-sucking poofter. I cry for an hour, and then I cry for another hour.

"You idiot. Why. Why. Why?"

And then I'm spent.

Empty.

Sliding into black oblivion.

When I next open my eyes, the room is dark. For once, my sleep had been dreamless. My limbs feel heavy, pressed into the overly soft mattress. In this nondescript box in an airport hotel, I've found a moment's peace.

# 17

The airport car park ticket machine is a squat, dark metal box with slots for cash, cards, and vouchers. When I push a button, I'm told to insert my parking stub. Noah must still have it. And he's two thousand miles away.

I hit a button for assistance.

A woman's voice crackles. "Can I help you, doll?"

"I lost my ticket."

"What's your licence plate?"

I've seen it so often in the past few days, but now my mind is blank. "It's one...something..." I rub my eyes. "It's...one..."

"Honey, we charge a full week for missing tickets. You got some way of paying?"

I fish a close-to-maxed-out credit card from my wallet, whisper a prayer to the God of unauthorised overdrafts, and slide it into the machine. The display goes blank and then spits it back out. Followed by a replacement stub.

"Use this to exit at the barrier. Have a great day."

Driving without a licence or insurance and no Oscar-nominated actor to charm the police is a risk, but it's not like I can take a bus. River Valley is a small town in the middle of nowhere. I already checked. The next bus leaves in four days.

No sooner am I out of the car park than the road opens up. There's traffic everywhere. Angry horns honk as I floor the accelerator and swerve across lanes, cutting up a truck driver who throws up his hands in fury. The speedo reads 25, 35, 40. And there's that familiar 50-mile-per-hour stench of something putrid burning beneath the bonnet.

I love this van.

The road straightens out and traffic thins, so I slow down, willing my heart to hammer just a little less. The sun is back where it's been since forever. High in the sky. I turn on the radio.

Billy Joel.

———

River Valley sneaks onto a signpost for the first time. A distant beacon of hope after almost three hours of driving like someone playing Mario Kart, trying not to attract attention. One hundred miles lie between me and Bo Hyson.

Probably.

I squirm, trying to find a comfortable spot, avoiding broken springs, as the road rises and falls, its curves hugged by towering trees.

By now, Noah will be back in Los Angeles. Do I call and check if he got home safe? Or would that be weird? What if Aaron answers his phone? Or worse, Dupree.

Then there's a clunk. And a rattle. And steam pours from under the hood, like a kettle boiling. The steam turns into black smoke, and a faint but enduring rattle intensifies. I steer to the side of the road. The engine judders to a stop, and when I turn the key, it answers with a click.

My knowledge of how cars and vans work extends to filling up with fuel and buying a Magic Tree air freshener. I fumble for a lever to release the hood, and there's a thud and a creek as it opens.

I peer into the darkness, squeezing random hoses. Some are hot. Some cold. Everything is caked in grease and stinks of burning rubber. I remember Dad teaching me to check the oil and stressing how it lies at the heart of almost every breakdown.

I unscrew a gunky cap, and more dank smoke pours out.

There's no service on my phone.

I'm officially screwed.

Surrounded by fields, trees, and open roads.

Do they have coyotes here? How big are they, anyway? I suppose I figured them to be like the cute little foxes that prowl around Birmingham back gardens, but what if they're the size of lions? And hungry

What are my options? Find help by walking to the nearest town, but that could take hours, and my feet already hurt. Bright stars already riddle the sky. I could stay here and hope a random mechanic drives by, agrees to stop, and knows how to fix an ancient VW Camper Van.

Who am I kidding?

Although I don't know why, I lock the doors and start walking.

———————

Darkness engulfs the lonely road, and my eyes strain for any sign of life, my ears pricking at each twig snap. Grit rubs between already blistered toes.

I have trainers in my bag. Why the fuck am I still wearing sandals?

Lights appear up ahead—an open-all-hours roadside diner.

A choir of Hallelujah angels sings.

Inside, it's like stepping back in time, with yellow vinyl stools and a vintage jukebox. I sit at the counter between men, taking a break from driving their perfectly functional cars and trucks.

"What can I get ya?" the woman serving asks, and I explain my situation.

"Is there any chance I could call for a tow truck? Or perhaps you know of a mechanic?"

She signals to the far side of the diner. "Our pay phone is in the back. Don's Garage is open late. There's a card. They'll send someone."

I sag with relief. "Thank you so much."

She stops wiping the counter with a rag that looks to have been around since the Civil War. "You plan on ordering something, or did you figure I'm running an information centre?"

I pay for a coffee and ask for 'whatever sandwich is easy to make' before searching out the phone. Don's Garage promises someone—almost certainly Don himself—will be out within an hour.

I sit and idly glance up at a television set, tucking into the best BLT ever. The news starts, and an over-tanned guy with super-white teeth bids a good evening.

Then, all at once, I'm not hungry.

"Aaron Biedermeier was today reunited with his fiancé. Actor Noah Winters cut short filming in Australia to be with the controversial director in a touching reunion, captured here on camera."

Noah appears relaxed and happy. He's had a haircut and is back to dressing like a Hollywood A-Lister. A designer-logo baseball cap, airbrushed skin, and a shirt that probably cost more than the monthly rent I pay Mum.

"You okay, honey?" The woman serving brandishes a jug of burnt coffee. "Don will be here any minute."

———

A battered pickup truck rumbles into the diner car park. A guy jumps out, short and squat, wearing dungarees. He raises a hand and comes inside.

"I guess I'm your knight in shining armour." He gurns through gappy, yellowed teeth. "Jump in, and let's go see what needs fixin'."

I slide into the passenger seat, and the truck lurches back onto the dirt track.

"I'm Kyle," I say, realising I haven't properly introduced myself.

"Don," he replies, not bothering to look my way. "So, what brings you out here?"

The cab reeks of stale cigarettes and sweat.

"A road trip," I say with a shrug. "Wanted to see a bit of the country."

Don sneaks a glance from under bushy eyebrows. "Judgin' by that accent, you ain't from around these parts."

We drive on, the only sound coming from the crunch of gravel beneath the truck's wheels. But conversation isn't what I need anyway. My mind is racing. When I reach River Valley, what do I say to win Hyson's support? That's assuming I find the guy. And why would he believe anything a stranger has to say?

We pass the same abandoned barn I gave wide birth on my trek to the diner. Rusted equipment leans against sun-bleached walls.

Don clears his throat. "Something about the desert brings out the worst in people."

I raise nervous eyebrows. "What do you mean?"

"Well, folk out here are unconventional. They live life on their terms, without interference from the government or anyone else."

I shuffle in the seat, unsure what he's trying to tell me.

"And sometimes," Don continues, "they take their

pleasures where they can find them. No matter how unsavoury."

A knot forms in my stomach. Is he coming on to me?

He shares a smirk. "Just a friendly warning, your Lordship. Stay on your guard out here."

I've never been more relieved to see a battered red Camper Van that appears to have driven its last mile, sitting by the side of the road, hazard lights still blinking.

Don parks up, and the air smells of dust and burnt oil.

"Shoot." He sounds impressed. "I can't recall the last time I worked on one of these beasts."

I try not to panic. "You can fix it, though, right?"

He reaches into his truck for a box of tools. "Never met an engine I can't beat."

Things get cold out here fast at night. I walk around, hugging myself to keep warm as Don digs under the hood, whistling.

"Here's your problem, your Lordship. Busted radiator hose."

He points at something, and I make understanding sounds.

"You're in luck," he says. "I can fix this."

Don gets to work while I try not to obsess about *unconventional people, taking unsavoury pleasures where they find them.* A strange energy emanates from the surrounding desert. The vast nothingness is alive and watching me.

When the job is done, I offer what little cash I have, but he refuses.

"Think of this as a favour to a fellow night owl. You

have to take care when you're driving alone on these roads."

Don's truck rattles back into the darkness. He's scared the living crap out of me. After jumping back into the van, I make sure every door is locked and search the glove box for Noah's starter pistol, not daring to turn off the engine in case it refuses to start again.

The fuel gauge flashes close on empty. I need to get moving.

———

Driving fast enough to cover the last hundred miles and just slow enough not to cause the engine to throw another tantrum is stressful, and by the time I see the first 'Welcome' sign for River Valley, my shoulders ache.

Nestled between mountains, the town seems trapped in a time warp. Smoke plumes from soot-blackened metal chimneys as I drive past wooden storefronts with faded awnings. Main Street is empty except for trucks slanted outside *Murphy's Bar*. An old theatre marquee advertises bygone show times.

I park outside a neglected General Store. The air is still, and the only sound comes from dawn chorus birds.

Across the way, a faded sign offers rooms to let, and I ring the bell. When there's no answer, I peer into a hallway. The carpet is worn through, and paint flakes from the walls add to the sense that this might be where I meet my maker.

I climb narrow wooden stairs, freezing at each creak.

My breathing turns heavy as I knock on a sturdy door marked 'Manager'.

A friendly older man greets me. Wrapped in a grey dressing gown, he stifles a yawn. "How may I help you?"

"I was looking for a room."

He reaches for a key from a row of brass hooks. "You're British?"

"I'm touring the area." I try to sound enthusiastic, but it comes out flat. "I figured I might stay a few nights."

He bobs his head as if taking in this information. "Welcome to River Valley. If you need breakfast, there's a place across the way."

The room he shows me is cosy and inviting, with a small fireplace and a single bed. A large bay window offers a street view and, beyond that, blue-green mountains.

"This is perfect," I say, and when I pull money from my wallet, he waves it away.

"Pay on departure." He signals to the narrow landing. "There's a shower and tub down the hall. No need to whistle or sing. You're my only guest, so nobody will walk in on you."

The walls are covered in faded floral wallpaper, and the floorboards creak under my feet.

"I need to see an ID." He pulls a *'don't blame me'* face. "State rules."

Hope dies. This had all been going too well.

"I left it in the van," I say. "I could perhaps drop it in later?"

When I return, I'll claim a window was broken and

my passport was stolen. He doesn't look like the kind of heartless stickler willing to evict a crime victim.

"You got an honest face," he says, his tone confidential. "Besides, it's not as if we're overrun with visitors here in River Valley."

My shoulders relax, and I let out a sigh of relief.

He takes a step towards the door. "I'll leave you to your business."

It crosses my mind that he could help me find Hyson and save a lot of knocking on doors.

"I figured I might look up an old friend," I say. "Does the name Bo Hyson mean anything to you?"

There's a flicker in his eyes, a slight pause, but then he glazes over. "Nobody I'm familiar with. Now, if you'll excuse me, I was fixing breakfast."

As the door closes, I sense that asking about Hyson wasn't my best move, and as I'm about to unpack, he appears again.

"I've thought about matters, and I *will* require ID. And I need you to go find it. Now."

———

The River Valley Diner is small and narrow, with a counter along one wall. Chairs padded with yellow vinyl surround worn wooden tables. Despite being well-lit, the place is anything but cheerful. The handful of patrons are all obviously local, and everyone says hello to everyone else and makes no secret of being curious about the stranger in town.

The aroma of bacon and eggs reminds me how it's

been a whole day since I ate, so I climb onto a stool and peer at a grease-spattered menu. A bell above the door jangles as a short, older woman enters, her steps slow and hesitant as she nods good morning. I startle when she taps my arm.

"Pardon me, but is this seat here taken?"

"Please, you go ahead."

She sits, pulls a compact mirror from her bag, and checks her hair. "You're headline news. Everyone wants to know who the handsome stranger that blew into town might be."

I put down the menu. "I'm nobody. Nobody at all." She doesn't push, so I relent. "My name is Kyle."

"Maggie. Ralph's my husband. You already ran into each. We run the guest house."

She pulls a rolling-eye face that suggests she's used to tracking down potential overnight guests and apologising. A young woman complains out loud about waiting too long for French toast and earns a scowl from the server.

Maggie chuckles to herself. "Nothing ever changes in River Valley."

I spy a row of lockers and hooks for jackets. One hook is empty. There are names on peeling stickers attached to each metal locker door. Louise, Enid, George, and Bo.

I double-take. Did I find Hyson without trying? Did my luck change?

"I planned on looking up an old pal," I say, at once turning terribly British.

Maggie blinks. "Ralph said. You're here for Bo Hyson."

"You know where I might find him?"

At first, she acts like she's about to give me the same cold shoulder offered by her husband, but instead, she nods and smiles.

"*Everyone* in River Valley knows Pastor Hyson."

# 18

It's not hard to find the River Valley Baptist Church. The town has one main street and three narrow alleys. A simple white clapboard church has a small steeple and chipped paint. Service times in folksy lettering are pinned to a board alongside details of bible classes, a blood drive, and the upcoming summer camp. Inside, rows of wooden pews are organised with hymnals and bibles. Morning sunlight filters through unstained glass across the scuffed hardwood floors. Near the pulpit, a plump woman in a calico dress is busy setting a vase of flowers on the altar cloth before stepping back to admire her work.

I clear my throat, and she starts.

"Excuse me," I say. "I'm sorry to bother you, but..."

She looks my way and frowns. "There's no service this morning. Pastor Hyson is away on church business. He's due back this evening. You want me to take a message?"

I shake my head. "I'm an old friend, and I was hoping to catch up."

She steps down from the dais. "You mind if I ask how you know the pastor?"

I scramble for specifics, cursing myself for not preparing a cover story.

"We lived in the same part of LA. I was at university there."

She cocks her head to one side. "You went to Antioch?"

I half nod, hoping this isn't a trap.

Her eyes grow wider. "Ain't that the funniest little thing? I lived in Culver all my life and don't recall your pretty boy face. You're from England, right?"

I snort. It's not dignified. "How can you tell?"

"You're not related to Belle Simpson?"

Something causes me to shake my head. "Bo helped when I was in a bad way. I sort of lost myself, you know?"

I'm trying to pull together a story. Should I be a reformed drunk or a drug addict? Did I steal stuff?

She purses her lips, studying me intently. "Well, I'm sure Pastor Hyson followed his teachings. But if you'll excuse me, I have work to do in the garden."

She picks up a basket and heads for a door.

"I'd love to see your horticultural collection," I say, and she's back to acting suspicious. Probably because nobody ever referred to what is likely a tiny vegetable patch as a *horticultural collection*.

"You know how to grow vegetables?"

"My father runs a market garden in England."

Dad grows runner beans up sticks near his shed and cucumbers on the kitchen window sill, so it's sort of true.

She leads the way to a small patch of dry soil enclosed by a weathered, wooden fence. Tomato plants, heavy with ripe fruit, are staked in the centre, surrounded by red and green lettuce, kale, and spinach. Baskets and tools sit along the wall.

"This is incredible," I say. "You must have to keep everything well watered in this heat."

She nods in satisfaction. "The tomatoes came in mighty fine this year. Of course, now I've got more than I can carry home."

I seize my opportunity. "I'd be happy to help."

She spares me the smallest of smiles. "Nobody turns down willing hands."

We work side by side, with her firing questions— how long do I plan on staying in town? And exactly where is it that I'm from? I keep each answer vague. Milly once said the worst liars tend to over-embroider. The trick is to keep things simple. When we've filled two baskets, she straightens up.

"I'll make tea, and you can tell me how you became friends with my eldest."

My instincts were spot on. This woman *is* Estelle Hyson.

———

She leads me down one of the three dusty alleyways to a small stone cottage with vines creeping up its pink-painted facade. Shading herself from the mid-morning sunshine, Estelle points to a nearby truck.

"My other boy hasn't left for work. Dwayne might not look much, but he's got a heart of gold. Been through tough times, but he always manages to be there for me and his brother. He might remember meeting you in Culver."

Obviously, that's not going to happen. "Bo never talked much about his brother," I say.

Her lips purse. "Boys can be that way."

The Hyson home is cramped but cosy, with hand-sewn quilts covering dark wooden furniture. Pressed flower art and cross-stitched bible verses adorn most every wall. It's a place where you remove your shoes without being asked. Estelle ushers me into a kitschy kitchen with chickens hand-painted on white tiles. Lace curtains filter sunlight. Ceramic canisters clutter the counters.

She calls out. "Dwayne, honey. We have a visitor."

A door swings open, and a hulking man all but fills the frame. Overweight, but muscular, and wearing oil-stained jeans. He looks me up and down.

"Kyle, meet my youngest, Dwayne. Kyle used to hang out with Bo. Back in Culver."

He strides over, eyes narrowed. "An old friend, huh? Funny, Bo mentioned no one called Kyle."

I shrink under his glare, my pulse quickening. "We, uh, lost touch years ago."

"How long ago?" He pokes at my chest. "You better not be troubling my brother with no nonsense."

I raise innocent hands. "I was passing this way and

made a detour. It just sort of crossed my mind to thank Bo for helping me through tougher times."

Dwayne carries on staring, and I try working out the best escape route should things turn ugly. If I dodge around furniture, he might trip. Fear brings speed, and I could make it to my van parked near the diner and wheel spin out of town.

"My brother has a generous spirit." Dwayne takes a beer from the fridge. "Even when it comes to strangers, he hasn't seen for years. Sometimes, he only sees the good in people. You be sure to show him gratitude and respect."

Estelle clicks her tongue. "I brought you up to have better manners. Offer the man a beer too."

"It's kind of early for me," I say.

Dwayne's lip curls "Some of us have already worked eight hours."

He vanishes back into what must be his room. A door slams, and muffled music plays. I'm still shaking when Estelle tells me she baked cookies and makes tea, adding that she knows British people prefer it with milk. There's a photo stuck on the fridge of what I take to be a younger Dwayne and a younger Bo. She catches me looking.

"I took that picture in San Francisco on a family getaway. It must have been six or seven years ago now. Maybe longer."

In it, Bo Hyson has a slender, athletic build with a defined jawline, high cheekbones, a straight nose, and striking eyes. This was the man serving drinks in Vegas.

"Bo will be so vexed he missed seeing you," Estelle says. "We don't get many visitors."

"How long has it been since he joined the church?"

"Gee, you got me there. I mean, he was always talking about God, and he loved his Bible, but...six years, I suppose. He's been in seminary for six years."

I swallow. "Am I mixing him up with somebody else, or did he ever work for a movie studio?"

She pauses midway through pouring boiling water into a yellow tea pot. "Most kids did some kind of part-time job to pay for their college fees."

"At Biedermeier Pictures?"

She turns around, and her eyes search mine. "Bo has long been a man of God. He devotes his life to preaching the word of the Lord and aiding those in peril. The other day, he told me about the wonderful things he's been doing with the youth group. They're great kids, and my boy makes a difference in their lives."

Dwayne is back.

"Kyle here was asking about Biedermeier Pictures." Estelle sounds jittery.

He towers over me. "Why would anyone care to know that?"

I force my voice to stay even. "Bo might be able to assist me with a concern."

Dwayne positions his face level with mine. His breath stinks of stale beer. "What kind of concern?"

"I'd rather wait and talk to your brother," I say. "When exactly are you expecting him?"

He stares for a second before straightening up with a grunt. "Bo is away on church business. All-day church business."

"But he's due home tonight?" I say, recalling what Estelle told me.

The idea of spending more than a few extra hours in River Valley sets my nerves on edge.

Estelle clears her throat. "I forgot to mention. Bo called first thing, to say he needed to stay overnight. He won't be home until morning."

She's lying. But I just nod and take the cup of tea she pours. We talk for a while longer. About Culver City, the weather in London, and growing vegetables.

———

I steer the van off the main street and onto a deserted stretch of scrubby wasteland. Remote enough that no one will bother me. I imagine word travels fast in places like River Valley, since everywhere I go, I'm met with curious stares. In the General Store, a woman ducks behind canned goods, watching as I pay for bottled water.

After a long day of avoiding glares, I huddle under a blanket in the van, desperate to pee. And hungry.

Bollocks to the good folk of River Valley and their stranger-in-town 'Deliverance' vibe. I've got as much right as anyone to eat at the local diner. Even if each mouthful clogs an artery. While there, perhaps I can ask who's in charge of the tourist board and pitch ideas about making visitors feel more welcome. For starters, they could take down what looks like a hanging noose near the shuttered town hall.

———

Fogged windows glow warmly under the almost black sky. The diner doorbell jangles as I step inside, my senses flooded by the smell of bacon, sweet maple syrup, and strong coffee. A different waitress from this morning tells me to sit anywhere and doesn't act like I'm the devil in disguise.

I slide into a booth, the cushion exhaling a puff of air.

"Coffee?" The waitress points to a cup she's already filled. She's an older woman with a raspy voice.

"It's quiet in here tonight." I fake an American accent, desperate for a non-judgemental conversation.

She nods, wiping the next table. "There ain't ever much action here, 'cept on Friday nights after the foot-ball game." The door clatters open, and she glances over her shoulder. "Back in a jiff, hon. You take your time and decide what I can get you."

Estelle's familiar laughter causes me to freeze—she's with Dwayne and some other man. I hide behind a menu as they pick a booth at the far end of the diner.

The place is empty, and their voices carry. Dwayne boasts about saving a cat, and the other guy laughs. Estelle mentions some stranger calling at the church but leaves out the bit where she lied about when her son might be home.

Their food arrives without them needing to order, and the waitress returns to me.

"Honey, I'm so sorry to keep you waiting," she says. "I always serve the pastor first."

The pastor who called to say he needed to stay out of town tonight?

"Honey?" she says. "What can I get you?"

"Eggs. Scrambled."

A lone fly buzzes aimlessly, bouncing off the window before zigzagging from table to table. Estelle mentions a bake sale, and my stomach grumbles. I absent-mindedly tap my foot against the vinyl floor.

"Tell me more about this guy that came to the house today," the man, I now guess to be Bo Hyson, says.

Dwayne huffs and speaks with his mouth full. "If you ask me, he was another one of those looky-loo reporters."

Estelle takes over. "Claimed he knew you from Culver."

There's a grunt and a sigh. "You tell him to go whistle if he comes looking for me again. Say, I'm away a while longer."

The waitress sets down my plate and refills my coffee cup.

The Hysons discuss an event at the church, and Estelle promises flowers from her garden. Dwayne agrees to help build a stage. They sound like an everyday family in an everyday town. Bo excuses himself.

"Louise, are you OK if I use the kitchen to make a phone call?" he says, and she laughs.

"Like I'm going to argue with the owner."

Bo Hyson owns the diner. I thought every man of God scratched a living, making ends meet and guilt-tripping parishioners into parting with cash. Mum says her local church WhatsApp group has become a digital begging bowl.

I let out a breath I didn't realise I was holding as Estelle laughs at something outside the window, and Dwayne calls someone a dumb mother. Hyson returns from the kitchen, and our eyes meet for the smallest of seconds before he sits back down.

I pay and leave, ducking through the door.

Outside, the night air is hot and muggy, with a hint of jasmine. Someone's television blares from an open window, and the laughter of a sitcom studio audience echoes through dark streets. I hide in the shadows to watch the Hyson clan eat dinner.

Except now, it's just Estelle and Dwayne.

Leaves rustle, and a finger taps my shoulder. I wheel around.

It's Hyson.

"I believe we know each other from Culver."

# 19

Bo Hyson moves fast. His strides are long. Keeping up has me out of breath. Neither of us speaks as he leads the way past where I parked and down a dirt track. Is this where Dwayne now waits to beat me to a pulp?

He points towards a tumbledown shed. "In there."

I've made it a life rule never to enter any wooden structures that belong to a man whose brother looks like he could crush my windpipe with one hand.

"I'd rather not," I say. "We could go back to the diner? Or the church, or..."

He gives me an almighty shove.

Inside, shafts of moonlight slice through gaps in the weathered wooden roof. Hyson latches the door shut before flicking a switch, and a single yellow bulb reveals bare floorboards. In the far corner, a rusty wheelbarrow sits, piled with mildewed sacks.

"Nice place you have here," I say, blinking.

He unfolds two white metal chairs that look wrong

against the shed's crumbling interior. I sit, and he stays standing, staring, his hands resting on his hips.

"Who are you working for?"

The question makes no sense. "I'm not *working* for anyone."

"What brings you to River Valley? I've grown to love this town, but it's no Walt Disney World."

He puts his face up against mine, and I breathe in an aftershave I remember from that night in Vegas. It turned my stomach, then. It turns my stomach now.

He groans, exasperated, and sits. "I'll ask you again. Who are you working for? The National Enquirer already offered twenty grand for me to talk shit about Aaron, and I told the slimeball to keep his money. That part of my life is ancient history." He pauses. "Did Carlton Dupree tell you I moved here?"

I shift uncomfortably. "That's a strange thing to ask."

He cocks his head, both eyes burning into me, and I wither under his gaze. Now he pauses. "This is going to sound dumb, but I know you, right? Your face, it's... familiar."

My mouth goes dry. Noah told me so many stories about so many kids at so many parties. Maybe he thinks I'm one of them. Out for some sort of revenge.

My palms sweat. "The last person in the world I trust is Carlton Dupree, but he *is* part of why I'm here."

Finally, Hyson sits. "I figured as much. Aaron got beat up, and two days later, Ralph had dudes in cheap suits renting rooms, asking what he could tell them about me."

The cold shoulder welcome I received at the guest house suddenly makes sense.

"So, come on," he says. "It's a fair enough ask. Why exactly are you here?"

I share an edited version of the story so far, and at the mention of Tim Larson, he looks down at the floor. "How is Noah holding up?"

"Still in love with a guy he watched die."

Hyson squeezes his eyes shut. "And Judah? I guess that was no accident."

The way he asks makes it clear he already knows the answer.

"We'd already left LA, but the circumstances were kind of similar."

He hangs his head. "Everything was supposed to end with that one night. That was always the agreement."

There's a heaviness in the air, and his expression becomes unreadable.

"When you say there was an *agreement...* was that between you and Aaron, or did Dupree get involved?"

For the longest of minutes, he stays silent, pressing his fingers together as if in prayer and searching for answers from his God, but then he looks me in the eye.

"After Tim died, Aaron changed. The parties stopped, and he made a big show of sponsoring rehab groups and giving breaks to kids who wouldn't otherwise have featured on anyone's radar."

I nod, not wanting to interrupt.

"He wanted to set up some kind of school. An Academy for the Performing Arts."

Hyson stops talking, face-palming like he made a connection, and only now does he hear it.

"That was him trying to work the guilt out of his system, right? Did anything change? Do the parties still happen?"

"Noah didn't talk much about that."

He groans, and his whole body slumps. "Dupree let me drag my family across the country for nothing. He paid me to leave town, just so that sick bastard got to carry on abusing more kids like Tim."

I want to tell him he's not to blame for whatever Biedermeier did after that night in Vegas, but that would be lying. By keeping his mouth shut and leaving town, he allowed a predator to fester. Monsters never stop doing what monsters like to do.

A question comes to me. One I don't want to ask. "Can I trust Noah?"

Hyson looks shocked. "Why would you doubt the guy? He's the only good thing to come out of this mess."

"You don't think Dupree maybe told him to get me out of LA so he could deal with Judah Eisenhart and perhaps pin that on me, too?"

"You guys were in a van heading for Georgia. How could he make it look like either of you had anything to do with what happened to Eisenhart?"

"By the same token, who is my witness? Dupree could write me off as a fantasist and stick to the story he already told the press that Noah was in Australia, looking at locations for his next film. Turn me into some crazed fan, making up stories."

It's Hyson's turn to look worried. "Noah won't let

him do that. The kid has demons, but he wouldn't sell you out. Not to Dupree."

I struggle to hide my relief, but he isn't done.

"Those parties..." He walks over to the door and peers out like he's checking nobody can hear. "Dupree was always working the room, making sure everyone got whatever they wanted. Boys, drugs. You name it. And there were cameras. Dupree has photos to keep Noah in line. The kind of material that ends careers."

————

I walk with Hyson back to the diner. We don't speak much, and I catch him looking at me like he's trying to remember the kid from that hotel suite six years earlier.

"Where are you sleeping?" he says.

"I was told there was no room at the inn," I nod over at the 'Rooms to Rent' sign. "I have a van."

"I can put in a good word. Talk Ralph into letting you stay."

I shake my head. "The van kind of feels like all I have left of Noah."

He turns and looks over at the diner. Estelle and Dwayne have already left. "He's a good kid, Kyle. Don't judge him. Sometimes you have to do shit that doesn't sit right. Because what's the alternative?"

I nod, making out like I get it. Like I understand why he chose to abandon me at the last minute.

"I'll wish you a pleasant evening," Hyson says. "Maybe we can talk again tomorrow?"

Time is short. For all I know, Noah could be trying on

his wedding suit tonight, tasting sample cakes, and ordering crates of white doves.

"I didn't get around to telling you why we were heading here," I say. "Noah said you have stuff on Dupree. Photos and recordings of phone calls."

Hyson's face hardens. "There was a fire. At the church."

He's lying. I've been around enough cheating ex-boyfriends to know. For one thing, he can't look me in the eyes.

"When was this fire?"

"Must have been close on two years ago."

"But the church building didn't burn. I was there today."

Hyson nods, still avoiding looking at me. "The fire was in a hall nearby. The sanctuary. The town raised money and paid for that shed. For storage."

I exhale. The one thing that angers me the most is when someone lies so obviously, treating me like I'm stupid.

"That shed predates me fitting into twenty-eight-inch waist jeans," I say.

He sighs and turns away. "Noah got it all wrong. There are no photos. No recordings. Nothing."

I'm tired. So very tired. My temper snaps. "What's the actual story, Bo? There was stuff, but some fire that never happened destroyed it. Was Noah telling me lies? *Straight arrow,* Noah Winters?"

A car drives past on the main street. Headlight beams light up our faces. He looks angry now.

"You're still married to Aaron," I say, deciding there's

little point in holding back my only ace. "Dupree never filed the divorce papers."

For the first time, shock registers on Hyson's face. Slowly at first, and then it hits hard.

"Asshole," he seethes through gritted teeth. "I shouldn't have trusted him. Not for one second."

I'm confused. "Trusted who? Dupree?"

Hyson slams his fist against a nearby fence. "It's not like we were ever in love. I was on the payroll. We had a business arrangement."

This familiar phrase causes my insides to tighten.

"The agreement was that we would marry, then separate."

I finish the sentence for him. "But you stay friends and say nothing but good things in public."

He starts pacing.

"OK. There was no fire." His voice has turned cold and hard. "I have stuff, and it's time to use it. That night in Vegas, I used my phone. I took photos and recorded what was going on. I can prove you were there, and I can prove when."

The biggest weight ever lifts from my shoulders, and I want to hug the guy. "

"I put them on a memory stick," he says. "In a safe deposit box. In a bank vault. In LA."

———————

Hyson has asked for time. Not long. Just one day to get things in order and talk to his family. His mother has been sick, he tells me—not so bad that she's about to die, but enough to need her kids around. Dwayne does all he can, and his car repair business keeps them afloat. But only just.

I'm in the van. It's cold and stinks, as usual, of damp and rust. Any hint of Noah has faded. I'll be so happy to leave River Valley—the kind of place people don't visit without reason because nobody bothers drawing it on maps. There can't be more than a few hundred living souls within its limits, and at least half are horses, cows, or chickens.

I pull out my phone, desperate to share my news. Milly picks up on my mood within two short words.

"Have you been drinking?"

"I located Bo Hyson. Would you believe he found God?"

A pause. "OK, Kyle. I'm not sure what you want me to do with that information."

My eyes sting, and the words come out choked as my throat tightens with unshed tears. "Dupree has been trying to set me up, but Hyson can actually prove I was where I said I was and that I had nothing to do with Tim Larson's death. Don't you see what this means? Noah doesn't need to marry the sick pervert."

For once, she's silent. I have done what the combined West Midlands judicial system, police force, and criminal community have so far failed to achieve. I've shut her up. I reveal everything, and when I'm done, Milly stays quiet for several loaded seconds.

"Kyle." Her voice is calm but firm. "Listen to me. As your friend and as a lawyer. What took place is tragic.

And from what you've said, Noah cares for you a great deal, but he's made his choice. Rightly or wrongly."

I lean back against a headrest and catch a last faint sniff of Noah's hair wax. Cedarwood and lemon balm.

"You were right about how I feel," I say. "I do love him."

There's a long pause.

"But you let him go, and now he's going to marry someone else."

How is she not getting any of this? "That was before I found Bo Hyson. Now I have proof Biedermeier knew about Larson."

She sighs. "Noah knew that anyway, but he still agreed to marry the guy."

"Only because he had no proof."

"You have one job to do, Kyle. Put an end to whatever those evil men did. Whatever they may still be doing. Then walk. The hell. Away."

———

It's midnight, and a pale moon hangs low over the church, casting long shadows. Something scuttles in the bushes nearby, and I check that every door on the van is locked. I can't wait while Hyson makes a deal with his family to vanish for a few days. I need to know what he's telling them. More than that, I need to pee.

The diner lights are low, but there's someone inside, standing near the till. Could I talk them into selling me leftover coffee or letting me use the toilets? Gravel crunches as I make my way along Main Street, my hand gripped around Noah's emergency can of pepper spray. Whoever is inside the diner heads for the door, steps out, locks it, and walks away.

I duck behind a bush to pee, hoping things here are different from Birmingham, where smart doorbells post photos to local WhatsApp Neighbourhood Watch groups.

Most houses are in darkness, but lights still burn in the Hyson home. I should know better. But creep into the yard to crouch beneath an open window.

"This is beyond messed up." Dwayne is saying.

"You could ruin everything." Estelle's voice is sharp and biting. "We signed an agreement. What happens if..." She trails off. "Did you hear something?"

Dwayne clears his throat. "Probably a raccoon. I'll check tomorrow. Make sure they're not nesting."

"But if he finds out about the money," Estelle says. "What then?"

My breath catches. She now knows why a stranger with a British accent arrived in town.

"Why didn't Dupree just pay that Eisenhart guy off?" she says. "Junkies always have a price tag. Now we need to clean up his fucking mess."

The blood drains from my face. So much for living off-grid, having nothing more to do with their old lives, and hiding in a desert town.

For the first time, I'm genuinely terrified as I scuttle back to the van to spend the night. Alone.

# 20

It's Sunday morning in River Valley, and for once, the sun *isn't* shining. Charcoal clouds gather as a bell tolls, its dirge calling everyone to worship.

A trashy paperback found under the passenger seat serves as a temporary distraction, but as the bell falls silent, I jump down from the van, intending to head for Main Street.

River Valley is a ghost town, with all the spectres kneeling in pews.

All except one.

Estelle is heading my way, loaded up with a thermos and Tupperware. She waves like I should be expecting her visit.

"The problem on Sunday morning is that everyone shuts up shop," she says, huffing at the effort of picking through scrubland. "I figured you wouldn't have been able to find any place to eat breakfast."

My mouth goes dry. There's no room to refuse her offer without inviting suspicion or, worse, a visit from

Dwayne. Estelle's floral cotton dress flutters as she approaches.

"That's kind of you." I try not to sound like I know she wants to *do something about me*. "But shouldn't you be at church too?"

She tilts her head. "I've already listened to just about every story my eldest has to tell from the Bible. Some of them three times over. I figured you might welcome my famous iced tea." She hands me two cups, removes the lid from her thermos, and pours amber liquid before reaching for the plastic box. "I baked these biscuits yesterday, so they're fresh."

The last thing I want to do is put one of them in my mouth. They're likely laced with whatever drug killed Tim Larson and Judah Eisenhart.

"Won't Dwayne wonder where you got to?" I say.

"I'll tell him I was helping others less fortunate than myself." She nods again at the biscuits. "That's what it says to do in the *big holy book*."

I hand back one cup. If the Hyson family has orders to do away with me, biscuits feel like a gentle way to go. Way better than being shot or punched unconscious. And this is a nice enough field. It's no Vegas, inner-city alley. Quite how Mum and Dad will take the news is another matter. Milly will think of something to explain how I wasn't in Manchester, and they'll forgive her for keeping secrets. She knows my funeral wishes. Nothing too churchy. Absolutely no hymns. I'll allow 'Morning Has Broken', just not as performed by Cat Stevens. Over-all, I want campy stuff like 'Keep Young and Beautiful'.

Buttery biscuit flakes melt on my tongue. This is

absolutely how everyone should die. There's another flavour in there. Is it lemon?

"Bo seems devoted to his congregation." I brush away crumbs, and Estelle beams like a proud mother might.

"The church is his universe," she says.

"Still, his work takes him away sometimes." I watch for a reaction. The smallest hint she might be waiting for me to get on with frothing at the mouth and tumble lifeless to the ground.

She waves a dismissive hand. "We get to have our Sunday dinners and nights in front of the television. The Lord's calling doesn't interfere with *America's Funniest Home Videos*."

I shift uneasily, unsure how to broach what I overheard last night. But given that she's almost certainly my smiling assassin, what do I really have to lose?

"What made you guys move to River Valley?"

"I guess my time in Culver City was over." There's a fond nostalgia in her voice. "We came into money and decided we'd had it with the fast life, and I'd always wanted to tend the land and grow vegetables. Dwayne was picking up odd jobs, and now he has a business. We thrive here."

I lean forward, feigning interest, waiting to start gasping for breath. "What about Bo?"

She exhales and peers up at the sky. "Even as a kid, California never really suited my boy. His skin was too pale, and I was forever rubbing his neck with Coppertone. But that's ancient history. Everything turned out just peachy."

My jaw aches from grinning. I take another bite of the biscuit. These are so good.

In the distance, a lone hawk circles, its shrill cry piercing the stillness. Estelle rubs her thin hands together, the papery skin rasping.

"The Lord has a way of putting our lives in order." She nods at my cup of sweet tea. And it's all so obvious now. That is how I'll die. The drugs are in the tea. I make out like a wasp or a bee came buzzing, dropping the mug.

She frowns. "What's troubling you, dear?"

"I thought I saw some kind of bee. And I have an allergy. My throat could constrict." The lie sounds feeble, even to me. I rake a hand through my hair, breaths coming fast. "Look, this has been lovely, and I'm sorry about the tea and everything, but the biscuits were delicious."

She smiles. "Don't worry, dear. There's more in the flask. Or perhaps you could visit with me while everyone praises the Lord?"

I look wistfully at the van. "I ought to hit the road."

She pulls a confused face. "You can't stay a while longer?"

"I'm done here," I say, determined not to sound scared.

Estelle touches my wrist. "If you give River Valley a chance, it might surprise you." She nods over towards the church steeple. "These biscuits. My iced tea. They're an excuse. I told my son I had to visit with a sick friend, so he didn't ask questions. I'm here today to tell you everything. The truth about what happened back in Culver."

The sincerity on her face gives me pause.

"What you heard last night," she begins, and then her eyes meet mine, smiling ever-so-slightly. "Oh, we have some video doorbell thing. I have no idea how it works, but Dwayne showed me how you were hiding out in our yard last night. And you must have questions."

I swallow, unsure whether to feel hope or dread about whatever *truth* she plans on spilling. Is Dwayne already on his way?

"It's not how it sounded." Estelle weighs her words. "We've lived here a while now, and word travels fast in a small town. People have said things over the years about Bo's old life. I tried to stay in touch with friends, but they had loose lips after a few drinks."

Estelle meets my gaze, regret playing across her face.

"I pieced together more than my boy ever realised. About the people he used to run with. The types of things they were mixed up in."

A thrumming echoes within as I process how she's colouring between lines already drawn.

Estelle stares down at her worn hands, twisting a wedding ring. "I didn't take hush money from Mr Biedermeier just to line my pockets. Lord knows I've tried to live a moral life. But when my Harvey passed, well, the bills piled up quickly. Dwayne did his best but could never get steady work. I made choices then to protect my family. Choices that I'll always regret, but we did what we felt we had to do at the time to get by. Bo set things up, but if you want to yell at anyone for moving to Georgia, yell at me."

She meets my gaze, her eyes glistening.

"You don't know what it's like to have to choose between putting food on the table or keeping the power on. Wondering if you can afford a doctor when your kid gets sick." Estelle wipes away a stray tear, shaking her head. "We've tried to bury the past. Start fresh. But it seems the past isn't done with us. Bo doesn't understand how much I know. I never let on. But it's time I came clean about everything, as best I understand it. I want to help make things right, for everybody's sake."

———

Hours later, I'm in the driver's seat. Trying to decide whether to stay and talk Hyson into coming with me to clear my name or find a way home. Estelle insisted that there was no memory stick in any bank vault. But what if she's wrong?

Either way, I'm what the experts call up shit creek, and I don't think I ever even had a paddle.

One phone call, and Bryn would sort out a travel permit. I'll call the school and say how I tested negative. Maybe apply for that full-time job. When Friday rolls around, I'll meet Milly for cut-priced drinks, flirt with the Pink Flamingo bar staff, get messy drunk, and wake up in a strange bed with an even stranger man on Saturday.

Life will return to normal.

I turn the key in the ignition, and the engine rumbles. My mind has cycled through the past few days. The people in River Valley live such disconnected lives, and maybe they're the ones who have everything sorted. No internet. No caring about who's in or out or who got cancelled.

The sun beats down as the miles tick by.

My phone rings, and I glance at the screen, and my chest tightens—it's Noah. I hesitate before hitting ignore.

He calls again.

And again.

Finally, I pull over, bracing myself before answering.

"Kyle." The voice I thought I might never hear again sounds close by. "Where are you?"

I falter, not wanting to carry on lying. "I'm leaving River Valley."

"Did you find Hyson?"

My pulse quickens. "I did, but...you know, what? Forget it. He says he no longer has anything you can use against Aaron. He lost everything in some sort of fire."

There's a pause.

"You need to talk to your lawyer," he says. "Dupree is talking to the cops and trying to implicate you in what happened to Tim. There's security footage putting you near where they found his body."

"Whaaa...?"

"Listen to me. I need you to think." He takes a breath. "That night, after you met Aaron, did he suggest going for a walk?"

"How else would we have ended up at a wedding chapel? You have to remember I was wankered."

"He's setting you up, Kyle. It's happening right now."

My blood turns to ice.

Noah isn't done. "Dupree also pointed out how you

happened to be in the country on the day Judah over-dosed. Six random years later."

"What?" I spit. "That's ridiculous. Why would I want to murder a reality star himbo with the IQ of a bale of straw?"

"The police are taking him seriously."

I grip the phone tightly. "I didn't do it."

"I know. But this was always his plan. That night in Vegas. You were the fall guy. You still are."

My mind reels. Noah's voice pulls me back. "You need to go back and talk to Hyson. He was in the room. He's your only hope."

———

The ancient wooden doors of the River Valley Baptist Church open with a groan. Candles flicker limply.

I spent two hours sitting in a lay-by, weighing the pros and cons of driving back here. Nothing Dupree has is actual proof of my involvement. It's circumstantial at best. The wedding chapel records will show the time and date when Fat Balding Elvis asked if I promised to be Aaron's *hunka-hunka-burning love* and never step on his blue suede shoes.

Even if Hyson was telling the truth, and there are no photographs. Perhaps, fat, balding Elvis might vouch for me.

I've no idea where and when Judah Eisenberg breathed his last, but cameras must have captured a red VW Camper Van cruising along Route 66 with Noah at the wheel and me riding shotgun. They have CCTV everywhere.

All Dupree has is my passport and, I presume, finger-prints on a champagne glass from the executive suite of a man I drunk-married six years ago.

Hours after Tim Larson died. The hotel's security tape will show that.

Still, Noah sounded to be at his wit's end.

I called Bryn. Then Milly. Then Bryn again, and he walked me through everything I needed to do to protect myself. And then I turned the van around and trundled along the potholed Main Street, parking outside the church.

———

Hyson is alone, kneeling at the altar, his head bowed in prayer. Is he searching for forgiveness? Justification for the way he sent his mother to warn me off? The closer I get, the more I see how his whole body shakes and his shoulders tremble with each whispered word. He clings to the base of a cross, his fingers ruddy with effort. Even in this dim light, I make out beads of sweat.

"Bo," I say, my voice gentle, and he looks up, startled. I take slow steps, each footstep barely audible.

"I didn't plan on coming back," I say. "Don't be mad at your mother. She did what you asked, and made me feel bad about asking you to help put a paedophile behind bars."

He ducks his eyes. I continue.

"I hoped we could talk under different circumstances, but fate wants us to have it out here. This is the house of your Lord, so I figure if there's any chance of having you tell the truth..."

I'm trying to put him at ease, but it clearly isn't working, so I keep a respectful distance from the altar.

"Come back with me and tell everyone what you know about Biedermeier. Estelle already told me there's no LA bank vault."

At first, his expression doesn't change, and then he points to the front row of chairs. We sit.

"I'm prepared to beg," I tell him. "I'm prepared to do whatever it takes."

He exhales. "You can't understand what you're asking. It would destroy my family's life. They don't know about what happened back then."

My fingers form fists. I'm biting my bottom lip. Does this man think I'm stupid?

"You didn't kill anyone," I say, "but by keeping quiet, you're giving the authorities a reason to charge you. I wasn't much more than a kid back then. I was 22 and with my best mates on a messy stag weekend. I made one shitty decision."

Still, he says nothing.

"I never stop screwing things up, Bo. When Dupree called, the only two words I heard were *Hollywood director*. My stupid ego told me fate was finally dealing me a good hand, and all I had to do was board that plane, waltz into a fancy hotel, and meet with sharp-suited lawyers to sign papers. And then, I'd be free. Free to scout around for open auditions. I was stupid enough to think saying I was once married to Aaron Biedermeier would be enough to get me taken seriously." I laugh. "Sure, that makes me naive, but how do you figure I deserve any of this?"

Bo's eyes connect with mine. "I found God because of what happened with Tim. It haunts me every day. I wanted to speak up." He glances away and up at the cross before bowing his head once more. "Except, of course, I didn't. I let myself stay afraid. Afraid of the machine, of the truth, of what Biedermeier and Dupree might do to me."

He gets to his feet.

"The weekend before all that crap happened, I posted bail for Dwayne after the cops pulled him in for fighting. Our apartment was falling apart. We had termites in the staircase and door frames. Ma thought I didn't hear her crying at night. Aaron offered me a way to make everything better."

"So you let him buy your conscience?"

Hyson stares, as if my words disgust him. "You've already judged me."

"I'm going to ask you one more time," I say. "Please come back with me. We'll go to the authorities together, and I'll support whatever you tell them. My lawyer will see that you get immunity."

He looks at me now, and there's something else in his eyes. Not fear. Not distrust. Something new. "Don't you get it? Tim's face would still be inside my head. Can your lawyer make me immune to that?"

"Noah lives with it, too," I say. "But what's the alternative? Stay here and wait for the entire house of cards to tumble. Because one day it will. Nothing is forever. Men like Biedermeier don't suddenly see the light. They get sloppy, and someone tells someone else what happened at one of his parties. How much longer do you think you can hide here? I can't even work Google Maps, and I found you."

He stays silent.

"This is your only chance to offer Tim Larson's family any kind of closure."

Hyson stares at the wooden cross. "Sometimes, ignorance is bliss. You think they want that sort of closure?"

"No." My voice softens. "But it might help them make sense of things. Tim's mother has probably spent years wondering if her son died because of something she did or said. Or didn't say. And what about Judah's folks? Or can you keep preaching the word of God with one side of your face and turning the other?"

He stares at a flickering candle, lost in thought.

"OK," he finally says, "first, I need to talk to Dwayne, and then I need Ma to know what I'm doing and why."

———

A clock strikes midnight. Estelle sits next to me at the kitchen table, clutching a pewter mug, her skin washed out under harsh lighting. Dwayne leans against the counter, his posture rigid and his eyes boring into me. Hyson is checking through his bag.

"Please." Estelle sounds frail. "You don't have to do this."

Muffled sobs wrack her frail body. The anguish of a

mother about to lose her child. Dwayne has to turn away, blinking back tears.

Hyson looks up from his bag. "I can't go on thinking I could have saved a kid's life. A soul departed from this world, and I did nothing. That kid's family deserves to know."

She shakes her head. "You seriously think they'll thank you for telling them how and where he died? For telling them what that evil man did to their boy."

Dwayne pushes himself away from the counter and rests a hand on his mother's shoulder. She nuzzles his touch.

"Bo's doing the right thing, Ma. We need to face up to the deal we made with the devil."

Now she grips my arm, her hands trembling. "Please. You mustn't ask this of him." Her eyes glisten. "Haven't we suffered enough?"

I hate that I'm adding to her pain by being here, even if I had suspected her of plotting to poison me.

"I wish there was another way," I say. "Only Bo can make things right."

Estelle gets up and goes over to her son, taking his face in both hands. "You've worked hard to build a good life here. This town needs you. The church needs you."

He kisses her forehead. "Don't complicate this for me, Ma."

Estelle looks between me and him. "I'm begging you. Stay here. With *your* family. The Larsons have spent six years grieving. If you open the wound, they'll only go through it all again."

Hyson's jaw tightens. War wages within. "I have to do this. For Tim and for Judah."

She stiffens. "Don't you give two hoots about the life we built here? Sure, I get how the cash was tainted, but we washed it clean."

Dwayne comes over to rest a hand on her shoulder. "My big brother is doing the right thing, Ma."

I wish myself invisible. I'm the ill wind that blew into town and spoiled everything.

Hyson swings his bag onto his shoulder. "We can't carry on building our lives on misery money. You'll have the church, the garden, and all your friends. Dwayne has his business. The only person losing anything here is me. And the thing I'm letting go of is guilt."

Estelle's eyes plead. "You've atoned. You found God. You changed your life around. This town depends on you."

He stays quiet for an entire minute. "But none of this erases what happened. It doesn't give Tim, Judah, or any other kid Biedermeier hurt, or might still hurt, the justice they deserve."

It's Dwayne's turn to talk. "I have always looked up to you, man. But yeah, I get what Ma says. Why poke at the hornet's nest if it's not in our backyard?"

My heart aches to watch this family tear itself apart.

Estelle rinses her mug in the sink and places it on the drainer. She looks at me and shrugs. "I know you think I'm some silly old woman, but I do understand. Two mothers get to say goodbye. What you're doing is so brave."

"And stupid," Dwayne chips in. "Don't forget, stupid."

Hyson lingers in the doorway, as if taking in the scuffed walls, faded furniture, and framed family photos one last time. Estelle presses something into his palm—a tattered bible. It looks to have been around forever.

"Keep close to God," she whispers, squeezing his hand.

Dwayne grips his brother in a fierce bear hug. "You got this, bro."

———————

The van stinks after serving as my home for two days. Dwayne ambles to his truck and returns with something in his hand. Hyson, quiet and solemn, sits in the passenger seat, clutching the crucifix that always hangs from his neck. Estelle refuses to meet my gaze. Instead, she focuses on her son, tracing the contours of his face with her fingers as if trying to memorise his features.

When he squeezes her hand, she leans forward to address me, her lips firm.

"I'm trusting you with something of great value to me." Her voice is low, almost a whisper. "Please be sure my boy stays safe."

I half nod but stay quiet. Why craft promises I'll almost certainly break?

Dwayne hands me a can of air freshener. "Take care of my big brother, dude." His raw emotion is unconcealed. "And of yourself. You both deserve better."

I'm thrown. He's shouldered a burden, too, forced

into playing the *man of the house* while Hyson searched for God.

"Thank you," I manage to say, and he claps me on the shoulder before stepping back to stand beside his mother as I turn the key in the ignition.

We can't have gone more than ten yards when there's a muffled call.

In the rearview mirror, I see Estelle running, her arms waving, her face pale under the street lamp's glow. I brake hard, and she wrenches open the passenger door.

Gripping his face, she speaks urgently. "You are my greatest joy. Do what must be done, but come home to me. Please. Come home soon. Come home safe."

He can only nod.

Estelle kisses his forehead tenderly, then steps away, making the sign of the cross.

Hyson stares ahead, his mother's figure shrinking into the distance. I turn on the radio. Tammy Wynette sings, and as the song ends, a news bulletin plays. He turns up the volume.

*In breaking news, the Las Vegas coroner has confirmed plans to re-open an inquiry into the 2017 death of actor Tim Larson, now linking the case to reality TV star Judah Eisenhart, who was found unresponsive in an LA motel room last week. The police have identified a person of interest.*

*Stay tuned for updates.*

# 21

Darkness shrouds the I-40 as we speed from River Valley. Hyson remains a silent shadow, staring out his window. He'd switched off the radio, and now only the hum of tyres fills the tense silence.

"You just speak up if you need me to pull over," I say. "Otherwise, I intend on driving through to morning and stopping for breakfast."

He doesn't answer, and my eyes stay fixed on the road, unspooling under yellow lines as mile markers flash by.

The first faint glow of dawn emerges as we cross into Tennessee. Across a sun-parched field, a featureless human shape waves—a scarecrow tied to a broken sign-post advertising apple cider. A pang of longing catches in my chest as I turn to point it out to Noah, and then remember he's not there.

There's a billboard.

*Rise and dine! Biscuits, sausage, bacon, eggs, and more—
next exit at Bobby's Diner.*

"You need to get some air?" I nudge Hyson's arm.
"Bobby's Diner does something called biscuits."

He opens his eyes, briefly disorientated, and then
half-smiles, shuffling up in his seat. "I'm cool for now."

He fingers the Bible he's held onto since leaving River
Valley. This isn't the same man who left Vegas six years
earlier. Pastor Hyson lives as far from Hollywood's glitz
and glamour as possible. A dust-covered row of clapper-
board houses became his refuge, and now I'm dragging
him away.

The green of the grasslands becomes the brown of
ploughed fields as we pass through towns and villages,
some little more than ramshackle sheds, others fancy
gated developments where smart homes nestle behind
high fences and cameras track the empty road.

The dashboard clock shows 6:47 a.m. My stomach
needs food, and I need to stretch.

Another flickering sign, this time for Dixie's Diner,
promising farm-fresh eggs, sausage, more of those
mystery biscuits, and gravy. I signal to pull off the highway. Hyson shifts and mumbles.

———

I park beside a weathered truck. When the engine is
done rattling, we hear the cicadas drone in the wind-
ravaged trees that surround a squat, flat-roofed building.
Hyson jumps down and heads across the cracked paving,
not waiting for me. I catch him up at the entrance.

The smell of fried bacon hits me. A handful of early morning risers huddle over breakfast, truckers mostly. The waitress, in her fifties, with kind eyes, points towards a booth by the window, where we slide into our seats as the sun paints nearby fields in a glow of oranges and reds. She brings a pot of coffee, fills two cups, and leaves us to read the menu.

"Ma sometimes makes pancakes." His fingers drum against the tabletop. "You think they might be good here?"

He's doing his best, making an effort to talk.

"Pancakes sound like good road food," I say, and when he wrinkles his nose, as if to say he has no idea what that means, I explain. "Fills you up and stays put."

It's the first time I've heard him laugh for real.

It makes me miss Noah all the more.

When the waitress comes, he asks for blueberry pancakes with maple syrup and extra cream. I order a Denver omelette. Then the silence sets back in, wrapping around us like a morning mist. The kitchen staff chatter and sing along to the radio. Hyson's eyes stay fixed on the window.

"Ever think about what might have happened if you never left LA?" I say, determined not to spend an entire day not talking.

His gaze stays thoughtful. "You already know the answer to that. I couldn't stop Biedermeier and Dupree. I just had to quit being a part of it."

There's something else I need to ask. "Are you regretting coming back with me?"

He takes a deep breath. "This isn't about regret. It's

about facing the past and hoping for a better future. But yeah, I can't stop myself from wondering if it was the right choice."

His honesty stings, but I appreciate it. If he'd told me everything was big, bright, and fluffy, I'd know he was capable of telling me what he thought I wanted to hear.

The waitress returns with our food. Neither of us eats much.

———

Hyson takes over driving, his hands steady, navigating the waking highway. A scorching sun beats down, and heat ripples blur as fallow fields fade, replaced once more by endless desert dust. The van's rattling AC wheezes. A blue car keeps pace behind, and a truck roars past, heading the opposite way. Sleep consumes me, and Hyson suggests a break when my head hits the dashboard for the third time.

"I know you want to get to LA, but maybe we should stop at the next town? Walk around a little. Energise. Find a place to stay. One night of quality rest might help."

"I still don't know for sure when the wedding is happening."

"It's a week from today."

My eyes widen. How come I missed this? I'm checking the news every few minutes.

"I made a call," he says. "Asked around a few old friends. It's at some place in the Hills. Black tie is optional."

Noah is going through with the wedding. I suppose a tiny part of me hoped he'd change his mind. A tiny, stupid part of me.

"We need to be sure of having some fight in us," Hyson says, as if he needs me to stay focused. "You're no good to anyone if you don't rest."

A sign comes into view—Liberty Hall: six more miles.

———

The asphalt gives way to a rugged dust track, and the van jostles with every bump and dip as the landscape shifts from desert plains to cultivated beauty. The road gets smoother, taking us past an unimpressive strip of flat-pack buildings and anonymous modern houses. A row of chain hotels compete on price.

Faded signs indicate a winding path leading to a rest area that's little more than an abandoned picnic ground, where weathered painted tables sit tatty and splintered, and rusted bins overflow. The debris spills onto out-of-control weeds. Hyson kills the engine but doesn't move from his seat.

"I get how you don't trust me." His words come out in a monotone mumble. "Why would you?"

I lean back against the headrest. "I hit rock bottom a while ago, and now I don't trust anyone. Not even myself."

He sets his hands on the wheel and stares at a town map tacked to a bulletin board. "For the longest time, I told myself I did the right thing that night. In Vegas. I figured kids do drugs, and bad things happen. I shouldn't even have been there. It was already over between me and Aaron. I'd given him an ultimatum. Stop the parties or stop pretending like we have any kind of relationship."

Birds flit between trees, calling to each other.

"The plan was to tell the press our lives had gotten too different and trot out the usual crap about staying friends. Wishing each other only the very best."

"So, why *were* you in Vegas?"

"Aaron begged me. CinemaCon was huge. Deals get signed there, and the last thing he needed was everyone talking about how Hollywood's biggest out gay director was getting divorced."

"People divorce every day."

"He was promoting some shitty movie about everlasting love. Can you even start to guess how the press conferences might go? The kind of questions that the hacks in the front row would throw his way. The movie wouldn't have mattered. Everything would have been about him. About me. About us. The way we planned it, I could vanish afterwards."

Dust eddies swirl, lifting leaves and litter into the air.

"When Tim got sick, I fell to pieces, and Dupree took charge. They said they needed to find a fall guy. Someone to take the blame. They needed fingerprints in the room and sent Aaron down to the casino. He found me a hotel uniform and said to serve drinks and keep my mouth shut."

My eyes close, transporting me back to the hotel casino, ordering drinks and watching a guy lose his money at a card table, when some handsome, craggy daddy-bear guy asks if he can buy me another beer.

"All the time, you were in that room," Hyson says. "I wanted to tell you to run like hell. Get the hell out. Save yourself."

I flashback to staggering around, trying to find the loo. I'd been fine one minute and smashed the next.

"Did you spike my drink?"

Hyson's face reddens.

"That night, I did a lot I'm not proud of. But you have to understand, Dupree didn't give me much in the way of a choice. All I can do now is try to make amends."

———

In Liberty Hall, sunshine glints off two-story buildings, and the pavements are busy with people going about their daily lives. Children play ball. Older kids walk, talk, and laugh. A woman lingers in front of a wedding dress store.

"Rock, paper, scissors to pick where we sleep," I say as we park across the street from three chain hotels.

He shakes his head. "The Marriott usually does clergy discount on account of the Mormon connection."

"But you're Baptist."

He laughs. "We're rivals, shooting for the same fish in the same barrel, and clergy discount is clergy discount."

It turns out he's not wrong, and a room advertised for 90 dollars morphs into one costing just under 50. We have to share but get two queen-size beds, a coffee-making machine, and a trouser press.

"Can't wait to press me some trousers," Hyson says

as the handsome desk clerk hands over key cards. It's my first time smiling in days.

———

I drop my bag on the pale beige carpet and flop onto a soft bed, staring at the dead mosquito-speckled ceiling. Hyson rummages through his bag, pulling out a laptop. He goes to sit at a small desk. "We should do our research."

"Research on what?"

He taps at the keyboard, curses about the Wi-Fi, and then sits back, folding his arms. "As of ten-thirty-two yesterday morning, I am no longer married to Aaron Biedermeier. Talk about cutting things fine. I guess Dupree needed to be sure Aaron pulled through before making any moves." He turns to me. "Do I look any different now that I'm a divorcee?"

"You look pretty much the same to me."

He makes a hissy sound. "I was kind of hoping for a handsome older guy that richer men would pity."

I laugh. I actually laugh. Bo Hyson isn't such a twat, after all.

"Come see the wedding venue." He clicks on another tab to access a *TMZ Live Stream* of a grand estate in the Hollywood Hills. Guys in smart grey overalls work to pitch a tent in lush gardens.

"I still have connections," he says. "I could get us onto the catering staff if you want to do the whole '*shoulda-been-me*' thing."

I don't look away from the screen. "What do you mean?"

"Every time you mention Noah, I see it in your face."

I turn away, my face is on fire. "He's a friend. Was a friend."

"And that's all?"

"Noah was someone I got carried away over." My voice crackles. "We all know guys like that, right?"

Hyson rubs his chin, like he's trying to find the right thing to say next. "In my case, that *guy* was called Aaron Biedermeier."

"Can I ask you something?" I say, and he signals for me to go on. "How old were *you* when Aaron first hit on you?"

"Was I just underage, you mean?"

It's obvious; that's what I'm asking. Aaron's official bio puts him at 58, and Hyson is in his mid-forties at most.

"I was grown up enough to know better, but too young to work out how bad people could be."

I sense pain. "Sorry. It's none of my business."

He gets up and sits on the edge of the other bed. "He took me nice places to eat, introduced me to all his big-deal friends, and let me watch what was happening on film sets. I was a kid who fixed up gardens and did odd jobs. Everything he showed me—his whole lifestyle—just kind of blew me away. And then, yeah, the parties started."

"You went to them?"

"Until Aaron made some excuse about loving me too

much to share me." He exhales. "And I bought that bull-shit, too. I only wanted to make him happy."

"How old were the kids at these parties?"

He looks to ponder my question. "How is any of this helping you?"

"Were they sixteen? Fifteen? Younger?"

"I guess, on average, sixteen."

"You mean some of the boys Biedermeier abused were younger than that?" My stomach churns, and I can barely get the words out. "Did you never try to stop him? You didn't think it was wrong, and you should tell someone?"

Hyson looks at me, his eyes darkening. "Aaron had connections. Money. And the ability to make people disappear."

"And that's where Dupree comes in?"

Darkness crosses his face. "I saw Tim die. When it all first happened, they said he was *'just sick'*, and Dupree was supposed to get him to the hospital." He trails off, head hung with shame. "After Vegas, Dupree came to the house and talked to Ma. He said he could fix things so we could start new lives someplace away from LA. I wanted out."

"You took his money and ran?"

He gets up and goes over to the window. "What Noah told you—the photographs. The recordings. I know what Ma said, but they do exist. I have them."

It's like someone sucked all the air from our room. He goes back to the desk, reaches into his bag, and pulls out a USB stick. "Nobody flies that close to a flame without taking precautions. I gave Dupree a copy and promised I already destroyed the originals."

A tiny light clicks on at the far end of a dark tunnel. "We can still go to the police."

He shakes his head. "You're underestimating Dupree. There's no way he'll roll over. Not without taking Noah down too. And yeah, if he has to go to jail, he'll make some sort of deal to score reduced time. But the lives he destroyed, they stay broken."

My fingers form fists, and Hyson places a placating hand on my shoulder.

"You have every right to feel betrayed. But try to see the impossible situation Dupree put Noah in."

In my head, I'm back at the airport, watching him walk up the ramp and through sliding doors. He's turning to wave, letting me watch as he turns away.

"I know it's a lot to process." Hyson is at the window again, his gaze fixed on the distant skyline. "But we've got a bit of power now with this. We'll need a plan— something airtight. And we have to be careful."

The room falls silent. We're bound by a common cause.

————

I'm woken from fitful sleep by my phone ringing. A lurid neon vacancy sign blinks outside, casting an eerie red glow through grimy, curtained windows. Muffled TV laughter echoes from a neighbouring room.

I find my mobile tangled in the sheets. Whoever called withheld their number.

It's 2 a.m., and the bed opposite is empty.

My first thought is to check that Hyson didn't take the van keys, but they're where I left them on a chair near a dresser.

"Bo," I call out, half expecting him to answer from the bathroom.

He doesn't.

It's two in the morning. Has he abandoned me? After everything he said, after all those confessions.

I dive from my bed and rummage in his bag, trying to find that USB stick. My phone starts up again, and this time I answer.

"This is Officer Willis from the Liberty Hall Police Department. I'm calling because we have an individual here who's given your name as a contact for bail. Am I speaking with a Mr Kyle Macdonald?"

My pulse jolts. "That's me."

"Sir, I'm sorry to say that one Bo Hyson was arrested for public intoxication and disorderly conduct. We have him in a holding cell if you can come on down and bail him out."

I exhale, feeling the weight of the world lift. "I'll be there as soon as possible."

It's early morning back home, and I need advice.

"Your best bet is to find a bail bond office," Milly says. "From what I know of how things work out there, they're all run by crooks, so nobody will ask to see ID. But they'll add a fee."

"How much of a fee?"

My wages cleared yesterday, meaning my bank

balance should be reasonably healthy, but that money buys my air ticket home.

Milly pauses. "Depends on the office, but usually around ten per cent of the bail amount. If your preacher man did something terrible, you could be looking at a few hundred dollars, maybe more."

———

My phone directs me to *Get Out Quick Bail Bonds*, wedged between a 24-hour diner and an apartment building. Debris skitters across the cracked sidewalk in the hot, dry wind. Laundromat steam-vents bellow as I pass, lending the night air a sour, chemical smell.

I buzz to be let in and push open a protesting door. Harsh tube lighting hurts my eyes, and the over-whelming stink is of disinfectant and puke.

I'm in the right place.

Behind an ancient computer at a counter piled high with files and coffee-stained forms, a middle-aged woman looks up from her magazine.

"Help you?" she asks, her voice loaded with fine gravel.

I put on my best Hugh Grant. "I need to post bail."

"Name?" Her long, fuchsia-coloured nails tap at a filthy keyboard, and an ancient computer screen flickers. She clicks the mouse, causing a printer to whirl into life.

———

Hyson stays quiet as we drive back to the hotel. The tension between us grows tangible. A voice inside wants to call him stupid and reckless and ask if he thinks this mercy dash is some kind of holiday. If everything he said before was bullshit.

Instead, I park, turn off the engine, and sit with my arms folded.

"What you did could have screwed everything," I say, trying not to lose it. "Not just for you. Not only for me. But for Tim's mother, Judah's folks. And for Estelle and Dwayne."

His eyes stay fixed on the dashboard. "I never meant for any of this to happen. I was blowing off steam."

Back in our room, Hyson doesn't shower. Just stumbles into bed and snores. Loud. I consider muffling his face with a pillow, but enough people have met an unfortunate end of late. Why add to the body count?

Through the open hotel room window, the night air buzzes with cicadas.

I stare at my phone. At more photographs of the happy couple.

*Noah Winters and Aaron Biedermeier celebrate with friends ahead of Hollywood's Wedding of the Year.*

I could call him.

I don't.

# 22

We pick at a complimentary breakfast of 'home-style' pancakes and rubbery eggs. The chipped Formica table is cold under my palms. Hyson's sallow complexion reflects a night spent drowning in cheap booze. He gulps black coffee, wincing with each mouthful, and I scrape my fork before deliberately clattering a knife and taking pleasure when his face tenses.

"I'll pay you back, Kyle. I promise." His eyes are guarded, not quite meeting mine.

I don't glance up; irritation still simmering. "How exactly? Do you plan on tapping into some secret Swiss bank account?"

He goes to speak, and I hold up a hand.

"Save it for someone who gives a flying fuck."

———

The morning drags, with one brief stop for fuel and a drive-through lunch. Occasionally, Hyson opens his mouth like he wants to either say sorry some more or assure me he's totally on board. But then he says nothing.

It's getting dark as we leave the highway and roll into another desert community with quaint houses, washed in soft, dusky light. The road takes us downtown, where the streets come alive and the air smells of fresh popcorn and barbecued meat. Strings of lightbulbs signal the main square, where makeshift stalls peddle everything from homemade bread to hand-knitted shawls. A banner overhead welcomes us to the *Holy Harvest Hoedown*.

"What the buggery bollocks is a hoedown?" I say.

Hyson shifts in his seat. "Some kind of harvest festival."

A preacher in a purple robe stands on a makeshift stage, his voice booming as he reads from a heavy-bound Bible.

"Let me guess," I say. "These are your people."

Hyson clicks his tongue. "I don't have any right to ask you for anything. And I promise I won't drink a thing, but do you think we might take a walk around?"

I'm tempted to refuse out of spite, and roll my head, causing my shoulders to pop and crack.

"The deal is you find us a hotel room," I say. "And you pay."

Hyson points to an empty parking space. "You wait here. Let me go ask around."

"Try not to get arrested," I call after him as he walks towards the main square.

I turn off the engine and roll down the window, letting in the humid summer air. The sound of a gospel choir grows louder, calling out to God.

Hyson is back. "I found a room, but we have to share a bed."

"Fine." I hold up my hands to signal I'm sick and tired of arguing. "Perhaps you won't snore so loud if you stay sober."

Over on the stage, voices rise in joyful chorus.

"Does this room come with a bath?" I say, and he grins.

"It's a four-star joint. Kinda fancy."

I'd expected him to have opted for a tumbledown boarding house with bedbugs on tap, but now I'm imagining fluffy white towels, brand-name toiletries, marble bathroom floors, and endless hot water.

"Listen, Bo," I say. "It strikes me this hoedown crap is more your thing than mine. Why not soak up the atmosphere?"

His eyes widen. "You're sure about that?"

"All I ask is two hours to soak in a bath."

He reaches out to touch my arm. "I promise to drink nothing stronger than apple cider."

————

Music and prayers drift through a hotel room window, opening onto the town square. I pull it shut and draw the curtains, craving instead the hiss of air-conditioning and the sound of an oversized bath filling.

Can I trust Hyson not to drink? No matter what, I've

decided if he gets into trouble, there will be no more middle-of-the-night races to jail bond offices. He can rot in a cell.

I sink into hot water up to my neck, breathing in eucalyptus bath oil, and drift away. I'm no longer mired in madness. I have no past. I have no future. Just this.

Two fluffy robes hang on the bathroom door, and I wrap myself in one, stopping to peer into the mini bar and slamming it shut after scanning the price list.

It's too long since I last got to flip idly through TV channels. Half are in Spanish. Almost all of them show ads. Red-faced men argue about abortion. Bible-bashers spew hate. Rake-skinny women boast about table-surfing all-you-can-eat buffets and staying thin thanks to a daily milkshake.

I reach for my phone, and there's a message from Milly:

Make sure you have a drink before you read this.

When I click, it's another photograph of Aaron and Noah. Side by side in wooden garden chairs set against trimmed hedges. The sky above is a too-perfect shade of blue, and Noah's wearing a too-white linen shirt with too many buttons undone. Aaron is a faded version of his former self—skinny arms poke out of his t-shirt. But his smile could rival the sun.

I hit play.

"So in love, right?" A woman in a hot pink dress gushes.

Noah bows his head. "We're enjoying this special time together. The future will unfold as it's meant to."

I think back on our journey and the late-night talks. Was everything one big act to keep me sweet? Something inside shuts down, and I harden my heart.

Hyson comes through the door and freezes at the sound of Biedermeier talking.

"What the hell is that?" he says.

"I have a kind of masochistic thing going on." I hold up my phone. "Just let me have this."

The interviewer fires more questions. "After everything, you opened your eyes in the hospital and saw Noah by your side. How did that make you feel?"

"He wasn't there," I say. "He was with me."

Aaron starts to speak, but then blinks and waves as if overcome. The camera swings back around to the host, and Hyson prises the phone from my hand.

"Why would you put yourself through that?" he says.

"I like to know how people I thought I cared about are doing. It's not like we're Facebook friends, and I can't see me scoring an invite to the wedding."

He stares at the freeze-framed screen. "For what it's worth, I don't think Noah wanted to be there."

I slump back on fluffed-up pillows. "He's happy now. That story he fed me..." I swallow tears. "He's a damn talented actor."

"Would something from the minibar help?"

"We could refuel the van for the same as they charge for a large vodka."

"This is all on me." He pours me a drink and fixes himself a glass of fizzy water. I down the vodka in one and hold out the tumbler for a refill. As he reaches into the fridge, his voice drops to a whisper.

"I had a call from Dupree."

Heat rushes to my face. "Did you tell him where we are?"

"He called to ask if you made it to River Valley. Wanted to be sure I didn't say anything to jeopardise agreements."

I scoff and stare at the swirly, patterned carpet. "What did you say?"

"I played dumb."

"I can imagine."

"He offered to wire money. Ten grand to keep my mouth shut." He settles on the arm of the couch, his brow furrowed.

"You should take the money," I say. "The church needs a lick of paint, and that diner wouldn't say no to a deep clean."

Bo ignores me. "Don't you see? This is a good thing."

I sigh so hard that it hurts my chest. "How do you work that out?"

"Dupree wouldn't be so worried about controlling the narrative if he trusted Noah. There's a reckoning coming. He senses trouble brewing."

My heart wants to believe, but I know what I saw. Noah kept touching Aaron's arm, and his face transmitted concern.

Looking me in the eye, Hyson lowers his voice to a whisper. "Dupree calling proves the entire house of cards could collapse any minute."

I don't look up. "What did you tell him?"

"That you tracked down Ma, but she covered for me."

I'm on my feet, hopping with fury. "He knows I was there?"

"Dupree only needs to make one phone call to the diner, and someone will say a British guy was in town. And then he'd know I was lying. What use would I be to you then?"

He's right.

"I told him you'd already left River Valley."

I glance at my phone. Noah has his hand on Aaron's arm. Every part of my heart aches.

"How could he just go back to him?" I try to keep my voice steady. "So much for making stuff right with the Larson family."

Hyson's breath comes out ragged. "You think he had any choice? The things that are bad for us are the hardest to give up."

"So...what? He's some kind of addict," I say. "Can't he call an *Abused Anonymous* helpline?"

Hyson's features tighten into a scowl. "Sometimes, the paths we choose lead to places we never meant to go."

My vision blurs with stinging tears. Does he mean me? Is this his way of explaining how I'm to blame? That I'm the one who wandered astray, winding up lost and alone through my own rubbish choices.

"You think Noah saw me as a mistake?" I say, and Hyson's scowl deepens, causing my stomach to sink.

"I think you and Noah are a risk. And taking risks is the only way we learn how to live truly."

I lie back on the bed, staring up at the ceiling. "What now?"

"As soon as we reach LA, we report your passport stolen. Sort things out and fly home. Put all that's happened behind you."

I try to steady my voice. "You make it sound easy."

"It has to be. You can't be the next Judah."

I think about when Dupree first called, and Milly showed me stories about Aaron on her phone. Stories I dismissed as *starfucker nonsense*. I wanted so much to believe fate had intervened and my luck was changing.

"Eisenhart shot his mouth off all over town," Hyson says. "Aaron was at the top of his game, and everyone loves it when the king's crown works loose. The spark took, and Judah lit a full-on dumpster fire. You saw what happened."

He pours me another drink, pulls over a chair, and sits, his posture rigid, as if bracing for impact. The white noise of the air conditioner fills an otherwise unyielding silence.

"How can you expect me to trust you?" I say, weighing each word. "When you first heard a British guy was in River Valley asking questions, surely you worked it all out? That night outside the diner. When you took me to that shed and lied about a fire destroying your proof. Forgive me if I say this, but you need a better continuity editor."

He nods, staring down at the floor. "Ma figured you'd hang around for a day or two at most."

I huff. "Yeah, she came to persuade me to leave town.

I meant to ask if she could get me the recipe for those biscuits. They were good."

He takes a sip of his water. The muted glow from a bedside lamp casts long shadows. Outside the curtained windows, the first hints of dawn appear—the faintest touch of silver lightening the night sky.

"You want to know why I expect you to trust me?" he says.

I nod.

"I've wanted to call the cops most every day since that shit happened in Vegas. I still have nightmares, Kyle."

I look for any signs he might be lying.

"Dupree never called for help. When the cops found Larson's body, he went downtown to help with enquiries. Told them Tim was last seen partying with some British tourist."

He sighs and shakes his head.

"Dupree flew Tim's folks to Vegas. He acted like he lost his own kid. Described you, while the cops took prints and swabs, and put on this act about how he couldn't believe Tim could be so dumb."

He wipes at his eyes, and my head spins. "They only had to check the security cameras. They'd have shown me coming back with Aaron. Way later."

"Yeah, except the hotel system had some kind of *white-out*." He surrounds the word with air quotes. "And Aaron was too busy on calls to talk to the cops. After they left, we boarded a company jet back to LA."

"But *you* knew?" I say. "You could have told the police what happened."

"Dupree told them I was with Aaron, so they never even spoke with me. Afterwards, he was fucking full of himself, expecting me to be grateful. I said I was going to the cops, and he reminded me he had photographs taken at parties."

"Wouldn't that have screwed Aaron?"

"Photographs of me with other guys. Guys that fell out of favour."

Hyson rolls his shoulders and groans like this was a secret carried around for too long.

"There's more.," he says. "Years ago, me and Aaron had some stupid fight, and I accused him of not trusting me. The guy hated to lose at anything. Including stupid fights, so he called a lawyer there and then. Signed everything he owned into my name."

I say nothing as the puzzle pieces slot into place.

"Right after the attack on Aaron, Dupree got in touch, screaming about the mess he was in and how he couldn't sign off production budgets or pay wages. Told me to fly back to LA."

I look up, wondering if I heard correctly. All the time we've been talking, something's been nagging at the back of my mind, and it's only now that it forms words.

"All this time, you had photos that could stop him from ordering you about, yet you stayed quiet. Did your God tell you it was fine to pass by on the other side of the street and ignore all the lives Biedermeier damaged?"

# 23

Heat radiates from the cracked asphalt in shimmering waves as the van bumps along a dusty, two-lane highway. It's late in the afternoon, but we're no longer speaking. Now that I know Hyson could have spared me all the pain, all the hurt, and all the falling for someone I couldn't have, I hate him.

He's map-reading and looks up. "Dude, I know you don't want to talk, but what's the plan when we get to LA? Do you think you're going to walk into the Biedermeier Pictures offices and demand to speak to Dupree and tell him you know everything?"

I shuffle uneasily in my seat, because that's pretty much how the scene has been playing out in my head. Possibly with great background music, the odd close-up on Dupree's face, and then on mine, laughing.

I rub clammy hands against my T-shirt as prickly heat creeps up my neck.

Hyson nods like he just saw inside my head. "I'm not saying we're in this together, Kyle, but we should agree on some kind of strategy."

"Such as?"

"I could call someone. A journalist."

I scoff. "Like I trust you to do anything."

"OK, when do you plan on making your move? The second we reach city limits, or maybe hold back until the big day. Crash the wedding. That way, you know you'll get TV coverage."

He's right. I hate him, but he's right.

"I want to talk to Noah first," I say. "I need him to explain why he did what he did to me."

Hyson pulls a concerned face but says nothing to change my mind.

————

Route 66 unfurls its last stretch, and up ahead, a sign welcomes us to Los Angeles. The city that was to have been my gateway to a world of endless possibilities. A symbol of hope. Now, even seeing it on a road sign fills me with dread.

"I guess we find a cheap motel?" I say.

Hyson leans forward to swat at an insect battering the windscreen. "I may have a place we can stay." He keeps his gaze fixed on the road. "I have a friend. Her name is Rosemary, and she's a devout Baptist preacher."

I try not to sound ungrateful, but I've had a belly full of his crap.

"If it's all the same with you, I'll make my own arrangements," I say.

He shrugs. "OK, but when they ask for ID, what story do you plan on spinning?"

I'm screwed.

"Is this Rosemary my only option?" I say, trying not to sound like the most ungrateful sod. "I just don't think imposing on someone out of the blue is good manners. When did you last visit?"

He squirms in his seat and clears his throat. "Look, I know it's not ideal, but do you have a better plan?"

Tension rises in my chest. Bunking down in the home of some Baptist preacher friend of the man who was part of why I'm in this mess doesn't sound like the first prize in any raffle, but he's right. I can't check in to any hotel.

"Fine," I say through gritted teeth. "But if she takes me to one side to explain how I'll burn in hell if my semen is used for anything other than the impregnation of a wife, I'm out of there."

Hyson tuts. "I can't say I ever heard Rosemary use the word *semen*."

"Is this like some preachers' network thing? How do you know her?"

"She was the senior minister at a church I attended when things got sketchy with Aaron. Ran a Baptist seminary, and when Ma announced we were leaving town, Rosemary put me in touch with the national convention."

"She knows about Dupree? And the parties?"

"I have to tell you something," he says, and I groan.

What fresh hell is he about to share? Do we have to get up at five and pray, or is it a silent home where they dick about with talking sticks? He reddens. "Rosemary never actually knew about my being gay."

"She's blind and deaf?"

He looks irked. "Half of River Valley thinks I'm straight."

I pull a quizzical face. "Are we counting pigs, cows, and chickens in that number? Because most everyone I spoke to knows you're a screaming queen."

Hyson juts out his chin. "I'm serious, Kyle. Rosemary has no idea. I never brought it up, and I don't think anyone else did either. But she's always been kind to me. And she's got a spare bedroom."

"Fine," I say. "But warn her, *this* guy isn't in the market for a conversion."

He pulls out his phone. "Be yourself. But maybe not so bitchy. Rosemary believes God embraces everyone."

He has her on speaker, and when she picks up, his tone is warm. They chat like they just saw each other last week. When he asks for help, she doesn't hesitate.

"You have to come stay."

After hanging up, Hyson pulls a smug face. "She truly is one of the best people I have ever met."

I grit my teeth. "Any friend of yours..."

————

We pull over outside a modest single-story house, with the lawn mowed and beds overflowing with pink roses.

This little town, just twenty miles east of the sprawling smog that cloaks downtown LA, could be a theme park, set up to recreate the swinging sixties, with an ice cream parlour flanked by striped awnings and a red brick coffee house shaded by trees.

"What's our back story?" I say, checking in with Hyson, nervous about meeting the woman who changed his life.

He jumps down from the passenger seat. "Rosemary only ever likes to know what matters. She doesn't need to care about who you are or why you are driving this Scooby Doo Mystery Machine."

He marches off, and I trail behind, feigning interest in the garden as the bright green front door swings open, and a petite woman with a halo of silver curls greets Hyson with sparkling eyes.

"Bo, sweetheart."

She pulls him into a warm embrace, then steps back and holds his hands in hers. His face softens, and then Rosemary turns her attention to me.

"This must be the friend you told me about."

Her voice is gentle and welcoming. I clear my throat, reminding myself to sound confident. "I'm Kyle. Training to be something Baptisty."

She wrinkles her nose and glances at Bo, who's busy doing a *shut-the-hell-up* face.

"Welcome to my home, Kyle." Her perfume tickles my nose. "It's such a lovely, warm day. We're sitting out in the backyard."

She ushers us inside and down a short hallway. My

fingers trail over vintage floral wallpaper. The pattern faded with age. We walk through a kitchen onto a patio with a small wooden table and ornately scrolled metal chairs. A modest garden is in late-summer bloom. Marigolds and zinnias sway in the breeze. A stone angel stands watch near a trellis arched with purple clematis.

We sit, and she pours from a jug of obviously fresh lemonade.

"How long has it been since we were last together here, Bo?" she says. He scrunches his nose but doesn't answer. "Tell me *everything* I've missed."

Her focus stays fixed on him, and as he talks about River Valley, skipping any mention of just why he's back in LA.

"And what about you, Kyle?" Rosemary's question jolts me. "What do you do when you're not adventuring with this rapscallion?"

I clear my throat. "I'm a teacher. Junior school. Young kids. In England."

Rosemary looks confused. "I thought you said…"

Hyson cuts in. "A Baptist school, and I first got to know Kyle when he came on a mission."

Rosemary's eyes glitter with enthusiasm as she tells me she once went to London and met with a couple called Smith, Jones, or Edwards.

"They were teachers. Perhaps you're familiar with them?"

He rescues me by reminding her we've had a long drive. "Right now, a shower would bring me closer to God. Point me towards your bathroom."

She shows us to the guest room, insisting I take the bed while Hyson sleeps on a foldaway.

"I'll let you boys get some rest. I left out fresh towels, and feel free to use whatever potions and lotions you find in there. I only ever shop at CVS, but they do the best things."

I go to thank her, and she holds up a hand. "No need to say anything. I hope you'll come to our service in the morning." It's a gentle invitation. There's no pressure. "Either way, French toast when you wake."

———

I wait until Rosemary turns on the radio downstairs before asking what happens now.

"Do you call Dupree and demand a meeting?" Hyson puffs out his cheeks.

"That's a little full-on. I figured we should take our time."

"We don't have time to take. By tomorrow afternoon, Noah will be married to that murdering paedo."

He huffs. "Isn't my calling Dupree the same as letting him know a storm is coming? This is a man whose entire reputation rests on keeping the garden green. Any hint of trouble..."

"Do I text Noah and invite him for coffee? Is that too risky?"

Each time I mention meeting up, Hyson changes the subject.

"You want to take a walk around the neighbourhood?" he says now. "It's kinda pretty. And if I remember right, there's a great place to get a beer down the block."

"I need to talk to Noah," I say.

Hyson gazes out the window, his jaw set in a firm line. "There's something I need to confess. Dupree already knows we're here."

I stare, glued to the spot. Surely, to God, no.

"Ever since you showed up in River Valley, I've been feeding him information. Let him know where you were, who you were talking to, and what you wanted me to do."

His shoulders hunch with shame.

"You've seen how my family lives, Kyle. Dwayne drinks the dough he makes, and Ma pours her heart into a patch of dirt behind the church. I'm working at the diner."

"You own the place."

"*Aaron* owns the diner. He uses it to launder money."

The bed creaks as I sit. Milly is right. I'm the worst judge of character. Every single person I've trusted since leaving Birmingham has turned out to be a big, fat *liar, liar, pants on fire*.

"What now?" I keep my voice even. "How do you plan on making it look like I overdosed?"

He glances away. "Dupree said to gain your trust and bring you back to LA. I'm supposed to deliver you to him." His tearful eyes meet mine. "I wanted to tell you sooner. This isn't what I want. But they have too much on me. I was at those parties."

Bile rises in my throat as this latest betrayal lands. "But you have stuff on them, too."

He reaches for me, but I shove him away.

"Don't." I keep to a whisper so Rosemary doesn't come running. "Was this your plan all along? Earn my trust, then hand me over to be stitched up and blamed for the deaths of two kids Biedermeier abused and then had killed."

"It's not like that. We can still..."

I'm already storming along the hall and racing down the stairs and out onto the street. Just up ahead, where the houses are painted yellow, a black car is parked. Its engine thrums.

A door opens, and Noah steps out.

He says something, but my brain fails to untangle the muddle of words. And then I see that it isn't him at all. I'm staring slack-jawed at a random guy, older than Noah. Same colour hair, same build, but taller. And he's holding up his phone, asking if I know where to find some street.

"I'm not from around here," I hear myself say.

I sound scared. Frantic.

And then I turn and run until my legs give out and collapse on the pavement outside a bar.

———

"Mum," I say when she picks up.

"Kyle? It's four in the morning. Are you OK? What's happened?"

"It's a long story. I just needed to hear your voice."

"Have you been drinking? I thought they didn't let you out at night on your course. You'll be in trouble, darling. Please…take my advice. Go back to your hotel room and get some sleep."

I take a breath. "I'm in Los Angeles."

There's a muffled noise, and Mum tells Dad to go back to sleep. Bedsprings squeak, and a door opens and closes. She'll be sitting on the landing. On the top step, under a framed photograph of the Queen, taken on the day Her Majesty came to Birmingham to open Millennium Point.

"It's a terrible line, love," Mum says. "All crackles and pops. I could have sworn you said you were in Los Angeles."

She laughs. I don't.

Where do I begin with my story? How about right back at the start?

"I had a phone call. Someone claimed I was married to a film director. And he was in a coma."

Hearing this out loud makes me officially as dumb as a box of hair.

———

At nine in the evening, Rusty's Roadhouse is mostly home to locals with nothing better to do but drink and stare glassy-eyed at TV screens. Low lights flicker, as if struggling to stay on.

"Beer," I mutter as I climb onto a rickety wooden stool. The barman turns, grabs a bottle, pops the lid, and hands it to me. I go to pay.

"Settle up when you're done, dude."

"Oh, right, thanks. I always forget."

"Brit?"

I nod. It's enough. We've said all we need, and he goes back to watching TV.

Why were Hyson's eyes full of tears when he told me what he'd done? When he admitted to taking the piss from day one. Is there a heart beating somewhere inside his chest, feeling something for the kids he let die?

And what about Noah? Conveniently discovering a conscience twenty-four hours before we reached River Valley. Hugging me with acting-school affection and kissing me with that perfect mouth. Telling me he's sorry.

It's all too absurd. A man who helped a paedophile abuse kids doesn't suddenly find God and become a pastor.

How could I have fallen for that?

Noah *was* told to get me out of town.

Hyson *was* the decoy.

Aaron waking from his coma was a nuisance, but they all needed me to carry on to River Valley because *Pastor Hyson had* stacks of evidence to help clear my name. The same Pastor Hyson, who jumped into a van, came with me all the way back here. The same Pastor Hyson who turned on the tears and lied about how he still saw Tim Larson's face every day and wanted to make things right.

I'm such an idiot, so pathetically gullible, swallowing every syrupy word any of those fuckers fed me. My own worst enemy, leaping blindly into Noah's arms like a love-struck kid, oblivious to the warning signs. I disgust myself. Trusting him was proof of what a naive, pathetic excuse for a gay man I am. Pitifully desperate for affection. Spineless and stupid.

And now, I'm a fugitive in a foreign city with nowhere to turn. No passport. No friends. And a mother climbing the walls with worry.

I didn't need to call her.

Add selfishness to that list of faults.

I should call 911 and give myself up. Tell the police everything, and pray a jury shows mercy. Because then, all the shit I shovelled on myself would be gone.

Milly tried to warn me. Hollywood directors don't have PAs who ring out of the blue and pay for first-class tickets and fancy hotel rooms. That isn't how dreams work.

My phone rings. It's Bryn.

Heart pounding, I answer.

"Kyle, there's been a development," he says, not bothering with his usual chitchat about the weather. "I can't go into details, but we have a credible witness ready to testify against Biedermeier. This could blow the case wide open."

I grip the phone tighter, scarcely daring to hope. "Are you sure? Who is it?"

"I can't say yet, but we have a real chance here if we move fast. Get yourself on the next bus or train back to LA. I'll explain everything."

Before I can tell him where I am, he hangs up, and I stare around the bar, possibilities churning in my mind.

Did I imagine that?

Or is Bryn in on this, too?

Is this yet another trick?

Except, how can it be? He's the boyfriend of a friend of my best friend. Friends are the only people worth trusting. Fuck everyone else. Fuck them all to hell.

The faintest flicker of hope sparks.

# 24

When I called Bryn back and owned up about being in LA, he sounded stunned. When I explained why and who I came here with, he went quiet and told me to get into a cab, texting directions for a nearby hotel where he'd already paid for the room. A place where you typed a number into a machine, and it printed a card to access your room. No ID needed.

I called him again after locking my bedroom door and dragging a heavy chair over to make sure it stayed that way. I turned off all the lights and hid in the bathroom. He texted details of where to meet up.

I slept on the bathroom floor.

Fitfully.

———

The Alchemy Café combines old-fashioned elegance with red brick simplicity. Arched windows let in the morning.

Background piano music mingles with the hum of conversation.

Despite spending the night on two thin towels, I overslept, and Bryn is already seated at a table, dressed in a blazer and chinos, staring at his open laptop. When our eyes meet, he jumps to his feet and gathers me in a bear hug. He smells of clean, of home, and of safety.

As he pulls away, his hand stays on my arm. "You've been to hell and back, man."

I sit, and he orders breakfast.

"What's this development?" I say as soon as I'm sure there's nobody in earshot.

Bryn leans away and grins. "Who's the most unlikely person to switch sides?"

"Noah?" I say blankly.

"Guess again."

"Aaron."

"Not even warm."

"Just tell me, for Christ's sake."

"Carlton Dupree."

It takes a minute to register, and even when it does, I shake my head. Surely, I heard him wrong.

"Dupree has turned on Aaron to save himself," Bryn says. "He wants immunity."

I know this is good news, and I should celebrate... and probably shouldn't do what I want to do and kiss Bryn's lovely mouth. Except...doesn't that mean Dupree gets away with everything?

"What about Tim Larson's family?" I say. "Or Judah Eisenhart's mother? Do they get immunity, too? Is

someone going to wave a magic wand and bring them
back to life?"

"Don't you see?" Bryn is still smiling. "This is great
for you."

He reaches into his pocket and pulls out my passport.
It's been so long since I saw it, I'm not sure it's mine.
I'm not even sure I want to pick up something recently
touched by Dupree's filthy, murdering fingers. I try to
push down the rage and sorrow boiling together in
my gut.

"I realise I should be OK with this," I say, swallowing
a deep breath. "Really, though, are you not bothered by
what's happening here? One man gets away with
abusing kids, and the one enabling him does a deal, and
hey presto, they become the hero. How is any of that
good news?"

Bryn's smile fades. "In my job, I've learned to take the
victories where I get them. There's a victim for every
crime."

I nod, trying to focus on the positive. With Dupree on
side, the police will arrest Aaron and bring down his sick
empire. Noah doesn't need to go through with anything.
Bryn's phone beeps, and when he glances down, his
cheerful grin morphs into a scowl.

"What's wrong?" I say, heart pounding.

He flaps his fingers into the 'phone' sign, showing
how he needs to make a call, and heads outside. I watch
as he walks up and down, waving his hands. Even before
he comes back inside, I smell disaster.

"Dupree was screwing with us." He slumps into his
seat. "Either that or he got a better offer."

———

Jet engines drone, and car horns bleat. Fluorescent lights flicker and hum. Harried travellers jostle, eyes trained on signs directing them to check-in zones. I've seen people in movies dash to desks and demand a ticket to go anywhere in the name of love.

Real life is nothing like that.

There's no single desk manned by a smiling blonde woman who wants love to conquer all. I'm in line for tickets at the British Airways counter, and things are moving slowly. When it's finally my turn, I pull out my best smile.

"I just need to get home," I tell a slender man with wire-rimmed glasses perched on his nose.

"And where might home be?" he says, without looking away from his computer screen.

"Birmingham. England."

Tappity, tap, tap on his keyboard.

"Nothing direct, but I can get you to London this evening, connecting through Chicago for $2200 with a seven-hour layover."

I suppress a groan, my stomach sinking. My bank account can't handle that.

"Would you mind holding the seat for ten minutes while I make a call?"

"That's not something we do."

He's already peering past me and beckoning the next person in line.

I squeeze my phone to stop my hands from shaking as I step aside, sweat pooling beneath my shirt.

Milly picks up on the second ring. "Where the hell are you? Bryn is going frantic."

I tell her everything, stumbling over words, leaving no room for questions.

"Can you cover the ticket for me, and I'll pay you back as soon as my next wages clear?"

The line goes quiet, and I hold my breath, shame burning.

"I just transferred two grand to your account. Get yourself home safe, OK?"

Tears prickle my eyes. "I will. Thank you. I owe you big time."

The airline guy pretends he doesn't remember me, so we go through the same routine, and I walk away, two thousand dollars down, with a seat booked to Heathrow, leaving in six hours.

I shouldn't, but can't help poking at my phone, searching for wedding coverage. The scab's already weeping. Why not pick a little more?

A live stream features drone footage of a glittering mansion in the Hollywood Hills. Huge limos line a driveway, and there's a marquee with ivory drapes and twinkling lights. Security personnel talk into earpieces, and uniformed guards patrol with slavering dogs. The press gathers behind a barricade near the main gates, jostling for the best position, eager to capture each high-profile guest.

Judah's mud didn't stick.

The Biedermeier-Winters nuptials are big box office.

My pulse spikes when Noah climbs from a black SUV,

smiling and waving at cameras. His cruel betrayal stings my every nerve.

He needs to hear how much this hurts. I want to stand in front of him and make him understand. He shouldn't be smiling, waving, and acting like this is any kind of OK.

I can make it there and back within six hours.

———

There's another long queue at the taxi transfer desk, so I do something shameful. I grab a wheelchair left by the doors and wheel myself over to where a line of new arrivals is waiting. They step to one side and let a driver help me into his cab.

"Where to bud?" he says, without really looking at me.

"I'm a guest at the Biedermeier-Winters wedding."

Now he's looking at me.

Now, he's weighing me up.

Now he sees how I'm dressed. Like someone getting ready to fly home. Sweatpants and a baggy T-shirt.

"I have an outfit in my bag," I say. "My flight was delayed."

We exit onto Century Boulevard and merge with the 105. Cruising west, the midday sun blasts. I'm sick of it. Never again, let me moan about a rainy day in Birmingham. How does anyone live like this, waking up knowing what the weather will always be?

The city blurs, and I leave a message for Hyson.

"You need to be there," I say. "If you have a single shred of decency."

The bumper-to-bumper lanes give way to an open road, snaking into the Hollywood Hills. Swooping curves carry us higher, and the air cools as the harsh sun softens behind veils of foliage.

I pull out my phone and send a text. Three dots fade in and out. And then I get my reply.

"Change of plan," I say, and the driver's eyes meet mine.

———

The Starbucks on Sunset hums with life. I'm wearing a red baseball cap pulled down low and five-dollar sunglasses. Indie pop filters through overhead speakers, and sunshine sneaks through vertical blinds, casting linear shadows on the polished wooden floor.

I half expected a silver limo with a motorcycle escort, but Noah jumps down from a black Jeep. He's wearing a worn-out hoodie, a size too large. I want to smile when he sees me and raises a hand. Instead, I muster a cold, staring nod.

He comes inside and slides into the seat opposite.

"Thanks for making time to meet with me," I say, sounding like he's the parent of some kid who put glue in another kid's hair because the second kid called the first kid a wanker.

He can't look at me. "I wanted to be here."

"Are you ready for your big romantic moment?"

His lips curve into a weak smile, though all I see is

sadness. "I guess."

I check to be sure nobody's watching. "Was any of what you said to me true? Hyson already told me he's still on the payroll."

Noah freezes, his shoulders tensing and a confused line forming between his brows, but I'm not done with the questions.

"Was I right all along, and the road trip was Dupree's way of getting me out of LA?"

He stares down at the table. "Is that *still* what you think?"

"That's not an answer."

He fiddles with a paper napkin. "Everyone tells lies. But nobody tells them all the time."

"Tell me one thing about the trip that was true."

He glances away. "Albuquerque."

The answer sucks every breath from my body. The kiss we shared was so short-lived that part of me still wonders if it happened. I want to believe him. Of course, I do, but what if this is just another lie?

Is he wearing a wire?

"I need to ask you something," I say. "And I promise, it's my last question."

He half-smiles. "Do I really give a damn about Aaron Biedermeier?"

"No." I take off my sunglasses, needing to see into his soul. "Did you truly love Tim Larson?"

Noah rubs his temples, looking exhausted. "What difference does any of that make now?"

I get up, but he stops me, grabbing my hand, his grip strong but quickly turning softer. I sit back down.

"You're the first person I've gotten close to since everything went wrong." Noah's voice cracks with emotion. "Being around you reminded me of who I used to be, and I don't expect you to understand the situation with Aaron. But never write off what we had. You and I." He looks past me through the window onto Sunset. "You've endured so much because of my dumb, selfish choices. All I have to tell you—all I can give you in return —is my word. That kiss mattered. It mattered more than I can say."

My chest aches, and I want to believe him. But he's about to marry the man who as good as murdered two young men. His first lover. His friend. God only knows how many more.

Noah pulls his hoodie up over his head, half hiding his face.

"People will wonder where I am," he says. "And I can't turn up dressed like this."

We hold each other's gaze, and I want to say much more. But what's the point? None of this is real. It's all make-believe. Welcome to Hollywood.

He turns to leave, then pauses.

"Whatever happens, you showed me myself again when I'd forgotten who that was. And you cared about Tim. Thank you."

And then he's gone.

———

Three local news networks livestream the Biedermeier-Winters wedding. The guests gather in a marquee on white benches adorned with blue silk and lavender lace. The grooms wear matching pink tuxedos. Aaron has a purple velvet bow tie and cummerbund. Noah sticks to classic black.

A string quartet plays as Aaron takes his place with the celebrant. Noah hangs back and waits with Dupree, who keeps tapping on the screen of his phone. Perhaps Aaron plans a 'party' later, and he's charged with finding 'childcare' for the guests.

A soul singer launches into her song, and Noah walks between the rows of smiling faces, exchanging nods and waving hello. He reaches the front and turns to face Aaron.

I shouldn't be watching this in an airport bar, but I can't tear myself away.

Hyson sets down a beer and sits.

We have spoken a little. I've told him I understood why he did what he did, wondering out loud how he slept at night. I'm glad he had the balls to show up, though. I wanted him here.

Noah's eyes lock onto Aaron's, and I search for signs of affection. He summed it all up for me that day on the road. In a battered red van. There was never anything to do with love in this business arrangement. It's all about the optics.

The celebrant begins with a reading from some book that can't be the Bible, judging by the f-bombs.

Aaron goes first with his vows, his voice husky with emotion.

"My heart..."

As he speaks, the camera zooms in on Noah.

He blinks and looks down, and his fingers bunch into fists.

When Aaron is done delivering vows that sound to have been workshopped by a room of writers, the celebrant turns to Noah.

He shifts to face Aaron, and his expression appears dark and stormy even on drone footage. He opens his mouth, but nothing comes out, and wedding guests shift uncomfortably.

Someone coughs.

Noah glances around, scanning the rows of faces.

The silence hangs heavy.

Finally, he looks at Aaron, resolve etched on his face.

"This man is special," he says. "Or rather, that's what he thinks."

Murmurs ripple through the crowd. Aaron's smile dims.

"Aaron Biedermeier is the reason Tim Larson died."

Guests gasp and exclaim before looking around to check if they're on camera before picking an appropriate reaction. Shock is good, but awe is better. Aaron grabs Noah's arm, his face contorted in rage. "Shut up, you little..."

Noah shakes him off and raises his chin. "I was too young to fight back. I was fifteen when it all started for me. I was one of the older boys Aaron Biedermeier abused."

Chaos erupts.

The celebrant rushes to intervene.

Security personnel converge on the altar, but Noah stands tall, defiance burning in his eyes.

# INSIDER

## UNLOCKING THE ENIGMA

Noah Winters reveals all in his most intimate interview yet

**When actor Noah Winters took the witness stand in the United States District Court for the Central District of California, he blew open Hollywood's biggest scandal since #MeToo rocked the entertainment industry. In gut-wrenching testimony, the former Oscar nominee exposed the rampant sexual abuse he endured as a teen actor at the hands of influential director Aaron Biedermeier.**

Winters is picking up the pieces of his shattered life. But rather than recede from view, he's emerging as an outspoken advocate for trauma victims. His harrowing journey from the abused to the activist is extraordinary and inspirational.

"For months afterwards, I was lost in shame, confusion, and fear," Winters tells INSIDER in an exclusive interview. "I convinced myself that hiding the truth was the only way forward. But you can't heal that way."

Winters' involvement with Biedermeier began after the director discovered the then-15-year-old acting hopeful and whisked him to Hollywood with promises of stardom. Behind the glamor, Biedermeier subjected Winters and other minors to ritualized abuse at drug-fueled parties.

"There were times I wanted to die rather than go back," Winters reveals, his voice raw with emotion. "I still have nightmares."

Unable to escape Biedermeier's clutches,

Winters agreed to 'date' the director to quash rumors, shielding him from backlash. Last year, allegations by former teen actor Judah Eisenhart against Biedermeier set off a chain of events that finally gave Winters the courage to speak up.

"Staying silent was destroying me," he reflects. "After what happened to Judah, I knew if I didn't speak, others would get hurt."

On the day he was to marry the director, Winters used his vows to expose a pattern of abuse, ending the day with multiple arrests.

With support from advocacy groups, Winters worked with prosecutors to build an ironclad case, testifying about the abuse despite the best efforts of Biedermeier's legal team to discredit him. Six other victims came forward, leading to the director's conviction on multiple counts of rape and child endangerment. He received a 25-year prison sentence.

Winters also implicated Biedermeier's long-time associate, Carlton Dupree. He arranged sexual liaisons and covered up crimes. Dupree was sentenced to ten years for obstruction of justice.

On the stand, Winters publicly apologised to the family of Tim Larson, a young actor who died of an overdose aged just fifteen. Larson's parents have credited Winters with finally giving their son a voice.

"Getting justice for Tim and the other victims

helped lift a weight off me," he shares. "Their pain haunted me for so long."

Winters credits intensive therapy for helping him process trauma suppressed since childhood. "I learned coping techniques to quiet demons that drove self-destructive tendencies." He credits being forced to confront his abuser in court with starting his journey towards healing.

Today, Winters channels his experiences into activism. He volunteers with organizations supporting abuse survivors, sits on a youth outreach program board, and regularly attends recovery meetings.

"Talking about my trauma openly and honestly has helped me reclaim my power," he shares. "I want to empower other survivors to find their voice."

Winters also works directly with male victims. "Boys face stigma admitting they've been abused," he says. "I want to end the shame." He has lobbied for legislation extending statutes of limitations for child sex crimes.

While continuing to raise awareness through public speaking, Winters has stepped back from Hollywood's glare. "I lost myself in that world. I'm rediscovering who I am away from the spotlight."

He lives modestly, sharing a Santa Monica apartment with his rescue dog, Zeke. He takes on acting roles selectively, and is drawn to projects promoting social change. There are still tough days, but his outlook has shifted. "Life will always have darkness, but it's how you cope that matters. Helping others helps me."

Close friend Kyle Macdonald stood by Winters during the trial and says his transformation has been profound. "Noah was dealt an awful hand but never gave up trying to do good. He's a survivor and a giver. His heart is pure."

Winters shyly acknowledges how far he's come. But his fight for victims, like himself, continues. "The justice system failed us for too long," he says, unbowed. "That changes now. I won't stay silent ever again."

# EPILOGUE

## 7.28 p.m. November 17, 2023 - London

This lavish hotel suite overlooks St. Paul's Cathedral. Noah is dressed in a black tuxedo, his hair slicked back and cheeks flushed from too much time in the sun. He's every bit the leading man I dreamed of.

I straighten his velvet bow tie and smooth his lapel.

"You do know this is an award for teachers," I say. "Everyone else will be wearing corduroy and cardigans with elbow patches."

Noah leans in and kisses my cheek. "I'm a movie star. People expect this."

He's not acted in over a year. All his time is spent talking to journalists working on projects for at-risk kids. Noah Winters has become the poster boy for the underdog.

And I love him for it.

"We'd best get moving before Milly empties the

minibar," I say.

He pulls me closer. "Let her celebrate. Tonight is about us."

My pulse races. I told myself that none of this mattered. Awards are just bullshit. But it does matter. I want to win this sucker. I want to win it bad.

We share a kiss before I step back, looking him up and down with admiration.

"You're amazing," I say.

Because he is.

In my smart grey suit and navy tie, I'm still his match. Linking his arm through mine, Noah guides us towards the door, and I hear that voice inside, screaming at me to wake up, that this isn't happening. People like me don't get happy endings like this.

Except it is happening. And this is my happy ending.

"Let's make dreams happen," he says, and as if sensing my doubt, he squeezes my hand.

"What if someone else wins?" I say.

He pretends to be unfazed, but a catch in his breath reveals otherwise. "It's the taking part that matters."

The thing I've come to learn about all actors is that they know what to say when push comes to shove. And my bullshit detector has gotten super sensitive.

———

After the not-really-wedding, Noah was placed under police protection and interviewed as a key witness. With no contact for weeks, I made peace with the likelihood of never hearing from him again. Maybe his people would send flowers. Though a small part of me clung to hope, I rebooked my ticket home.

And then a letter arrived. Handwritten. I'd never seen Noah's scrawl, and it surprised me just how neatly he formed each word. Obviously, I ran samples through websites that analyse handwriting and personality.

Don't judge me.

*'The uniform, well-spaced letters indicate someone methodical and cautious who cares about how they present themselves to the world. A right slant suggests he is open to new ideas and connections. Strong vertical strokes imply ambition.'*

He explained how he was entering a residential trauma programme, and the rules stipulated zero contact with anyone associated with the court case.

My heart ached, feeling like I'd lost him all over again.

The trial, when it happened, was, of course, a media circus.

Over there. And at home.

Protesters gathered outside the courthouse, demanding justice for Biedermeier's other victims. For the men who dared speak up in the weeks after Noah broke his silence. And there were many other men.

The accused walked past jeering crowds each morning, grinning and acting like it was some kind of publicity thing. Aaron wore a baseball cap and shades. Dupree stuck to his signature blue suit. I saw in their faces how both men believed they'd walk free. Because straight white men with straight white money always did.

And then there was Bo Hyson.

Estelle held his hand as he walked past the same placards. Dwayne too. I wanted someone to speak up and say something that proved that Bo wasn't to blame.

Not really.

Except he was. I'm not stupid. I know what he did, even though I know why.

All three men were guilty.

Noah's testimony proved damning. As did the words of 32 other young men. Most of them broken. Some only able to give evidence long-distance by video. Details of horrific abuse were laid bare. I didn't get called to speak. The prosecution kept things simple and let me be one of the lucky ones.

Biedermeier was sentenced to 25 years on multiple counts of child sexual exploitation. His empire crumbled, and his assets were seized. True to form, Dupree turned on his former boss in a plea deal that earned him reduced time. Ten days into his sentence, his bloodied body was found at the foot of a stairwell.

Bo Hyson struck no such deal. Estelle didn't cry in front of the cameras. Dwayne held his head high. And then it was over, and I was nervous about reaching out.

"He made it clear we had to accept things were over in that letter," I said, but Milly insisted.

"He also told you he loved you."

"He signed it *with love*. That's different. I put that on birthday cards for people I can't stand at work."

She was having none of it. "You can afford to fly cattle class and stay in a cheap motel."

I could, and I did.

We met for coffee. Same place as always. Same table.

The conversation started out stilted, and then Noah took my hand and looked into my eyes with a warmth I told myself couldn't be real.

"I'm sorry," he said. "I should have trusted you."

He cracked my heart of stone.

We talked for hours, reconciling our stories and feelings, and it felt like no time had passed. Like it was yesterday when he boarded that plane in Memphis, heading back to LA, and I checked into an airport motel to scream and scream into a pile of pillows.

Noah turned down deals to write books or script his story, instead using his platform to advocate for trauma survivors. He still struggles with PTSD, but helping others has brought meaning.

Last month, we put in an offer on an end-of-terrace house in Moseley, Birmingham, and truth be told, I'm not sure how the neighbours will deal with a movie star living on their street, but who cares? There's a lawn out the back, and roses grow around the front door. It's everything I've always wanted.

We're taking things slow and healing together.

*CumDump64* still texts with photographs, which demonstrate remarkable athletic prowess.

Milly refuses to let me block his number.

Noah too.

"Teacher of the Year." Noah picks at a piece of lint from the collar of my jacket. "It has a nice ring."

"I just know that smug nun who taught a blind kid how to read Braille is going to walk it," I say. "Why couldn't I have chances like that? The judges love strength against adversity."

"Twelve months ago, you helped crack a grooming operation."

"The blind kid always wins." I shake my head, a one-track mind. "It's the first law of award ceremonies."

Noah turns and takes both of my hands. "Don't worry, babe. You've got this."

We make our way to the elevator and ride down to the lobby, and as soon as we step out, we're greeted by flashing cameras. And Milly.

She's very, *very* drunk.

"Darlings!" She grabs both of our arms. There are crumbs in her hair. "You guys give off an amazing vibe. I'm excited. And guess what? The nun is wearing couture. So much for giving up her worldly goods and living a life of poverty. I've already tipped off one of the judges."

Noah and I exchange a knowing look, and I can't help but feel a little jealous of Milly's drunkenness. It's been 53 days since my last drink. Noah has six months. I wish I didn't need to care, but tonight isn't about anything that happened in Vegas or River Valley. Tonight is about picking up the Best Teacher award, waving it in the face of that Dior-wearing nun, and proving something to myself.

I'm winning at life.

# GHOSTED

This is a preview of my previous novel 'Ghosted' - available most anywhere they sell books and almost certainly in a fair few clearance bins.

Professional Santa Silas French fills out the same application as always for his regular stint at a New York department store. Ellen Gitelman hangs her jacket behind the counter at the East Side Diner and smoothes out her waitress uniform as she waits for the coffee pot to stop percolating.

> *"Fanning's prose and dialogue are crisp, brisk, and incisive, and the characterization is strong in this novel that's ideal for readers who love diverse casts, surprising connections, and healing relationships, with much comic complication."*

**Publishers' Weekly**

*Three dots.*

That means Joey is writing a message. Silas French squints at a telephone he isn't certain he knows how to operate, but he can't go back to the Verizon store again. Last time, the sales staff acted so busy, so important, so far above him. One said how he should read the instruction manual, implying he didn't already do that. From cover to cover, skimming foreign language versions, in case bits didn't get translated.

*Three dots pulse; first gray and then white, fading in, fading out.*

Thirteen years is too long not talking to your kid. Joey's life turned out fine. A guy at Ziggy's bar had shown Silas how to use Facebook, and he saw photographs. Joey married some guy called Zach. They have two kids, Apollo and Lumen. Not names he loves, but they're healthy and happy.

He pulls at a loose thread on the sleeve of his sweater, and it runs a hole. Nancy would never let her husband leave the apartment in such a disheveled state. She'd say he looked like a bum and needed to clean up his act, before blowing a kiss and insisting she'd have him no other way. He ought to get his beard tidied up and maybe his hair too. He's too old to wear a thrift store knitted beanie, but New York in November is colder than Siberia.

*Three dots.*

Dr. Malinowski's waiting room always has the same smell, a mix of disinfectant and eucalyptus. A calendar shows early crimson chrysanthemums and is set to October. Silas wants to flip it onto November, but that would be rude, and perhaps Malinowski likes the picture. He glances at the clock. The doctor's assistant knows he needs to leave on time, so how come Malinowski is with some other patient? Thin walls muffle their voices, but whoever it is, her voice stays even, and her words sound measured. This isn't someone getting bad news.

*Three dots.*

What's the doctor going to say that Silas hasn't already heard a hundred times? Exercise more. Take your pills. Eat better. Who has the time to shop for home-cooked meals? He tried a plant-based burger because the packaging claimed it would bleed like real meat. It left a red slither on the plate, and he managed one bite before digging through takeout menus to order Chinese.

At their last appointment, Malinowski made it clear, it's more than eating better and exercising. Silas needs a stent. A tiny tube to keep his arteries open and carrying blood to and from his heart. A stent means surgery, and he already checked, Medicare won't cover everything.

Laughter from the next room suggests some Upper East Side tootsie inviting the doc to drop by for Christmas cocktails. Silas tends a garden on East 78th and the lady of the house never suggests he joins her for after-work drinks.

*Three dots.*

There's a nick in the knee of his pants. He ought to buy new ones. Pants that fit, not pants that used to fit a larger body. After losing thirty pounds in the space of a year, he hammered new notches into his belt.

It's ten after nine. When you book to see a doctor,

you stick to your allotted fifteen minutes out of consideration for whoever is next in line. In under an hour, Silas is due at Goering Brothers department store to sign up for his regular holiday season job as Santa. Four men work shifts: Sam, Justin, Marty, and Silas. Except not Marty. Not this year. His wife got in touch to say he passed, and Silas opened the letter too late to make the burial but sent flowers. Yellow roses. He hopes it was the correct thing to do. Nancy would have known.

*Three dots.*

Come on, Joey. Say you're good with me flying down to Florida for New Year. Your mom wouldn't care to think of us not talking. Before she died, I promised to put things right. I should have done this before now, but we can fight about it some other time. Like when we see each other.

The thing is, Joey, I come from a different generation. I said what I said to protect you. We live in a shitty world, and I didn't mean that because you're gay it automatically meant you'd die of AIDS. How could you think that of me? Anyhow, things have changed with cures and vaccinations and stuff. I talked to a guy selling coffee in the West Village, and he told me how he's living with HIV, and it no longer means a death sentence.

*Three dots.*

And then they're gone.

# about mo fanning

Part-time novelist, part-time stand-up comic, and full-time ageing homosexual, Mo Fanning lives in a Black Country backwater town better known for its drive-through Gregg's than its thriving literary scene. He aspires to someplace more  rural, where his nearest neighbour has four legs and is hard of hearing.

With a unique talent for blending romance and comedy in intriguing settings, Mo is an emerging voice in contemporary fiction with lofty ambitions of becoming the *go-to quote monster* for anything to do with LGBTQ romance novels.

Beyond writing, Mo displays a passion verging on unhealthy when it comes to the Eurovision Song Contest and will happily discuss the waning value of a key change.

# also by mo fanning

spring street books

# GHOSTED

"Just the tonic for these times"
VERA CHOK

**Professional Santa Silas French fills out the same application as always for his regular stint at a New York department store. Ellen Gitelman hangs her jacket behind the counter at the East Side Diner and smooths out her waitress uniform as she waits for the coffee pot to stop percolating.**

A double whammy of bad news leaves Silas jobless, with no money to pay for a planned trip to reconcile with his estranged gay son Joey in Florida. Cutbacks at the diner cost Ellen her job.

A chance tip from his local bar gets Silas a job as Santa on a cruise ship that happens to be docking in Florida, where Joey lives with his husband and kids. Ellen heads to a café across the street and spots a bulletin board ad selling tickets for a cruise. Her riotous friend Julia volunteers as a travel companion.

The MS Viking just happens to be carrying 3,000 gay men in the mood to party.

**What could possibly go wrong?**

# REBUILDING ALEXANDRA SMALL

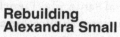

**Rebuilding
Alexandra Small**

MO FANNING    #romcom

**Alexandra Small has it all - a thriving career, a beautiful home, and a loving family. But when a devastating setback shatters her world, she's left to pick up the pieces and find her footing again.**

Unsure of her path forward, Allie embarks on a journey of self-discovery that will challenge her, make her laugh, and open her eyes to the possibilities that lie ahead.

As Allie navigates the complexities of life, she forges unexpected friendships, rekindles lost passions, and faces the ghosts of her past. Through it all, she learns that sometimes, hitting rock bottom can be the catalyst for rediscovering your true self and finding happiness where you least expect it.

**Join Alexandra Small on her moving journey to rebuild her life and embrace the power of change.**

# THE ARMCHAIR BRIDE

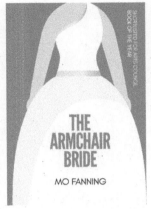

**Lisa Doyle is almost forty, single, and ready to take charge of her life. Fed up with being the girl most likely to die alone, eaten by feral cats, she's got a plan to shape up and find love.**

But when her childhood BFF asks her to be maid of honour, Lisa's world implodes. The bride's new bestie? None other than onetime school bully Ginny.

Things go from bad to worse after a video of Lisa's office party from hell goes viral.

With the wedding getting closer and former classmates parading their perfect lives alongside smartly dressed husbands on social media, Lisa invents an astronaut husband. When her roommate bails on pretending to be this man of action, Lisa talks her recently divorced boss, Brian, into standing in.

With Ginny taking charge of wedding plans, Lisa must decide whether to stand up to the bully or run for the hills.

Full of zany mishaps and family drama, The Armchair Bride is a laugh-out-loud romcom about shedding baggage, embracing independence, and learning that happiness comes from within.

**Because the only person you need to please is you.**